AN UNCIVIL WAR

The Medieval Saga Series
Book Three

David Field

SAPERE
BOOKS

AN UNCIVIL WAR

Published by Sapere Books.

20 Windermere Drive, Leeds, England, LS17 7UZ,
United Kingdom

saperebooks.com

Copyright © David Field, 2022

David Field has asserted his right to be identified as the author
of this work.

All rights reserved.

No part of this publication may be reproduced, stored in any
retrieval system, or transmitted, in any form, or by any means,
electronic, mechanical, photocopying, recording, or otherwise,
without the prior written permission of the publishers.
This book is a work of fiction. Names, characters, businesses,
organisations, places and events, other than those clearly in the
public domain, are either the product of the author's
imagination, or are used fictitiously.
Any resemblances to actual persons, living or dead, events or
locales are purely coincidental.

ISBN: 978-1-80055-679-9

I

November, 1120

On the quayside at Barfleur, all was chaos and debauchery. King Henry had already departed on an earlier vessel, having graciously declined the invitation of its captain, Thomas FitzStephen, to travel on his newest refitted vessel the *White Ship*, and was probably now somewhere mid-Channel on his way back to England. This was the signal for polite behaviour to be abandoned, and those who rolled out of the alehouses to piss against their walls, or vomit on the flagstones, were still accompanied by hopeful whores clinging to the cloaks they had donned in order to step out into the all-pervading drizzle.

'The priests wish to give the customary departure blessing,' FitzStephen was advised by a deckhand who was still capable of rational thought.

FitzStephen adjusted his hose and stepped back from the inn wall. 'We can dispense with their righteous drivel for once,' he muttered. 'This vessel is the finest in the family fleet, and God will preserve us from harm, given our precious cargo. See to the loosening from the bollards, since we are bidden to overtake the king's vessel. We make full sail as soon as we clear the harbour wall — no point in looking for the headland on a night like this.'

Once the vessel began to respond to the roll of open water, some of the noble guests leaned over the side to spew back the wine they had been generously gifted by the king. The deckhands were therefore finding it difficult to make their way along the gunwales in order to keep a lookout through the murk. Full sails were being hoisted in the bid to overtake the king's barque, and Captain FitzStephen could not hear anything above the riotous clamour as, somewhere for'ard, a whore who had jumped aboard was shedding her garments and performing a lewd dance. He therefore missed the yell of alarm from the port lookout as the partly submerged *Quilleboeuf* rock loomed out of the squall.

The sharp edge ripped a massive hole in the side of the vessel, which rapidly began taking in water. Few of the inebriated passengers were aware that their last moment of life had come until the planking under their feet began to heave and buck, and even then many of them took it to be the effect of the wine they had consumed. Then waves of water covered their boots, and it was too late. In the mad scramble for the small boat lashed to the stern board, several panicked fights broke out. When it was eventually launched overboard, it was followed by too many of those who could not swim even when sober, and it foundered at the same time that the *White Ship* went down.

The shrieks and pleas to God became fainter and less frequent as the unforgiving ocean claimed three hundred lives. They were men and women from all stations in life, from the nobility down to the seadogs, but the loss of one in particular was to have devastating consequences for the future of England.

The footmen, ushers and messengers drew lots for the unenviable task that might cost them their lives, but eventually it was a lowly page who ventured into the chamber in Windsor Palace in which King Henry was seated. The page prostrated himself on the carpet that lay in front of the roaring fire.

'What means this, you oaf?' the king demanded as he stared down at the boy. 'Did you trip?'

'No, sire. By your leave, I've been sent in with the worst of messages, and I fear for my life once I deliver it.'

'If you be only the messenger, why should you fear for your life? Am I portrayed abroad as a tyrant, say you?'

'No, sire. They speak of you as a loving family man, which is why my message is so dreadful to bear.'

'What about my family do you have to impart? Is the prince returned from Barfleur?'

'No, sire. But truth to tell, he left the port of Barfleur some days since.'

'Has he been captured and held to ransom by pirates?'

'No, sire.'

'Then *what*? Speak plainly, boy, and no harm will be visited upon you. But if you delay further, I will have you taken out and boiled.'

'It is the Prince William, sire.'

'Obviously, but what of him?'

'Sire, the *White Ship* foundered as it left the harbour, and all aboard were tipped into the raging ocean. There was but one man saved.'

'And?' King Henry persisted as the colour left his face.

'And that man was not your son, sire.'

'So William Adelin is lost?'

'So it is said, sire. I bring only the message, and I have no confirmation of its truth.'

Henry stared back at the hapless youth with unseeing eyes, before waving him away. 'You may leave me. You may *all* leave. Go! Now! Such tears as must be shed may not be shared with subjects. Away with you all!'

The chamber emptied hurriedly, as those who had been present sought a more sheltered location ahead of the threatened storm of grief.

II

Sir Thomas Walsingham, in his capacity as Captain of the Palace Guard, was not summoned until the following morning. Although he had anticipated the summons ever since the news had reached Windsor two days ago, he had been kept from King Henry until the previous evening. He left off his daily inspection of the outer motte, leaving the remainder of the detail to a second in command, and made his way to the Audience Chamber in the Windsor Tower.

Although prepared for what awaited him, he was concerned at the apparent depth of the king's depressed and anxious state, clearly a reflection of his heartfelt grief at the loss of William Adelin, his only son and the obvious heir to his English crown and his estates across the Channel. But Thomas was even more worried by the first few questions levelled at him as King Henry sipped from a wine goblet and stared distractedly out of a mullioned window down at the distant River Thames.

'You are well, Sir Thomas?'

'Middling so, thank you, sire. These early December winds cause me much sniffling, but otherwise I do not yet begin to feel my fifty odd years.'

'I am pleased to hear it. And your family? You have a son and a daughter, do you not?'

'Indeed, and might I express my admiration for your powers of memory, sire? I have a daughter Elinor, my first-born, and a son called Richard, two years younger. Since the death of their mother some years ago, they grow restless on my father's estate at Walsingham. He is of course an old man now, and given to frailty. You will perhaps remember him?'

'I could hardly forget him,' Henry smiled as he continued staring through the glass. 'I owe him my throne.'

This was in many ways an exaggeration, although Thomas was not about to correct his Majesty. But it was beyond contest that on the last occasion that King Henry's older brother Robert had attempted an invasion, it had been Sir Wilfrid Walsingham's military strategy that had saved the day. Before that, Thomas's father had laid to rest the ugly rumour that Henry had become king by organising the death of his older brother Rufus in a hunting accident in the New Forest. But no doubt the determined, if somewhat bookish, Henry — the youngest remaining son of the great invader William of Normandy — would either have survived by his own wits, or would have found another military commander with the same experience and guile as Sir Wilfrid Walsingham.

'Did your father ever tell you how, when my brothers and I were mere boys, he hauled Rufus off me by the seat of his hose?'

'Many times, sire,' Thomas smiled nostalgically. 'It was one of his favourite tales for a winter's night by the fire at Walsingham. But my father paid dearly for that when Rufus became king and imprisoned him for almost two years. It was only your brother's untimely death, and your merciful intervention when you assumed the throne, that preserved his life.'

'So our two families have ever worked in harmony, each to preserve the welfare of the other, could one say?'

'Indeed, sire,' Thomas agreed with a sinking sensation in the pit of his stomach. A favour was clearly about to be traded in.

'You will have been mourning the death of the heir to the English throne, William Adelin?'

'Indeed, sire, and I have issued instructions that the Palace guards are to wear black armbands on their tunics for the next week.'

'My thanks for that,' Henry muttered, before turning from the window and calling for the page to bring an extra wine goblet for Thomas. Then he beckoned him to the seats that were located before the roaring log fire, waited until the page had withdrawn to a corner of the Audience Chamber that was beyond earshot, lowered his voice and continued. 'The death of William Adelin brings more grief to the nation than it does even to me.'

No response seemed called for, so Thomas waited.

'As you will be aware, I have only one other remaining legitimate child, and that is my daughter Maude, married these several years to Henry of Germany, the Holy Roman Emperor. The barons are hardly likely to accept, as my successor, either a woman or one of my illegitimate sons. The queen, Maude's mother, died two years ago, and I remain unmarried with no immediate likelihood of siring another legitimate son — so you will appreciate the chaos that could follow any untimely death of mine?'

'You are, sire, if I might make the observation, in seemingly robust health.'

'Seemingly, Thomas, seemingly. But there are days when my stomach rebels at what I send it. And since it is a somewhat generous stomach, this in itself is a serious rebellion. No, do not pretend to smile, since that was not meant as a witticism, and the matter I wish to raise with you is far too serious for levity.' .

'Sire?'

'Tell me about your wife's ancestry,' Henry demanded out of the blue.

Thomas's heart leaped into his throat as he prayed for forgiveness for the lie he was about to tell. 'She was from Blois, where she served at the Court of Count Stephen. I believe that you and he were related, sire?'

'Indeed,' Henry confirmed. 'He was married to my sister Adela, although not very happily, or so I am informed. He had many mistresses, and several illegitimate offspring.'

Thomas waited politely to learn where all this was leading.

'The death of William Adelin has had two unfortunate diplomatic consequences. The first is that clearly he cannot now marry Matilde of Anjou, to whom he was betrothed. Her father, Count Fulk, has already sent an urgent messenger across the Channel demanding the return of the lady herself, who was residing at Winchester this past year, along with her dowry, which took the form of certain estates in Maine. We have long been in dispute, Fulk and I, over whether those estates were his to give in the first place. He now threatens to marry one of his daughters to William Clito, the son of my older brother Robert.'

'It was my belief that both he and his father were in safe custody following the battle at Tinchebray,' Thomas observed, but Henry shook his head.

'The father, certainly, and he will never see daylight again, even though he *is* my brother. But my nephew William Clito was allowed to escape due to treachery on the part of the man who was meant to be guarding him, and who was bribed by Louis of France. I had the man done to death very publicly and painfully, but the fact remains that Clito is at large, and enjoying the support of Louis, who is offering him estates in the Vexin, which of course brings him close to the borders of my own Normandy. Among Clito's other protectors may be listed Duke Robert of Flanders, and if Clito acquires the estates in Maine he will be well placed to mount a pincer attack on my Normandy lands from two sides, with assistance from Flanders to the north-east.'

'And what is it that you require of me?' Thomas enquired, relieved that the topic of conversation had moved on from his wife, whose true identity might be crucial to the direction in which the king was heading.

'First and foremost, I wish you to form a company of your most reliable men to escort the Lady Matilde safely back to her home in Anjou. That will at least remove one of the grounds for complaint from that Duchy. Then I wish you to accompany my ambassador down into the Vexin, and, more specifically, the estate of Evreux, which lies strategically across the main route from the French base in the Île de France to the coast of Normandy. And in the opposite direction, of course. I wish to learn of the current loyalties of its count, who is of the House of de Montfort, and who inherited the estate by virtue of marriage to my Aunt Agnes. In these uncertain times we must make what we can of family loyalties.'

'Indeed, sire. Talking of which, do you anticipate that I will be abroad for any length of time? And when would you wish me to depart? Only I must visit my father, and see to the proper management of the estate that I regret that I have been neglecting during my royal service.'

'The need is urgent, clearly, but you will not be making the journey alone. Nor will you be at the head of the entourage. You are a fine soldier, Thomas, but not, I suspect, suitable ambassadorial material. The delegation will be led by Robert of Gloucester, who has more than once displayed both his loyalty and his skill in such matters.'

King Henry was clearly not exaggerating about the importance of family ties in the pursuit of political and military outcomes. Robert Fitzroy, Earl of Gloucester following his marriage to its heiress, was the oldest of Henry's illegitimate sons, born before the king's marriage to the late queen, Matilda of Scotland. Now aged thirty, he was in the prime of life and well placed to negotiate matters on behalf of an English crown that would have been his, were it not for his illegitimacy. But he was fond of his younger half-sister Matilda, known as 'Maude' to distinguish her from her mother, and Robert had more than once vowed allegiance to the father who had sired him and seen to his education and welfare. He had also been close to William Adelin, without any obvious indication of jealousy or rivalry.

'Has Lord Robert been advised of your wishes, sire?' Thomas asked.

'He has indeed, and he knows more than you of the nature of the business he must conduct across the Channel. Your role will be to provide an armed force for his protection, and no more. But while you are in Anjou, it will be but a short detour on your part to venture into Blois in order to relive some memories and determine the current allegiance of Count Theobald, who now rules Blois. You were highly regarded by his father in your youth, were you not, before he threw his treacherous hand in with my brother Robert?'

'Indeed, sire. It was he who knighted me in the field, and it was Your Majesty's generous and gracious pleasure to honour that title when I returned with news of that impending treachery.'

'You had earned it by your loyalty to me. But what of any loyalty you may have towards Blois? After all, your wife was from there, and once had connections at Court.'

'My wife died some five years since, sire, so why is it now so important that I visit Blois?' Thomas enquired, anxious to change the subject once again, but his heart sank at the answer he received.

'Because therein lie other claims to my throne following my son's death. As I already reminded you, Stephen of Blois was married to my sister Adela. He has three sons, of whom the current Count Theobald now rules in the stead of his older brother William, who is said to be witless. There is another brother, Stephen, and countless daughters, in addition to the former Count Stephen's illegitimate brood. They are all related to me by blood, as nephews and nieces. Following the death of William Adelin, and since the barons are likely to reject Maude as my successor, my preferred choice to rule England in my stead would be either Theobald himself, or his brother Stephen. I wish to know if either of them intends to pre-empt my decision by making a claim with the support of Louis of France.'

'Do you think I would be safe in Blois, given my part in undermining the former count's intrigues? He was forced into a peace treaty on terms that obliged him to marry his favourite, albeit illegitimate, daughter Emma to your Royal Treasurer Herbert of Winchester,' said Thomas after taking a deep breath.

Henry smiled conspiratorially. 'Therein lies another mystery that you might wish to probe, Thomas. Herbert died a year or so ago, and it was expected that the Lady Emma would seek to return to Blois, given that there were no issue and that she was beloved of her brothers. Instead she simply vanished into the countryside, and when young Stephen ventured over here to seek her out, he received certain information that sent him back across the Channel within the week. I thought perhaps that you might, through your late wife, have had some inkling as to what may have caused the wealthy widow to take such a course, given that your good lady served Emma when she was at the Court of Blois. "Melusine" — I believe that such was her name?'

'Yes, sire,' Thomas replied after swallowing hard to suppress bile that owed nothing to the quality of the wine. 'Her name was indeed Melusine, although given the difficulty experienced by those on the Walsingham estate in pronouncing such a name, she took to calling herself "Emma", in memory of the lady she'd served so loyally.'

'But the real Lady Emma has not appeared at Walsingham?' Henry enquired as he looked hard into Thomas's eyes. 'You have not been harbouring her there, knowing that she might be a valuable asset in our relations with Blois, in which are located two possible claimants to the crown of England and my estates in Normandy?'

'No, sire,' Thomas replied hastily, 'but I shall of course make additional enquiries when I am able to return to my long-neglected estates, which hopefully can occur ere I depart for Anjou and the Vexin. But I may need to send another in my stead to Blois, given that I betrayed the former count to his enemy.'

Henry tutted loudly. 'You forget yourself, *Sir* Thomas by my grace and favour. The so-called "enemy" to whom you refer was the very king to whom you owed allegiance, and still do. In short, *me*. You can now see why I choose not to entrust you with any diplomatic duties? Your loyalties are suspect in the matter of Blois, and do not lose sight of that fact when you accompany Robert on his mission.'

'No, sire. Now, if I might be permitted to withdraw, go about my duties, and make arrangements to visit the family estate ere I depart?'

'Yes, do so, but ensure that you leave someone competent to command my Palace Guard while you are away.'

As Thomas walked slowly back across the yard, he was breathing heavily and attempting to come to grips with what he had just learned. The secret that he and his late wife had been carefully guarding for the past twenty or so years was about to be revealed unless he trod very carefully during his return visit to Blois. If her true former identity were to be revealed, he faced the prospect of a treason trial at worst, and disgrace and dismissal from office at the very least.

The lady who had borne him first a daughter called Elinor, then a son called Richard, was of the House of Blois itself, and she was the half-sister of the man who now ruled the Duchy. Emma, the illegitimate daughter of the former Count Stephen, had been pledged to marry the Royal Treasurer Herbert of Winchester. However, on the vessel bringing her across the Channel, she had swapped identities with one of her ladies in waiting called Melusine, so that she could make a life with Thomas and Elinor, the daughter she had already borne him.

Melusine had been the one wedded to Herbert of Winchester, posing as Emma. The real Emma had assumed that name for several years, until those residing on the Walsingham estate had been encouraged to call her 'Emma', ignorant of the fact that this was her true name. Only Thomas's cousin Elston, who had married them before his untimely death, and Thomas's parents had been aware of her true identity, along with his sister Matilda. His mother, Joan, had died five years previously, and his father, Wilfrid, now well into his seventies, would shortly take the secret to his grave. This only left Matilda — or Tilly, as he called her — childlessly married to a former physician from Blois who had accompanied Emma across the Channel. He had died only last year, leaving Matilda a middle-aged widow dedicated to the work of the orphanage that had been created at Walsingham.

Thomas had one more shock to the system awaiting him as he headed towards the Gatehouse, intent on making a spot check of its alertness. He heard his name being called, and turned to where his lieutenant, John Loverseed, was striding after him.

'I heard you were with the king, so I sought you there. You have a visitor. He says he is your son, so I bade him wait in your business chamber. I have had the fire lit.'

'Thank you, John,' Thomas replied as he tried to keep the surprise from his face. *Richard, here at Windsor?* It was a four-day ride, even by fast horse, and the tidings could not be good. He lengthened his stride and hurriedly opened the chamber door to reveal the figure warming himself by the fire, long, lean, mud-splattered and white of face. They embraced, then Thomas pushed Richard back to gaze into his distraught eyes. 'What is it, Dickon?'

'It's Grandfather,' he was advised. 'He's taken to his deathbed, and is refusing food and drink until he has spoken with you. For pity's sake, ride back with me! I have already spent two horses, but we can make it back by the third day, if we foreswear sleep.'

III

Thomas and Richard reached the doorway of the manor house and dismounted. Richard immediately collapsed into the inch or so of snow that had fallen during their final night forcing their way north from Cambridge, and he lay there giggling with exhaustion. Thomas moved with stiffened thighs that made his gait resemble that of a child's toy soldier, and he leaned down to pull his son from the ground just as a cry of welcome was heard from the doorway.

'So soon!' Tilly called as she scuttled across the light snow in her outdoor sandals and embraced her brother.

Thomas smiled into Matilda's eyes, and noted the extra wrinkles that had formed around them since he'd last seen her. 'Widowhood has given you care lines,' he remarked.

'They were there already, given that my brother regularly embarks on journeys that take him far away and endanger his life.'

'How is Father?'

'He'll be all the better for seeing you again, anyway, and perhaps we can persuade him to eat. Brother Benedict from Ely, who's their Infirmarian, has tried every ploy he can think of, but the stubborn old warhorse refuses to partake of a morsel until he's spoken with you. Whatever it is, he clearly deems it to be of the highest importance. I'll let him know that you're back with us, and then ply him with some of my broth, but by the look of you two it will be tomorrow before you get to speak with him. Go inside and fill your stomachs from the gruel pot — there's fresh bread on the griddle. I'll have bolsters taken into the guest chambers and order that fires be lit. Now — inside, both of you!'

Thomas slept like the dead for a day and a half, and it was the late afternoon of his second day back at Walsingham before he stepped quietly into his father's bedchamber and all but tiptoed towards the bed.

'I'm not dead yet, so no need for the respectful footfall,' came the stern response from the grizzled old veteran.

Thomas chuckled as he lowered himself onto the side of the pallet and took his father's hand in his. 'I only hope that God grants me as many years as he has you,' he murmured, a tear forming in his eye, at which Wilfrid tutted.

'There's such a thing as living *too* long, as I'm beginning to learn. Your brain arises from slumber before your body's ready for another day's challenge, and you spend the first hour of the morning checking which parts of you are still in service.'

Thomas chuckled. 'You've seen so much in your long life, have you not?'

'I've lived through the reigns of four kings in all. First there was Earl Harold of Wessex, who become King Harold for long enough to die just above the village where I was raised and taught to grind corn by my father, God rest his soul. Then the dreadful William from Normandy, who slaughtered anyone who wouldn't fall down and worship the ground under his mailed foot, even though they couldn't understand a word he was saying. We thought he was bad, but then his dissolute son Rufus took matters even further, and saw his people simply as a means of raising revenue for his vile games.'

'It was he who imprisoned you,' Thomas added. 'I remember that well enough, since I determined to raise an army and lay siege to the Tower. If Rufus hadn't died when he did, I would probably have been executed as an enemy rebel. But our current king had you released, the Lord be praised, and we both went into his service.'

'You're still a hothead,' Wilfrid admonished him, 'and that son of yours is no better. Worse, if anything. He spends all day, every day, reminding me of you — constantly demanding to be allowed to go out in the world and achieve fame and fortune. But as it transpires, it did you no harm — a beautiful wife and a daughter to match her in looks. A pity about my hot-headed grandson, all the same.'

'A case of a branch falling too close to a tree,' Thomas smiled. 'I was told by Aunt Elva — or "Mother Grace" as of course I must call her now — that when you were only the same age as Richard, you thought you'd killed the son of a thegn in your village and ran away to become a soldier. Then in later life you deserted the king's service to come here. Were those the actions of a level-headed man?'

'Do you remember first coming here?' Wilfrid enquired as he propped himself up against the bolster head with assistance from Thomas, who shook his head.

'My first memory is of being here, and fighting with Geoffrey. I remember that his mother was in charge here at the time.'

'Richeldis de Faverches was a wonderful lady, and a truly spiritual person,' Wilfrid reminisced. 'She truly believed that the shrine that sits in the manor garden was built by the Virgin Mary herself. There was no craftsman around here who would admit to having constructed it, so perhaps it was true. It was already here when we arrived, fugitives from what they called "The Harrowing of the North". The Lady Richeldis took us in, and we formed our own little army, or "Fyrd", as armies were called in those days. Then your Uncle Selwyn was killed when

21

we rode out against a brigand called Hereward, and your Aunt Elva became a nun, then eventually progressed to being "Mother Grace" when Lady Richeldis died. Then in recognition of our action in ridding the nation of Hereward, King William granted me the estate. But now the time has come to give it back, which is why I summoned you here.'

'You're handing the estate back to the Crown?'

'No, to Sir Geoffrey, your old childhood rival. Although in one sense it will be going back to the rightful King of England. You know of his ancestry, of course?'

'Indeed, he never stopped reminding me of it in our younger days, before we went on those Crusades to which he was so devoted, and his mother revealed the truth of his birth to him. His father was the King Harold to whom you referred earlier, was he not?'

'He was indeed, in the days when Lady Richeldis was known as "Edith Swan Neck". But that isn't why I'm bequeathing him the estate. I'm doing so for two reasons. The first is that neither you nor Richard have shown any interest in maintaining it, and the second is that it is lawfully his anyway, in right of his mother Richeldis. Being the wonderfully generous and spiritual lady that she was, she never once demurred when King William gave it to me. Now I intend to honour that purity of spirit by ensuring that it goes back to her son.'

'He's no farmer, any more than I am,' Thomas protested.

'But he would seem to have inherited his mother's religious fervour, and he wishes to found a priory here.'

'And what will happen to us? For that matter, what will happen to the existing convent, and the orphanage?'

'That is for you all to work out,' his father advised him. 'I am down for death fairly soon, as my old bones constantly remind me. By my calculation you have less than a year in which to sort your own destinies, so I recommend that you begin to do so without delay.'

The following evening, those whose futures hung in the balance sat around the long table in the main hall of the manor house, too nervous to do true justice to the magnificent spread that Cook had produced on instruction from Matilda. She was generally regarded as the true head of the estate, given her father's frailty and bed-bound condition. Thomas announced their father's intention of bequeathing the estate to Sir Geoffrey de Faverches, and it was Sir Geoffrey who was the first to speak.

'I realise that this will have come as a great shock to you all, but none of you need have any apprehension regarding your futures. My sole ambition is to found a priory on the estate land that lies across the river, and matters on this side may remain as they are. Mother Grace may continue with the excellent sister house founded by my late mother of blessed memory. Given that these uncertain times seem destined to create a steady flow of orphans, I'd be grateful if Matilda could continue to maintain the orphanage, perhaps under the spiritual guidance of Mother Grace. I know that Tilly has for some time been contemplating taking the veil, and I would welcome Sister Matilda into our spiritual fold with open arms.'

The contented sighs from the senior ladies in question left little doubt that this arrangement was acceptable, but clearly it did not cover everyone, and Geoffrey continued.

'The ones hardest hit by Sir Wilfrid's bequest will of course be his son Thomas, his grandson Richard and his granddaughter Elinor, and they must of course choose what course to take. I wish there to be no doubt that they still have a home here should they wish, and that their chambers in the manor house are theirs for as long as they need them. But my childhood friend and former Crusade companion Sir Thomas will, I imagine, wish to continue his honourable career as Captain of the Palace Guard, so it remains for Richard and Elinor to choose a future that best accords with their ambitions.'

'So I can become a knight at last?' Richard demanded.

Geoffrey burst out laughing. 'Spoken like your father before you!' he guffawed as he leaned to one side to clap his hand on Richard's shoulder. 'He and I would set about each other on the grass above the shrine with make-believe swords made of tree branches, while our mothers looked on proudly and Thomas's father shook his head in disapproval.'

'See?' Richard responded with a look of triumph towards the head of the table, where his father sat, grimacing down at Geoffrey.

'What Sir Geoffrey omitted to mention was that I usually won,' he grumbled, 'and he's waited all these years to repay me by encouraging my son to make the same foolish mistakes that I did. Be wary of what you wish for, Richard.'

'So I may return with you to London and begin to make my fortune in battle?' Richard demanded eagerly, and his father gave a reluctant nod.

'Fortunes may indeed be made on the battlefield, but it is also the place where arms, legs and lives may be lost. If you are pig-headed enough to pursue your idle dream, then I would that you do so under my supervision and training. You may accompany me as my squire, that is all, and I will control your every engagement in the field.'

'And what of me?' Elinor pouted from further down the table, where she was seated next to her Aunt Tilly. 'You men are all mouth and bravado. It is as if the world has only one sex in it, until it comes to marriage, childbirth and heirs to fortunes. You speak as if only plunder and battle honours came back with Father from Blois, when in fact he came back with my mother. She may have been dead these five years, of the same fever that took my grandmother Joan, but she passed on as much wisdom to me as Father seems to have done to Richard. She taught me that women may acquire fortunes of their own by marrying into the wealthiest houses of the realm. My mother's beauty earned her my father, and it has been kindly spoken by many that I have inherited some of her appeal. I would therefore wish to be presented at Court, in order to test my ability to become the lady of some well-endowed lord. And by "well-endowed" I do not just mean money.'

Her father all but choked on his venison. Geoffrey blushed bright red, while Mother Grace tutted and Tilly suppressed a giggle. Then it fell awkwardly silent until Thomas picked up the conversation.

'Never let it be said that this father abandoned his daughter to the perils of maidenhood on an isolated Norfolk estate. Particularly not a daughter who seems to already possess too much worldly knowledge. I give you the same words of caution as I gave to your brother, Elinor, namely that the world out there is wicked and dangerous. The Court of England, albeit blessed with a benign monarch this time around, is nevertheless as pitted with opportunities for a fatal end as any battlefield. The courtiers who hang around the throne are, in their own way, as vicious and rapacious as any warrior, and their objectives are no more honourable. I will of course take you with me, and let us see where your beauty may lead you. But be advised that your loving father will ever be looking over your shoulder, and any unwanted hand that may be laid upon you will be removed from the arm that accompanies it.'

'Spoken like a true father, not that I have any experience in that regard,' Geoffrey beamed. 'It would seem that we are all sorted into our future roles, so let us give thanks to God, not just for this excellent repast, but for the love that He beams down on us all.'

Upon their arrival at Windsor, where Thomas lost no time in resuming his duties, they learned that King Henry was due to remarry. His new bride was Adeliza of Louvain, a beautiful eighteen-year-old with German connections who, it was rumoured, had been chosen for Henry by his daughter Maude in the hope that it would strengthen England's alliance with the Holy Roman Empire.

Like other royal officials, Thomas had been well aware that Henry was courting the entrancing, if somewhat naive, beauty, as a replacement for the dead queen. But there had been no wedding announcement prior to the recent death of William Adelin, and it was being mooted around the royal palaces that the sudden announcement was due in no small part to Henry's need to sire another male heir while he was still capable. He was now in his early fifties, and time was running out for the continuation of the dynasty founded by William of Normandy.

Thomas was fully occupied in the duty of securing the safety of his Majesty and his new bride when they were married in the chapel at Windsor in January of 1121. He was able to leave Richard and Elinor to settle into the somewhat cramped apartments he commissioned for them inside the south wall of the Bailey. The traditional honeymoon period of two weeks, spent largely indoors due to the inclement weather, meant that it was well into the first few weeks of spring before the family were granted an audience, and King Henry and Queen Adeliza smiled encouragingly at the new faces.

'You bring another warrior to my banner,' Henry observed as he gazed appreciatively at Richard. 'And one, what is more, that is even longer in the body than his father. Can he fight yet?'

'Only with shadows and blunted blades,' Thomas smiled. 'But he comes from a long line of those who can, and once could, so there is hope for him. However, if I might make so bold, I would offer him as a fit companion for your ... for Robert of Gloucester. He will ride in my train, but will be rostered into the earl's bodyguard as both a protector and a student of diplomacy. I hope that by these means he will progress his career in such a way that his head will not be cleft from his shoulders ere he reaches his thirtieth year.'

'It shall be as you wish,' Henry nodded sadly, 'since I know only too well how the loss of a son sits heavily on the heart.'

'But what of the elegant young lady?' the queen enquired. 'Does she seek to serve in the royal house in some capacity? I fear that her natural beauty will be her undoing, since few of the ladies here at Court could tolerate being so outshone in looks by those who braid their hair or assist them into their gowns.'

'I have a suggestion in that regard,' Henry offered. 'We have received word from our daughter Maude that she is headed for Normandy for a brief period, in order to meet with us and share our grief for the loss of William Adelin. She is unlikely to bring many of her German ladies with her, so perhaps the Lady Elinor might wish to be considered as a companion for our royal daughter upon her arrival?'

'I feel sure that she would,' Thomas replied, 'since she is already so gifted in matters of dress and decorum.'

'She is also capable of speech on her own account,' Elinor replied, bridling, 'and she would be delighted to accept such a gracious opportunity.'

Henry chuckled. 'You sired a fiery one there, Thomas.'

The queen smiled and added, 'You and Maude will be well matched, Elinor Walsingham. She also declines to let her sex get in the way of her wit.'

As they walked back out into the early spring sunshine, Thomas placed an arm around each of their shoulders.

'You would both seem to have taken the first steps on your chosen careers. But be warned — it will not always be that easy, and I will not always be at your backs.'

IV

Thomas stood diplomatically in the shade of the Guardhouse doorway as he watched Richard thrusting, parrying, lunging and side-stepping with all the skill of an experienced swordsman under the tutelage of John Loverseed, Thomas's lieutenant and second in command. He smiled with fatherly pride at the speed with which Richard had taken to knightly activity, then felt a chill up his spine when he realised that this could only result in Richard demanding to be at the forefront of any future military action.

Thomas was committed to taking Richard with him everywhere as his squire, and allowing him every opportunity to earn his knightly spurs, but as a father he could only pray that future events would not necessitate renewed conflict across the Channel, which in recent years had proved to be never-ending. Hopefully any future disputes that King Henry got himself involved in could be settled by diplomacy.

He stepped out of the shadows as the two men rested their swords. Richard walked across to the armoury while John walked back towards the Guardhouse, grinning at Thomas.

'For someone raised at the Shrine of Walsingham, your boy shows great promise and much in the way of existing skill, sir. Is it in his blood, or do the nuns of the convent there teach swordplay as well as fingering their beads?'

Thomas gave a wry chuckle. 'My Aunt Elva — "Mother Grace" as she now is — would box your ears were you to suggest that she would engage in anything so unspiritual.'

'So Richard owes his prowess to you?'

'So it would seem, although I've spent all the eighteen years of his life thus far trying to dissuade him from developing it. You know as well as I how even the strongest knight can fall in battle due to some ill fate that was not of his devising. I fear for Richard, as you would no doubt fear for any son of your own. It is to be hoped that future bloodshed may be avoided by the employment of oily tongues.'

'Talking of which,' John replied, 'when will you leave for Normandy, and will I be left in charge in your absence?'

'You may rest assured of that, John, but as for when, that may depend upon the king's health, not to mention his mood. His spirits have been lifted somewhat by news that the Empress Maude is journeying to the *Château de Caen* in order to join her father in mourning. This should speed his departure, and we simply await the arrival of Robert of Gloucester in order to assemble our company for travel.'

'So this will not be simply a family reunion? If Robert Fitzroy is in attendance on his father, then this bodes further diplomacy among the nobles of Northern Europe, does it not?'

'So it is to be hoped, rather than further warfare. I am to command the royal escort, while offering my son Richard as a bodyguard to Robert as he learns something of the duties and skills of an ambassador. Has he sufficient martial ability to act as a bodyguard, would you say?'

'Without doubt, but you must surely wish him to be more engaged in diplomacy?'

'Fervently, John, fervently. While he is developing an oily tongue, he will have no use for his sword arm, and may hopefully progress to old age with his limbs intact.'

Two weeks later, Thomas stood on the ramparts above the gatehouse of the *Château de Caen* — in reality a heavily fortified castle built by King Henry's father Duke William of Normandy — alongside Robert of Gloucester as they watched the imperial train passing under them and into the outer bailey that gave access to the main dwellings. The Empress Maude was in the centre, riding side-saddle on a white palfrey and surrounded by men at arms in the livery of the royal house of her husband, Henry V of Germany.

Robert snorted quietly. 'As usual, she wishes our father to believe that she has become the demure lady, when she would much prefer to ride astride like the men around her. When we were growing up under the care of Archbishop Anselm, while our father was clashing steel with my Uncle Robert, we would often steal out into the countryside, where she would challenge me to race. I've seen her clear a six-foot hedge and remain on the back of her mount — believe me when I advise you that she is a wildcat in a gown.'

Thomas reminded himself that although they were only half-siblings — and no-one was sure who Robert's mother had been — they had been close friends for most of Maude's eighteen years, even though for the past decade she'd been married to Holy Roman Emperor Charles V, a man sixteen years her senior, and resident in the Palatinate that came with the imperial title. Although Robert was from King Henry's loins, his illegitimacy ruled him out of the succession, yet he had never once been known to display any enmity towards his half-sister Maude, or before her the former heir to the throne William Adelin. This made him a perfect ambassador for his father, and Thomas had no doubt that his services were about to be employed to the maximum, if all-out war between the rulers of Northern Europe was to be avoided.

'Wildcat or no, she is fair of countenance,' Thomas observed, not entirely diplomatically.

Robert nodded. 'More's the pity that she was married off at the age of eight, before her true beauty revealed itself. Now she is bound to an old man.'

'A man merely of your own age, surely?' Thomas teased him gently.

'Indeed, and believe me, there are days when I feel much older than my thirty years. But my point was that had Father waited until her mature beauty was on full display, he might have put that to greater use.'

'Surely, an alliance with the Holy Roman Empire is of considerable value to England in its ongoing disputes with Louis of France?' Thomas argued.

Robert snorted. 'Louis the Fat — "*le Gros*", as even his subjects call him? These days he can barely mount a horse. No, my friend, the current danger comes not from Louis himself, but the many minor monarchs who surround our estates here in Normandy. Blois, Maine, Flanders, the Vexin and so on. It would be far better if my sister were married off to one of those, to prevent them forming alliances under Louis' nominal banner. That is why I am summoned to attend this reunion between father and daughter — that I might then journey into neighbouring lands and report on the state of their loyalty to my father.'

'Taking my son with you as your bodyguard,' Thomas reminded him ruefully. 'I would deem it a personal favour if you would refrain from putting your life in such danger that he is obliged to unsheathe his weapon.'

Robert looked sideways at him. 'I need little persuasion not to hazard my own neck, Sir Thomas. That is what diplomacy is all about — conveying unpleasant messages from one ruler to another without reaping the consequences. I am fortunate that it is no longer traditional to kill the messenger, as it once was.'

'Hopefully you will impart those skills to Richard, so your father might think of him as more of an ambassador than a warrior.'

'No doubt your own father had similar hopes for you,' Robert smiled, 'and yet you fought your way to high office as Captain of the Palace Guard.'

'This is true,' Thomas admitted, 'and I defied him, as Richard seems determined to defy me. But circumstances were different in those days when my father served yours, and the royal brothers were forever feuding.'

Robert sighed. 'It has never really ended. Little did William of Normandy realise, when he sired three sons, that their squabbles would render the northern lands of the former Kingdom of Francia into a permanent battlefield.'

'Not just the brothers,' Thomas reminded him. 'At least one sister caused further unrest when she married into the House of Blois.'

'Indeed,' Robert chuckled. 'My Aunt Adela's marriage to Count Stephen was the cause of your need to defend our southern shores against Duke Robert, was it not, when the two rose up against my father?'

'Indeed, but it was Count Stephen who first knighted me, when I served by his side on Crusade. Your father graciously endorsed that title when I fought alongside my father against the joint invasion.'

'And you married into the nobility of Blois, did you not?' Robert probed.

Thomas felt the familiar chill as he hoped that Robert's sources of information had not gone more deeply into the matter of his marriage than that. 'Indeed, but no more of that, since the death of my wife still pains me, five years after the event, and the mere mention of those days is like to reawaken my grief. For that reason I shall not travel to Blois with you, should you be sent there. Given our current peaceful relations with Count Theobald, you should be in no danger.'

'As you wish. Now let us leave this windy spot and seek some dinner ere we venture to intrude upon the family reunion down below us.'

As it transpired it was the following day before Thomas, Richard and Elinor were summoned into the Great Hall, where they stood alongside Robert of Gloucester to offer their formal welcomes to the Empress Maude. Thomas's only memory of her was as a slim, agile, flaxen-haired girl of five or six years of age who was forever attempting to sneak a small horse from the stables at Windsor. More than once he'd been obliged to take her by the hand and return her to the governess from whom she'd escaped. He smiled as he looked up at the self-assured lady that she'd become.

For Richard and Elinor it was a first meeting. Elinor was entranced by the elegance of the blue gown that was draped around Maude, who sat on a padded bench beside her father, with her new stepmother on the other side. Maude saw the wide-eyed look on Elinor's face and smiled as she beckoned her over.

'You would seem to like it,' she smiled at Elinor as she indicated the gown with a wave of her heavily jewelled hand, then noticed that Elinor's rapt attention had transferred to the rings and bracelets. 'You are in awe of beautiful things, but surely men must besiege you with such finery, given your own beauty?'

When Elinor remained tongue-tied, Maude reached out and took her hand as she drew her down onto the bench. Queen Adeliza shifted slightly to make way for her, and Thomas and Richard stood, open-mouthed at the familiarity.

'You see — I don't bite,' Maude assured Elinor. 'You may speak your mind.'

Elinor finally found her voice. 'You must forgive me, Your — my lady — but it's my first time at Court, and I'm unsure of how one is expected to behave.'

Maude grinned. 'Would that everyone behaved as you do, since then we could be assured of their sincerity. Let's begin with your name, shall we?'

'It's Elinor,' Thomas advised.

Maude's eyes flashed. 'Did I ask you?' she demanded. 'The girl can speak for herself.'

Thomas dropped his eyes to the floor, and King Henry chuckled.

'You have spirit, daughter, but I will thank you to leave it to me to put the Captain of the Palace Guard in his place. He is Sir Thomas Walsingham, and the lady whose hand you have taken for ransom is his daughter Elinor. The young man with Sir Thomas is Elinor's brother Richard. Father and son serve me, and we had hoped that Elinor could be taken into your service.'

'I would be delighted to have her in such a capacity, but I fear that her beauty would outshine me wherever we went. Whence come those dark eyes and that shining black hair, young Elinor?'

'From my mother, my lady,' Elinor all but whispered. 'She was from Aquitaine, or so she advised me. Seemingly the dark features are normal among ladies there, unlike our own women, who tend towards white skin and red hair.'

35

'Like mine, you mean?' Maude teased her, then chuckled at the look of horror on Elinor's face. 'I must apologise for my puckish humour — I did not mean to appear offended. I simply state the obvious, namely that all of us from the original House of Normandy seem to come with the same hair colour and florid countenance. In my childhood I wished that it were not so, but it has not betrayed me. I am Empress of Germany — did they tell you that?'

'Yes, my lady. But you are also heir to the English throne, are you not?' Elinor enquired without any sarcasm.

Maude smiled. 'You must have noticed that I am a woman, so how can I be heir to England?'

'Because your father is the king.'

'My husband is the Holy Roman Emperor, but that does not mean that I will inherit that. Has life not taught you that this world is ruled by men?'

'Our estate certainly is,' Elinor smiled back. 'It is in Norfolk.'

'So why do you wish to travel to Germany?'

'I do not. I simply wish to serve you at Court.'

'And you shall, but not the German Court, since it is a dreadful place. The food is vile, the conditions are brutal, the men smell worse than their horses, and the weather is dreary. I would not subject someone as naturally beautiful and delicate as you to such torture, but when I am in England you may indeed attend upon me.'

Elinor's face lit up as she turned triumphantly to her father and brother. 'When do we travel back?' she asked eagerly, and Maude gave a ringing laugh.

'Would that it could be soon, but I must return to my husband within the week. I am allowed here only for long enough to bring comfort of sorts to my father, then I am bidden to return.'

'You have no choice of your own?'

Maude shook her head. 'That is the way for all married women, whether they marry kings, emperors or woodcutters. They must do as their husbands bid them.'

'Then I shall take no husband,' Elinor insisted with a grimace.

'You will live your life without a man or children?'

Elinor turned slightly pink, dropped her gaze and whispered, 'I said only that I would not marry.'

Maude burst out laughing and patted Elinor's cheek playfully as she looked across at her father. 'I would have this one awaiting me when next I journey to my homeland. Would that I need not return to Germany!' With that she rose and walked sedately out of the chamber, leaving the remainder of the company to gaze after her.

King Henry was the first to break the silence. 'As wilful and determined as her grandfather, as you can see. Would that she *could* inherit, but the barons would feel too greatly challenged, I fear. However, she would seem to have taken to your daughter, Sir Thomas. Does Elinor always form such easy bonds with those of her own sex?'

'To tell the truth,' Thomas replied uneasily, 'she has rarely journeyed beyond our estate, where there are none to be found who can so easily engage her interest. But our daughters would seem to be content in each other's company.'

'Indeed, and I shall give instruction that she is to be added to those who attend upon my daughter when she is in England, although as you heard for yourself that will not be either soon or often. In the meantime, I would have Elinor accompany the Lady Matilde when you return her to her home in Anjou. Robert, you and I must discuss the terms of your stern message to her father, Count Fulk. The rest of you may withdraw.'

'Don't let it go to your head,' Thomas advised Elinor as they crossed the ground towards their temporary apartments. 'Maude has a reputation for being headstrong and wayward, and may well have forgotten you ere she sets foot back in England. We must now look to our immediate duties, and we are, it would seem, next destined for Anjou.'

It was a journey that took almost a week, given the slow pace necessitated by the litter carrying the young Lady Matilde back to her homeland following the death of her intended bridegroom William Adeline. The track took them south out of Normandy through Maine, large portions of which had been intended as Matilde's dowry, although King Henry of England had long maintained that Maine was under the suzerainty of Normandy. Any fractious warfare that these competing claims might have generated had been averted by the intended marriage, but given recent events there was now a distinct risk that Anjou and England would be meeting on a battlefield somewhere within the pleasant farmland through which the procession was picking its way. Elinor was riding alongside the Lady Matilde and chatting away in her best French, the product of many hours in the schoolroom at Walsingham under the stern tutelage of Brother Francis from the nearby Abbey of Ely.

'What instructions did the king give you?' Thomas enquired casually of Robert on the final day of their journey. The castle at Angers had come into sight on the hill that rose above the wetlands through which they were meandering.

'My message is for Count Fulk only,' Robert replied with a diplomatic smile, 'but it would be as well for you to make great display of these men at arms who accompany us, in case the old tradition of killing the messenger has suddenly been revived by these peasants. Certainly I will require both you and your sword alongside me when I impart what I have to say. You might also invite Richard to attend with us, for his first lesson in wrapping the unacceptable in a pleasant package.'

Thomas was holding his breath later that evening when they were admitted into the presence of Count Fulk. Robert delivered first the deep regret of his king that the two houses were not to be united in matrimony, and second the fact that while the Lady Matilde had been safely returned, Henry of England did not intend to return the estates that had been her dowry, since they rightly belonged to Normandy anyway.

Fulk appeared to have been forewarned of this, since there was only a slight frown on his face as he nodded his acknowledgment, then replied, 'You may advise your king that his claim to the lands of Maine is, as ever, disputed, and furthermore that they will now form the dowry of my second daughter Sybilla to William Clito. This match has the blessing of Louis of France.'

'Since William Clito is my master's nephew,' Robert replied tactfully, 'then at least Maine will remain notionally within the family. But its physical occupation is of course another matter.'

'Is that a declaration of war?' Fulk demanded as the colour rose in his face. 'If so, then I shall be obliged to regard you all as my first prisoners in the engagement. And tell your man to remove his hand from his sword hilt, or it will be cut off by those of my own retinue who surround you.'

'Do as he says,' Robert whispered hoarsely to Thomas, whose actions had been instinctive. As he whispered an apology, Robert turned back to Count Fulk with a smile that was as pleasant as it was false. 'I am merely an ambassador of his Majesty King Henry, and the man by my side is merely my personal bodyguard.'

'And the taller one attempting to hide behind you?' Fulk demanded with a stern glare at Richard.

'His son,' Robert replied, 'who is merely in attendance to learn of the burdens borne by ambassadors.'

'Tell your father that his continued refusal to acknowledge the right of Anjou to occupy Maine will be reported to Louis of France. You have safe escort from my lands, provided that you depart on the morrow. And tell King Henry that his bastard son is a poor ambassador.'

'That could have been worse,' Robert chuckled the following morning as they set out on their return at a much faster pace. He turned in his saddle to address Richard. 'You showed greater restraint than your father, who was rash enough to finger his sword hilt in the presence of our surly host. There is hope for you in the ambassadorial service. Let us see how you fare in Blois and Evreux, where we are bound next.'

'I shall leave you to undertake that portion of your journey with only Richard as your companion at arms, and I'll board a ship back across the Channel from Barfleur, taking Elinor with me,' Thomas announced. When Robert raised an enquiring eyebrow, while Richard allowed himself a satisfied smile, Thomas explained, 'For one, I need to return to Westminster, in order to ensure that the Palace Guard is in all ways prepared for the intended return of King Henry. Secondly, I believe that Elinor has seen enough of France for one season. And, most importantly, I left Blois on the most recent occasion under something of a cloud, and later stood at arms against its former count, Stephen, when he invaded England along with Duke Robert.'

'As you wish,' Robert replied stonily, 'and let us hope that your son has learned sufficient in the matter of swordplay to guard the king's ambassador — *and* bastard son, as we were recently reminded.'

V

Five days later, Robert and Richard were the honoured guests at a banquet hosted within the ducal palace of Blois by its current duke, Theobald. Richard was particularly intrigued by everything he could see around him, given that these halls must once have been home to his late mother. According to his father, she had been a lady in service to the Lady Emma, allegedly an illegitimate but much favoured daughter of the late Count Stephen.

The usual diplomatic overtures were exchanged. Robert conveyed messages of love and affection from King Henry to the ducal brothers Geoffrey, Theobald and Stephen, given that they were all his nephews by virtue of their mother having been Henry's sister, Adela of Normandy. Richard had been warned in advance that these genial formalities were merely a cover for a much more important message that Robert had for the older brother and Duke Theobald. Therefore, Richard was to amuse himself as best he could the following morning.

He was doing precisely that, strolling casually along the southern battlements and gazing admiringly down at the River Loire that flowed some sixty feet below him, when a liveried page appeared. 'Master Stephen wishes audience with you,' he advised.

Somewhat surprised that it was he, and not Robert, with whom the count's younger brother wished to converse, Richard followed dutifully behind the page, and was led into a luxurious chamber on the second floor that was part of Stephen's private apartments. He nodded appreciatively when Stephen, who was alone, offered to have wine brought in for their consumption, and waved Richard into a padded and highly decorated bench seat by the window. Stephen then sat down beside him, leaving only a few feet between them.

Richard felt obliged to say something. 'To what do I owe this honour? I am merely an attendant to the man who represents King Henry.'

'You are more than that,' Stephen smiled back knowingly. 'You are my nephew, and I am your uncle.'

Richard was open-mouthed and incredulous. 'How can *that* be?' he demanded. 'My father has no brothers and only one sister, who is a childless widow devoted to operating an orphanage on our family estate in Norfolk.'

'And your mother?' Stephen enquired with a conspiratorial smile. 'What do you know of her?'

'That she was from here in Blois, certainly. But she was a lady in waiting to the Lady Emma, and travelled to England when Emma married the royal Treasurer.'

Stephen's smile widened, but took on a faint look of pity. 'So you were told the same as everyone else on your estate, clearly. The time has come for you to learn the truth of the matter. You may wish to consume some of that wine, if only to mellow the shock of what you are about to learn.'

Richard took a deep draught of the wine in his goblet as Stephen gazed out of the window glass and continued as if talking to himself.

'It is true that the Lady Emma travelled to England as the intended bride of Herbert of Winchester. She was of course my sister by blood, although a bastard who my mother — the Countess Adela — would never accept or recognise, despite her being our father's favourite. She was beautiful, with the dark eyes and hair typical of the women of Aquitaine, where her mother was residing when my lusty father bedded her.

43

What do you remember of your own mother's appearance, pray?'

'Just as you describe,' Richard conceded. 'Dark hair and eyes, which both my sister Elinor and I have inherited, although in Elinor it is deemed beauty.'

'Precisely,' Stephen nodded. 'And you were told that your mother's true name was "Melusine", and that she had been a lady attendant upon the Lady Emma, were you not?'

'Correct, but what of it?'

Stephen gave a triumphant smile as he swirled the last of his wine in his goblet, drained it, then held it out for the page to refill. The silence lay heavy as he awaited the page's return to his corner of the chamber. Then he continued quietly: 'Melusine had bright red hair and blue eyes, and she was the biggest whore at the Court of Aquitaine.'

'You call my mother a whore?' Richard protested as his hand flew to his sword hilt, but Stephen remained unmoved as he gently shook his head.

'No, because she was *not* your mother. Your mother was Emma of Blois.'

'How can *that* be, if Emma married Herbert of Winchester?'

'She didn't. The woman who married Herbert of Winchester was Melusine. Given her skills in the bedchamber, she no doubt gave such great satisfaction that the old fool never thought to question his good fortune.'

'And this miracle came about *how*, precisely?' Richard demanded sceptically.

'On the vessel that brought the two women to your shores at Portsmouth, they exchanged identities. No-one in England, other than your father, knew what Emma looked like, and both were beautiful women in different ways. But Emma already had a child in her arms — your sister Elinor.'

'So ... that is ... my father and she...?'

'Indeed, many times — under this very roof, as it transpires. When the terms of the Treaty of Alton — between King Henry on the one hand and my father and Duke Robert on the other — incorporated the marriage contract between Herbert of Winchester and Emma of Blois, there was clearly a need for urgent action, and the exchange of identities was the one selected by your mother. She and your sister were smuggled north to your estate, where no doubt she called herself "Melusine" for the remainder of her life.'

'No,' Richard replied hoarsely. 'We were told that those on the estate found her name difficult, so she asked to be called "Emma". But did Herbert of Winchester never come to realise how he had been deceived? Surely, when Emma's — my mother's — family came to visit, or she journeyed back here, the secret would have been revealed?'

'Which is why Melusine never returned, and also discouraged any visits from us. It was not until Herbert died two years ago, and his widow failed to return to us, that our suspicions were aroused, and I was sent across the Channel to investigate.'

'And?'

'And I quickly learned two things. The first was that the widow had received a generous endowment, which she took in the form of coin. She then headed north in the company of the former under-steward with whom she had, it was confided to me, been consorting for some time. I also received a very detailed description of her — a voluptuous seductress with flowing red hair and the sort of bodily curves that would set your teeth on edge. My sister Emma was beautiful in her own way, but not like that.'

'But how can you be certain that this "Emma" was my mother?' Richard enquired.

Stephen smiled. 'The so-called ambassador in whose train you travel has a loose tongue for someone of that calling. I was suspicious that there might have been some sort of false practice at the time of Emma's arrival in England, so I simply brought my conversation with Robert Fitzroy round to the family background of his companion — yourself. I was hardly surprised when your father chose not to show his face back in Blois, and I had already noted your dark features, so when Robert spoke so enthusiastically of your sister's dark beauty, I was left with no remaining doubt. We are uncle and nephew.'

'And why are you advising me of this? For that matter, have you disclosed your knowledge to your brother Theobald, the current count?'

'Not as such, although he was able to confirm what our father had confided in him, namely that our beloved sister had consorted with your father during his visits here on behalf of the young King Henry. It was known that she had travelled back to Aquitaine in order to give birth to your sister, and that she was carrying her in her arms when she finally departed Blois to go to England. There was also a physician in her train who specialised in the rearing of infants, but what eventually happened to him I have no idea.'

'His name was Armand, and he married my Aunt Matilda,' Richard replied quietly. 'He died two years ago, of a fever.'

'Thank you, that would seem to complete the picture. More wine?'

'No, thank you, my head is already reeling with what you have disclosed. But presumably you did so with some purpose in mind other than a joyous family reunion?'

'Perhaps you should be the ambassador, rather than the over-garrulous Robert Fitzroy. You perceive correctly, and for reasons of my own I have not disclosed the full extent of my knowledge even to my brother Theobald.'

'Why not, pray?'

Stephen looked quickly around the chamber, to ensure that only the page was in attendance in the corner. He lowered his voice. 'Robert of Gloucester came bearing portentous tidings regarding the future of the throne of England.' He pulled at Richard's sleeve in order to engage his full attention. 'How would you like to occupy high office in your native realm?'

'That would be my ultimate ambition, certainly, but what had you in mind?'

'You are aware that your King Henry is now without a male heir, and that his only legitimate offspring is the Empress Maude?'

'Indeed — it must be common knowledge throughout all nations. So what?'

'Well, it would seem that Henry is desperate enough in his search for a male heir to have cast his net sideways. In the same way that you are my nephew, my brothers and myself are his, since our mother was his sister Adela.'

'And he offers you the crown?'

'So we were advised by Robert when we met with him privily yesterday. One of us will in due course be declared his heir, if there is no further male issue.'

'You are of course aware that he has recently taken a new bride, and that the current queen is not only of childbearing age, but also most comely of feature?'

'Of course, but your king is now entering those years of his life in which his seed will not flow either so freely or so fruitfully. There may well be *no* new male heir.'

'And then your brother Theobald will become King of England as well as Count of Blois?'

'And why should he, simply because he emerged from between our mother's thighs two years before me? Why should one brother inherit everything, while the other is left a comparative pauper?'

'So you would wish the crown of England for yourself?'

'Clearly, and you will be richly rewarded for assisting me in that.'

Richard allowed himself a hollow laugh. 'You should be approaching my father, not myself. It is he who is Captain of the Palace Guard, and close to King Henry. I am merely his squire, and am possessed of no influence at Court.'

'No, but you *are* possessed of eyes and ears, are you not? Eyes and ears that may be put to my service?'

'You wish me to become your spy? Your conspirator? Your ferret down the rabbit hole?'

'And you would no doubt wish to become the Duke of London, or Canterbury, or wherever you may wish to name?'

'What would you require of me, precisely?'

'I would wish to know of the relations between King Henry and his new Queen Adeliza. As you may know, I have already spent several years as an honoured guest at the English Court, where my uncle Henry has shown me considerable favour and affection, almost as if I were his son. I remain here in Blois only in order to better manage my attempts to regain control of my Normandy estate of Alencon, gifted to me by King Henry, but overrun by Fulk of Anjou. But I shall make regular visits across the Channel, and when I do so I shall require from you a detailed account of what prospects exist for the birth of another male heir who would put paid to my ambition. Also, during those times when I am absent, I shall require regular despatches through an ambassador who I shall appoint in due course. In return, on my accession you will receive such titles and estates as you shall desire at the time. Are we in agreement to all this?'

'What of your brother Theobald?'

'What of him? As I already advised you, I consider that I am more entitled than he to the English throne. What is more, I believe myself to be more in King Henry's favour than my surly brother, who only became Count by virtue of his seniority when our older brother proved to be lacking in either wit or wisdom. That was our mother's choice, and for once she got things right. So no more mention of Theobald — you are my man, and nobody else's, understood?'

'I take it that my father is to remain ignorant of your plans?'

'Naturally, since whatever he knows he will report back to King Henry.'

'But you are not planning on overthrowing him,' Richard pointed out. 'You seek simply to remain in his favour until there is no prospect of a further male heir.'

'You are talking about a son of William of Normandy,' Stephen reminded him. 'The brothers fought like dogs over a deer carcass, and each of them learned to regard close relatives as their most deadly enemies. Were any word to reach Henry that one of his nephews was seeking news of how things fared in his bedchamber, what would he be likely to think?'

'I suppose I must defer to your greater experience,' Richard conceded, 'but it will be hard to keep matters from my father.'

'Then I recommend that you maintain such distance from him as you are able,' Stephen counselled him. 'Where next are you bound?'

'Back into Normandy, so far as I can deduce, although I am at a loss to understand why. Why should we need to reassure ourselves of the continuing friendship of the Count d'Evreux?'

'Amaury de Montfort?' Stephen laughed. 'You have much to learn of affairs on this side of *La Manche*, clearly. Good luck in Evreux, but look to the small change in your money purse. As for your life, be sure to keep your mouth firmly sealed, and leave it to Robert Fitzroy to oil the waters.'

VI

Richard remained largely silent as the small group trotted comfortably north-east through Vendôme, Dunois and Chartres towards the southern borders of Normandy on their way to their final destination, Evreux. They subconsciously held their breath and kept well to the western boundaries of Chartres, on the other border of which lay the Île de France that was the stronghold of Louis of France, who was in a long-standing dispute with Henry of England over his refusal to pay homage to Louis for Normandy. There were only six men at arms remaining in their escort, after Thomas had taken four of them back as protection for himself and Elinor, and they would not last long against any routine French patrol of their borders.

Richard had enough reason to reserve his counsel, given the change of direction that his life had suddenly taken. If Stephen of Blois was correct in his belief that he would be named as England's heir, and Richard performed, with distinction, the tasks he had been set, then a noble title would be his for the asking, along with vast estates that would obviate any need for him to grow wealthy on the battlefield. But his curiosity got the better of him as the spires of Evreux Cathedral came into sight along the flat plain through which the straight road was leading them at a steady pace.

'Stephen of Blois cautioned me to take care for myself and my possessions when we arrive at the de Montfort estate,' he advised Robert. 'How can that be, when the lands lie within Normandy, and our master King Henry must therefore be its liege lord?'

Robert snorted. 'You do indeed require considerable education before you will be fit to send on any diplomatic missions, young man. What do you know of the de Montforts?'

'Next to nothing,' Richard admitted.

'So I surmised from your previous remark. They hold the land out of family loyalty, but by a thread only. It is strongly believed that the current count will throw in his hand with Louis of France at the slightest indication of renewed conflict between him and King Henry.'

'There is obviously a history of which I must be made aware.'

'How long have you got? It began, as did most of our recent upheavals, with Duke Richard of Normandy, the great-grandfather of the William who conquered England. He had many bastards, as seems to have been the family tradition, and the lords of Evreux descended from one of those. But the line expired two years since, with the death of the final lord, Count William, who had no heir. His sister Agnes claimed right and title to it, although she was already married to Amaury de Montfort-l'Amaury, who already held, and still holds, estates in the Île de France, the ancestral lands of the French king.'

'So much information to absorb.'

'You need not commit all that to memory. What you *must* bear in mind is that two years since, Henry seized suzerainty of Evreux in his own name, although he allowed the sister to remain on the land. But her husband, "Amaury III of de Montfort", as he styles himself, is adamant that he holds his estates for no Englishman, not even the king. However his original estate in Montfort-l'Amaury is held direct from Louis of France, and curiously he seems to have no quarrel with that. But should warfare break out again on the southern borders of Normandy, it may be confidently expected that the de Montforts will throw in their mailed hands with Louis. Do you now understand why we have been sent to sound out the current loyalties of this treacherous mob of ingrates?'

'Yes, I think so. But I will leave you to do the talking.'

'That was what your father insisted. So why were you in private conversation with Stephen while we were in Blois?'

'He was enquiring as to why my father had not accompanied us, and I advised him that he wished to see my sister Elinor safely back across the Channel,' Richard lied.

'If he believed that, then he is more of a fool than I would expect of a cousin of mine. But no matter — we must ask directions before much longer, if we are to reach Evreux before those looming clouds drop their load. That *is* a task I shall leave to you.'

The reception they received at the château at Evreux was warmer than they had anticipated, although the seasoned diplomat Robert sensed that the Lady Agnes was nervous regarding the absence of her husband, Amaury de Montfort. He was on his estate only a few leagues north of the *Île de la Cité*, the part of Paris in which Louis of France had his residence.

'Did your husband feel sufficiently satisfied regarding your safety during his absence?' Robert enquired politely as they sat sipping mulled wine while two serving maids set the board in advance of the delivery of supper.

Lady Agnes smiled. 'I am not without a protector, and we have enjoyed many peaceful years here. The only threat might come from further uprisings against Henry of England, who is of course our overlord.'

'And were there to be such an uprising, by whom would it be stirred up?' Robert enquired as Richard listened in amazement to the smooth way in which his mentor could divert a conversation to his chosen destination.

'That would of course depend upon the nature of the grievance. But when I spoke of my protector, I was referring to this gallant young knight who is joining us.' She nodded towards the doorway, and Robert and Richard turned in order to view the latest arrival.

He stood a clear six feet from the ground — perhaps an inch shorter than Richard — and was gifted with the broadest shoulders that could have been dreamed up by any artist. His long fair hair cascaded onto the neck of his brightly coloured tunic, and a pair of piercing green eyes shone out defiantly as he shook hands with the visitors, making a determined effort to crush Richard's in the process. Then he smiled, sat down, and graciously accepted the goblet of wine held out to him by a simpering serving maid.

'May I introduce my brother, Guy de Garlande?' Agnes purred. 'He has journeyed from the family estate of Rochefort, many days' ride from here, on the coast beyond Poitou.'

'But surely not simply to protect you during your husband's temporary absence?' Robert probed gently.

'Indeed not. He seeks his fortune in the world, since the life of a fisherman does not appeal to him, and it is all that may be available to him where we spent our childhood. Guy is only a year younger than me, and even when we were children his seemingly limitless energy knew no bounds.'

'And he hopes that your husband can find him a suitable position at the Court of King Louis?' Robert enquired with a hint of disapproval.

Agnes shook her head. 'Our liege lord is King Henry of England, is he not? Might Guy not find a position of service in his Court?'

Robert's eyes narrowed as he gave Guy a suspicious look and addressed him directly. 'You travelled here for just that purpose, did you not? You knew that we were bidden to visit Evreux by our master King Henry, and you took the opportunity to be here. You are not here to defend your sister at all, are you?'

Guy spread his arms in a gesture of surrender and flashed the sort of smile that left maidens swooning, although it was wasted on the two men. 'I have clearly been caught out by those wiser than myself, so there is little point in denial. But you should know that I have already seen service in Poitou, Angouleme and Périgord, in the train of those who would employ me. I have a strong sword arm and an even stronger desire to live to an old age. If King Henry values such attributes, then I would travel back with you to Caen.'

'Henry will no longer be there,' Robert advised him, 'but I would be happy to escort you back to him in England. We would benefit greatly from having such a strong and seasoned warrior at our side in any renewed contest regarding the overlordship of Normandy. I have no doubt that my master would be more than happy to grant you some English estate in return for your undertaking to serve his cause here in Evreux.'

'How do you know that he is "a seasoned warrior", as you flatteringly called him?' a very jealous Richard demanded as they walked along the upper corridor of the east wing on the way to the chambers they had been allocated. 'You have only the word of a braggart who clearly thinks very highly of himself! For all you know, he has been sent to spy at the English Court!'

'For all we know, he has,' Robert smiled back as they reached the doorway to his chamber. 'But if you are to be a true diplomat, you must not allow your personal feelings to get in the way of a skilled manoeuvre. He is obviously handsome and dashing, and has no doubt enjoyed many a village maiden, but such vanity may be employed against him, should the occasion merit.'

'And if he really *is* a French spy?' Richard demanded.

Robert lowered his voice. 'Two things. Firstly, we may feed him false information that he may carry back to Louis in Paris. Secondly, we may hold him hostage against any false action by his brother-in-law de Montfort. While we have custody of her pretty brother, we may rely upon our hostess to persuade Amaury where his best interests lie, if he wishes to maintain a happy house. And so I bid you a good night. We leave at daybreak.'

VII

When Richard and Robert returned to Westminster with Guy de Garlande in their party, Thomas reacted with angry disbelief.

'I felt exactly as you do!' Richard protested. 'But Robert was adamant that it was a wise strategy to bring him back with us, since he will prove a useful hostage against any aggression by Amaury de Montfort against our southern Normandy borders.'

Thomas snorted derisively. 'Robert Fitzroy will not be the one responsible for him while he wanders freely through the hallways of the various royal palaces. For all we know, he has been sent to assassinate the king!'

'But you guard the king, do you not?' Richard fired back. 'Are you admitting that you cannot protect him against one French peacock?'

'Don't be impertinent!' Thomas yelled back. 'How do we know that he is a mere idle boaster? You and Robert were sent to Evreux because King Henry suspected that the de Montforts might be plotting an uprising against his Norman estates, and what do you do? You bring back a member of the family who may well be skilled in the use of weapons, and may even be sworn to die in the attempt to kill Henry. Do you call *that* diplomacy?'

'It was not I who was charged with the ambassadorial duties,' Richard reminded him hotly. 'If you have a complaint regarding what has been done, take it up with Robert himself, rather than venting your spleen on me. But I doubt that you will, given that he is a royal son.'

'I will do what you should have done,' his father replied. 'I will put his boasting to the test. The first test will be of his prowess with a sword. You are still in knight training, but John Loverseed remains at Windsor, in charge of the Guard in my absence. What could be more natural than your seeking sword training from one who claims skill in such matters?'

'And how will I be able to judge that skill?' Richard challenged him.

'You will not — I will. While you and he are cutting and thrusting up and down the stable yard here, I will keep watch from my chamber above, and form my own opinion. It is fortunate that we were thus accommodated on the first floor here.'

'And where will Guy be assigned a chamber?'

'That will be a matter for the Chamberlain, once Guy has been presented to King Henry, which is set for the hour before supper. We are both bidden to attend. Your sister will be there anyway, in attendance on the queen, with whom she has earned great favour during your absence. Now see to the amusement of our unwanted guest in the hours that remain before that meeting, and in the process ensure that he learns as little of the layout of the palace as possible. Perhaps you might consider taking him for a walk along the riverbank.'

The hour before supper came soon enough, and Robert was waiting for them by the door that led into the Audience Chamber. Guy had taken the opportunity to change from his riding clothes into a fine purple silk *bliaut* cut short to reveal his long legs, which were attired in black hose stretching into his ankle-length boots. His head remained uncovered, to allow his long fair tresses to swing with every movement of his body. There were several gasps as he walked confidently alongside Robert of Gloucester, bowed the knee a few paces from the throne, and looked back up with a broad smile that seemed to light up the entire chamber.

'Sire, may I present Guy de Garlande, brother-in-law to Count Amaury de Montfort of Evreux?' Robert also bowed, but only from the waist. 'He brings loving greetings from that estate, and wishes to serve his overlord as may be seen fit — perhaps among his armed forces?'

Henry smiled and indicated with his hand that Guy was to rise, although he did not offer him a seat. Thomas and Richard likewise remained standing behind Guy.

Henry looked him up and down before speaking. 'It would seem that the fashions in Normandy are changing rapidly. Has purple silk replaced brown homespun?'

Guy appeared unfazed by the veiled criticism of his choice of dress. 'I clearly do not dress thus on the battlefield, sire, and it is there that I would seek to be of service to you. I have taken on many men already in the theatre of war.'

'And how many of those did you despatch?' Henry enquired.

'All of them clearly, sire, else I would not be here to offer my strong arm in the defence of your throne.'

'And what thinks your brother-in-law of your sudden change of allegiance?'

'I was not aware of any such change, sire,' Guy oozed diplomatically, 'since my sister advises me that you are our overlord for the Evreux estate.'

'As indeed I am, although *Seigneur* Amaury might dispute that. What of his estate closer to the Île de France?'

'Of that I have no immediate knowledge,' Guy assured him, 'since I have never visited it. My own family estates lie far to the west, in Poitou.'

'But Amaury approves of your journey here?' Henry persisted.

Again Guy's smile was intended to be placatory. 'He was not consulted, sire, since he was on his southern estates when I took my leave of Evreux. It did not occur to me that I might require his consent, and he may still be unaware of my departure.'

'And one wonders at his likely reaction to it,' Henry mused, before something else seemed to occur to him, and he diverted his gaze to Robert. 'Has the Chamberlain seen to our guest's accommodation?'

'Indeed, sire. He is installed in chambers on the abbey side of the first floor, adjacent to those allocated to the Walsingham family, and a few paces down the hallway from my own, on the riverside.'

'This is good,' Henry nodded, then looked at Thomas. 'And the Palace Guard is fully manned, I assume?'

'Indeed, sire,' Thomas confirmed. 'I have left John Loverseed in command at Windsor.'

'Then there would seem to be little to delay our supper,' Henry smiled. 'Perhaps Guy de Garlande might wish to join us?'

'Do the men now outshine the women of Normandy in their choice of attire?' Queen Adeliza enquired of Guy as she sat with him to her left and Elinor to her right. Thomas and Richard were further down the table, on the other side of the king.

Guy flashed her one of his smiles. 'You must forgive me my Poitevin ways, Your Majesty. In my country, the men have adopted the style and manners of the troubadours who have emerged from neighbouring Aquitaine. They write ballads pertaining to courtly love, and they dress to impress the ladies who have captured their hearts. I must own that when I saw how the men dress in Normandy, my heart sank to my knees.'

'It would nevertheless have remained intact,' Elinor said quietly, 'since your knees are a good distance from the ground.'

The queen chuckled, but nevertheless turned with a look intended to admonish Elinor for her impertinence. Her father glared at her from down the table, and Richard blushed with embarrassment, but Guy seemed amused by the observation.

'Again, in my country men are bred tall, in order to impress the ladies and strike fear into their enemies.'

'Might you consider taking this courtly poet into the Palace Guard?' King Henry enquired of Thomas, who shook his head vigorously as he suppressed a look of horror.

'I think not, by your leave, sire,' he replied deferentially. 'It is, as I earlier advised, at full strength, and I have another task for our honoured visitor. My son still requires something in the way of sword training, and since the young man from Poitou has already advised us that he possesses such skills, I would deem it a great favour if he would pass some to my son Richard. The day cannot be far away when they will be needed in England's defence.'

'I would be honoured,' Guy replied. 'And perhaps his beautiful sister will, in return, give *me* advice on how best to ensure that the ladies at Evreux can outshine the men in the matter of their attire.'

Two days later, Thomas's eyes were glued to the mullioned glass through which he was staring down at Richard and Guy, thrusting and parrying in the stable yard below him. Guy had not been boasting when he claimed prowess with a blade, but Thomas was both relieved and somewhat surprised at the degree to which Richard was holding his own. The day was not long distant when he would have to remove the fatherly restraint and allow the boy to go out on his own in battle. He trembled with fear and loathing as he recalled some of the sights he had been forced to witness during skirmishes and sieges along the Normandy borders in his days as a captain in the royal livery.

From an adjacent chamber window in her own apartment, Elinor was also watching the encounter — trembling, flushing hotly and wondering what on earth was happening between her thighs.

VIII

Two weeks later, Richard was instructing the groom in the brushing of his horse after his daily canter, when he heard a large party of horsemen galloping into the stable yard as if pursued by the hounds of Hell. The man at its head called for grooms, and all the available stable boys rushed out to take hold of bridles as heavily armed knights clad in the blue livery of Blois jumped from their saddles. Their leader removed his battle helm, and Richard had no difficulty in recognising him. He strode quickly across the yard and hailed the man.

'Count Stephen, welcome to England!'

'I am not yet Count of Blois,' Stephen replied curtly, 'and this is by no means my first visit to England. But if Alencon is to be preserved as an English possession, I must seek the support of my uncle. Take me to the king without delay!'

Richard was forming the necessary words to explain why he was interrupting King Henry's meeting with his father when Stephen brushed past him and saved him the task.

'That slimy rat of Anjou has invaded Alencon, Uncle, and is laying siege to the town!'

'So soon?' Henry enquired, looking up.

Thomas's military brain kicked into action. 'How many men has he?'

'Difficult to say,' Stephen replied. 'But he has siege engines and cavalry, and the walls lack recent repair. I was in pursuit of Count Fulk once I received word of his crossing of the Normandy borders from Maine, which of course he regards as his to cross in peace since he gifted it to William Clito upon his betrothal to his daughter Sybilla. Then from an adjoining hill I

63

saw the full extent of his forces, and rode hard here along with my personal guard.'

'So you require English forces to lift the siege?' Thomas enquired urgently. 'Are the northern borders of Normandy still secure for a landing at Barfleur?'

'They were when last I was there, which was only days past. But there is worse to relate — there has been an uprising of discontented barons to the south, in the region of Evreux, and they are said to have been fermented by de Montfort.'

'Bastard!' Henry spat, then turned to Thomas. 'Do we still have the brother here at Westminster?'

'Indeed, sire,' Thomas confirmed. 'I believe that it was Robert's intention when he brought him here that he should be held as a hostage to fortune and good behaviour for such an eventuality as this.'

'He is to be close confined, but not yet trussed in irons,' Henry ordered. 'Place a permanent guard on his chamber and allow access only in order that food and drink may be supplied to him. Then gather as many hardened soldiers as you can muster at short notice and join me in the stable yard as soon as dinner is over. Before we ride to the relief of Alencon, I wish to make a prisoner of de Montfort, then bring him back here to be hanged and drawn as a traitor.'

'And the matter of the Palace Guard in my absence, sire?'

'You have seconds in command, do you not? If it comes to that, you have a son.'

'Very well, sire. If you will excuse me, I will set about the necessary arrangements without delay.'

'Why me, and why may I not come with you?' Richard demanded, but Thomas had no time for argument.

'Because I'm your father, and you will do as I say. In my absence, the Palace Guard will be commanded by Alan Thoroughgood, but *you* will be responsible to him for the secure guarding of our prisoner — the man you brought over here in the first place. His brother-in-law is stirring rebellion in the south of Normandy, and when it is appropriate Guy de Garlande will be hung from the Tower walls. In the meantime, he is to be kept fed and watered like a prize horse, but no more. He is not allowed beyond his chamber door, his pisspot is to be emptied regularly, and his only exercise will be walking up and down the floor of his chamber. I have given instruction for his windows to be barred, and the guard will be changed twice daily. You will supervise that guard, and should Guy not be available for a hanging in due course, the king will look to you for an answer. Is that all clearly understood?'

'Has Robert agreed to this?'

'He has not even been consulted, since the matter of palace security falls within my bailiwick. Now see about your duties, after you have hugged me farewell — we leave in time to catch the tide from Portsmouth, and I have much to see to in the meantime.'

Before the sun had moved into its afternoon quadrant, a massive contingent of armed men led by King Henry in full battle armour clattered out of Westminster Palace yard and onto the track that lay westward towards Windsor, and the open countryside beyond that. An English army was on the move, and once again the serenity of Northern France was destined to be shattered by the sound of metal clashing upon metal.

'Why was it necessary to have Guy confined?' Elinor complained to the queen as they sat in her Withdrawing Chamber, working on their tapestries.

'You've taken quite a shine to him, have you not?' Adeliza observed.

Elinor blushed. 'He's such a wonderful treat to the eye, and his manners are all that a lady could wish for in a man. As for those long legs — well, I hesitate to continue.'

'You do not need to, since I am a woman myself, and one whose passions have not yet begun to dry. As for why he is confined, he is clearly now to be regarded as an enemy, given that his family are rebelling against his Majesty's rule in Normandy.'

'Surely he cannot be held responsible for what his sister's husband chooses to do?' Elinor argued. 'And a man of his physical energy should not be confined to a narrow chamber like an errant horse that needs to be tamed.'

'How do you know his chamber to be narrow?' Adeliza enquired with a teasing grin, and again Elinor flushed bright red.

'I was there — once only, I might assure you. It was when my brother sought the loan from him of a suitable wrist guard for his sword arm, ahead of their regular martial exercise. I was sent with the request that Guy bring the item with him when they met, and the chamber is furnished merely with a narrow bed and two chairs. Not sufficient for a man of such sensitivities and refined tastes.'

'I wonder what might be his tastes in womenfolk,' Adeliza mused.

The English army approached the third rebel castle that week, and rapidly overpowered the gate guards. They then thundered into the courtyard, jumped from their horses and raced inside. It was by now a practised routine, and as Thomas and his men ran through the living quarters, rounding up the domestic staff and herding them outside to watch, Robert held the lord at sword point and escorted him to the battlements. There, a grizzled and bored-looking man at arms tied a rope to his waist, put out his eyes, then threw him over the side, leaving him swinging and squealing in sightless agony. Before they finally departed, carrying as much portable wealth as they could stuff into their saddlebags, Robert of Gloucester made his usual farewell speech.

'Put out the word that this will be the fate of anyone else who chooses to defy the authority of your liege lord King Henry of England.'

Thomas was sickened by it all, and was counting the days until they finally reached Evreux, their ultimate destination, and could hold Amaury de Montfort to account for his part in provoking the uprising. But once they reached the castle at Evreux, they were met at the entrance to the castle keep by his wife Agnes, their three small children gathered pathetically at her skirts.

'Where is your treacherous husband?' Henry demanded.

She shrugged. 'No doubt where he has been these past few months, skulking on one of his estates to the south of here. They are Montfort-l'Amaury, Épernon, and Houda, but you enter the Île de France at your own peril, since it is the stronghold of King Louis of France. Should you have occasion to meet with my occasional husband, pray advise him that it has been a poor harvest, and that his children are hungry.'

'He is under the protection of Louis the Fat?' Robert demanded.

'Under his shadow, perhaps, if he kneels below the king's waist. But he holds his French estates from the King of France, in the same way as he holds this estate from whoever rules Normandy this week. It is so difficult to keep track of the changes.'

'He holds Evreux for *me*!' Henry bellowed. 'I am the King of England, and I hold your brother captive in my palace of Westminster. Tell your ungrateful and traitorous pig of a husband that if there are any more rebellions among Norman barons that are the result of his stirring the pot, his brother-in-law will be hanged and quartered.'

'There is no love lost between them anyway,' Agnes replied with another shrug, 'but I will see that he receives the message. For myself, I have always believed that my brother would die the way he has lived — with a great deal of show. If you really wish to cause him pain, make him dress like a field labourer and cut off all his hair.'

'We are done here,' Henry advised the company as he turned his mount and dug his heels into its flanks. 'Robert, you ride with me.'

Later that night, in their temporary camp, Henry called for all the plunder they had acquired during their brutal campaign to be piled in the centre of his tent. He then turned to Robert.

'Take a small escort, and carry this fortune south to Rome. Seek an audience with Pope Callixtus and offer him the entire amount if he will annul the marriage of my nephew William Clito to the daughter of Fulk of Anjou, Sybilla. While you are about that, we shall teach Anjou a lesson in diplomacy that it will never forget.'

Elinor was a familiar enough sight in the palace kitchens, since it was one of her duties to enter it daily with the order for Queen Adeliza's frugal meals. While her husband took great delight in guzzling his way through large sides of cooked meats, Adeliza's delicate constitution required more in the way of grilled fish, milk puddings and cheese crepes. No-one therefore challenged Elinor's presence beside the hatch through which the dishes were handed to the servers who would carry them to the upper rooms. She spoke urgently to Alys, the queen's own server.

'Who carries the food to the prisoner on the first floor?'

'What, the real 'andsome one wiv the long legs? The French beauty?'

'Yes, him. Who carries his food to him?' Elinor repeated in a whisper.

'It depends, dunnit? We draws lots ter do it, 'cos 'e always gives us a little reward, an' there's always a smile and a chuck under the chin. We 'opes fer more than that, o' course.'

Later that day, her gown covered with a mantle as if she had just entered the palace, and with her giveaway black hair well hidden under a serving cap, Elinor accepted the serving dish through the hatch and hurried to the first floor chamber. The guards moved aside to give her entrance. One of them knocked on the door with the butt of his halberd, then reached inside his tunic for the key that unlocked it.

Guy was looking dolefully out of the window at the west wall of the cathedral as Elinor put down the tray and hastily shed the mantle and cap, allowing her luxuriant black locks to tumble down to her shoulders. Guy half turned in order to gruffly acknowledge the arrival of his solitary meal for the day, then whipped fully round in amazement.

'Aren't you — you know — *her*?' he enquired clumsily. 'The queen's lady — Elinor, isn't that your name?'

'It is,' Elinor confirmed with a dry throat.

'Why are you ordered to bring me my frugal repast?'

'I was advised of your forward behaviour towards the serving maids from the kitchen.'

'They complained?'

'Only that you took it no further,' Elinor smiled back, and Guy burst out laughing.

'So you are here to place a request on their behalf for more unseemly behaviour?'

'No.'

'Then what? A request on your *own* behalf, perhaps?'

'That rather depends upon your actions when I bend to place this tray on your table,' Elinor replied as her heart threatened to burst through her thin gown. A moment later she felt the hand rest where she had hoped, and straightened up with a delicious shudder. 'As I suspected. You take advantage of helpless young maids.'

'And are you still a maid?'

'I was when this dinner was handed to me. But that condition may not last until supper.'

IX

Thomas was finding it increasingly difficult to keep his men in order. They had travelled for days across first Maine, and then Anjou, without meeting any resistance. Every castle they came to, and every estate that they trotted across, seemed to possess a local lord who was only too willing to acknowledge the suzerainty of Henry of England. Consequently, there was no need to give battle and no plunder to be had. By the time that they sat overlooking the fortress at Angers, the men were muttering that they had not signed up in order to ride peacefully across Northern France like pilgrims on their way to Rome. If they were not allowed to break loose soon, Thomas feared desertions, which would not look good for his leadership abilities.

His heart therefore sank when he saw the gates being opened to admit the exit of a small group of horsemen who even from a distance seemed to have in their centre a man so richly dressed that he had to be of the nobility. King Henry, riding to Thomas's left, with Robert on his other side, made a noise that was something between a sigh of relief and a snort of derision as he squinted in order to improve his vision, then announced, 'Here he comes, the skulking rat! We've ridden all over his alleged lands of Maine, and his undoubted home territory of Anjou, without him raising a hand against us. Now he no doubt trots out to swear his false allegiance. Even rats turn and fight when they are cornered!'

If Fulk was feeling intimidated by the sudden arrival of an English army, it didn't show in his face as he greeted the royal party with a broad smile. 'Welcome to Anjou, Henry. I had hoped to receive a visit from you as the father-in-law of one of my daughters, but God clearly had other ideas. You are most welcome, nevertheless.'

'Spare me the mealy-mouthed falsities,' Henry growled. 'I am here for an explanation of your recent actions in attacking Alencon, which is clearly within the boundaries of my estates of Normandy, whatever doubt there may be over who governs Maine. Although I am obliged to advise that as we passed through Maine it seemed to be the general belief of its various lords that they held their land of me, and not yourself. Since you have been collecting the rents, I assume that you have done so as my representative in those lands, and that therefore you have a sizeable amount in coin awaiting collection.'

The smile did not leave Fulk's face as he replied, 'Regarding the feudal dues from Maine, they have been employed in order to equip me to take a force on Holy Crusade, upon which I will shortly be departing, with the Pope's blessing. Since you seem to be on such friendly terms with him that he was persuaded to annul a perfectly good marriage between my older daughter and your nephew, I feel sure that you would not wish to incur his ire by depriving Jerusalem of a fighting force under his banner. As for Alencon, you might wish to reign in your other nephew Stephen, whose brigands have taken to crossing the border into Maine in order to pillage. I will ever defend what is mine, as no doubt will you.'

'Enough of this canting drivel,' Henry replied testily. 'We are tired, hungry and thirsty, and I hear good things about the quality of your pink wine. We may talk further while we eat.'

Three hours later, the two men were chuckling over ribald jests like two old friends in a dockside alehouse. Thomas bit back the angry words that threatened to break free when he reminded himself that he had marched an entire army of men for five months without any meaningful armed engagement, while the only tangible plunder had gone into the coffers of the Church of Rome. He was itching to return to his duties in England and had no time for the sight of two ageing drunks filling their guts with rich food and gallons of the local wine while they made slurred promises of ongoing friendship that neither of them was likely to honour.

'We are both too long in the tooth, and fond of the softer life, to be constantly engaged in bickering over Maine,' Fulk declared as his face glowed with the effects of the third flagon. 'It was a pity that we never became united by the marriages of our younger family members. The death of William Adelin was tragic, but clearly ordained by God, whereas it was you yourself who put paid to your nephew's claim by marriage with my daughter Sybilla. But you have another nephew, of course — the one who rules in Alencon — and he would no doubt welcome the opportunity to share a marriage bed with a lady of Anjou.'

'Stephen?' Henry hiccupped back. 'I think too highly of him to order him to take second place to someone else's ambitions, and I may confirm what you no doubt already suspect — namely that he will one day inherit England as well as Normandy. You would be bartering one of your daughters for the opportunity to inherit an empire, Fulk, my friend. Concentrate on saving Jerusalem for God, because as a diplomat you make a fine crusader.'

Before much longer, both men were assisted to their bedchambers, and it was a very bad-tempered Henry who summoned Thomas the following morning and ordered him to assemble the men for the long ride back to Caen. As they camped south of the village of Conde on the road back across Normandy, where a more northerly track led to the traditional harbour of Barfleur, Thomas entered Henry's tent with a request for leave to return to England.

'You no longer require an army to accompany you, since all would seem to be quiet among your subjects on this side of the Channel,' Thomas argued. 'It has been almost seven months since we departed from Westminster, and I must ensure that all is as it should be for your return in due course. We have heard nothing regarding rumblings among the English barons, but our constant travels have made it more difficult for messengers to find us.'

'You are wise to be cautious,' Henry nodded, 'but I would prefer that Stephen and Robert remain over here with me. I have a proposal that I wish to put to Stephen, and if he is in agreement then I would seek the approval of my vassals on this side of my kingdom. As for Robert, I have no doubt that his services will be required in the near future, since I do not believe for one moment that Louis of France will rest once he learns that William Clito is no longer married into Anjou.'

'As you prefer, sire,' Thomas nodded, content to be allowed to return home on any condition short of arrest and imprisonment. 'You will find the Palace of Westminster all secure upon your return.'

'I left you with one simple task — one that even you should have been able to discharge without difficulty,' Thomas was complaining to Richard two weeks later. 'And what do I find? Your sister has been cavorting with a man deemed to be an enemy of England, while you sat back and allowed it! Quite apart from the threat to the nation, thought you nothing of your sister's honour?'

'She is well over twenty years of age,' Richard reminded him, 'and perfectly capable of guarding her own honour — or not, as she may choose. Guy is still secure in his chamber, which is the only task you set me, so where is your ground for criticism?'

Thomas tutted loudly. 'If, unbeknown to anyone, Guy has inveigled Elinor into some sort of devious plot against the throne, where stand we? Both of us were entrusted with ensuring that he posed no threat to the security of the nation, so why did your sister suddenly take herself off? She has been missing for some months, according to what I have managed to learn. What I do *not* know is where she might have taken herself off *to*!'

'Grandfather is dead,' Richard announced sullenly. 'I would have told you minutes ago, had you not begun our first meeting for eight months with criticism of my actions. Seemingly he passed peacefully in his sleep, but Mother Grace has taken it ill, and it is feared that she will not long outlive him. I would have travelled with Elinor, but she insisted otherwise, and of course I had to see to the security of our prisoner.'

'Well, now that I am returned, you may leave the security of Guy de Garlande to me,' Thomas replied, 'and lose no time in returning to Walsingham. Pay my respects to the memory of my late father, and bring such comfort as you can to your Great Aunt Elva, if she still answers to that name. But above all, bring your sister back here without delay. There is now even more urgent need of her at Court. Queen Adeliza may well have excused her lengthy absence, but the Lady Maude will not. If you recall, Elinor was chosen by Maude to be her

Senior Lady, and she will be back in London before the winter sets in. For good, it would seem.'

'She is estranged from her husband?'

'In a sense, yes. She is widowed. Her husband Henry of Germany, the Holy Roman Emperor, died several weeks past. He had been in considerable pain, or so it was reported by those who brought the message to Alencon as we journeyed back to Caen. Robert of Gloucester has been sent to bring Maude to her father's side, and the final order I received was to ensure that her chambers here at Westminster are reopened, suitably aired, and equipped with adequate servants. Henry will not take kindly to Elinor's unexplained absence, after he has shown her such favour. See to it — and do not fail me this time.'

X

Richard was still burning with resentment as he left the track that led from Fakenham to the coast, and saw the familiar manor house of Walsingham glowing in the late afternoon sun. One solitary ray beamed down on the shrine that he had known since boyhood, as if welcoming him home and reminding him that the Virgin Mary had blessed this land. On the near side of the river was a new structure that rose many feet into the air, and was clad in the wooden poles that the stonemasons employed to gain access to the higher levels. Sir Geoffrey's priory was clearly well on its way to completion, and the cluster of buildings ranged around the main structure no doubt housed the monks' various activities when not at prayer.

There was no sign of any life across the river on the manor house side. As Richard clattered across the wooden bridge that spanned the stream and urged his horse to the left, he felt uneasy, as if some pestilence had overcome those who resided here. Then he breathed more easily as he saw the familiar, if somewhat stooping, figure of his Aunt Tilly leave the shrine and bend her back against the stiff breeze as she made her way back to the manor house.

'Aunt Tilly!' he called out, and the figure turned. She smiled uncertainly as he dismounted and hurried towards her, then something made him stop. He realised what it was when he saw that Matilda was wearing the black veil that he associated with his Great Aunt Elva, as the head of the convent. He raised his eyebrows and Matilda nodded sadly.

'I'm Mother Angelica now. Mother Grace died of a broken heart last week. She and her brother were very close, and the death of Sir Wilfrid seemed to draw the very life from her. She's buried over there, with her husband, who of course you never knew.'

'I would have returned to mourn Grandfather's passing when Elinor did, but I was guarding an important prisoner in the service of King Henry.'

'Elinor grieved enough for both of you,' Angelica smiled, 'although of course she had a reason of her own for being here. Have you come to escort her back to her duties at Court? You may find that she is reluctant to leave here now.'

'And why might that be?'

'She must disclose that reason to you herself. But come inside and partake of some sustenance, since from memory it's a long way from London. Mind you, it's been many years since I was there.'

As Richard entered the main hall of the manor house, he saw Elinor waiting for him with her back to the window that looked out over the vegetable garden. She had obviously been aware of his arrival, yet had made no effort to leave the house in order to greet him. Now she stood facing him with defiance written all over her face.

'Did Father send you?' she enquired bluntly. 'I cannot imagine that you came here of your own choosing. You've missed two important funerals, by the way. I'll take you to view the graves when you've eaten.'

'Father *did* send me,' Richard replied, 'in the sense that it was his order that led to my coming north. But the real reason why we seek your return to Westminster is that the Lady Maude is widowed, and is travelling back to London, where she will expect you to be waiting to serve her.'

'And she will wait for long enough,' Elinor grimaced. 'I have good reasons for wishing to remain here now.'

'Please don't pretend that you're going to take the veil and devote your life to God,' Richard sneered. 'Not after the way you behaved with Guy de Garlande. The guards on the door eventually confessed that on some occasions it took you an hour or more to serve his dinner, so I think we can surmise what it was that delayed you. May I deduce that he then rejected you, having robbed you of your honour, and that now you seek to hide your shame under a wimple?'

Elinor's mouth turned down as she gestured to the view through the window behind her. 'After that cruel barb, perhaps I shall make you wait before I summon food and drink from the kitchen. Since Aunt Tilly became the abbess on the death of Great Aunt Elva, she's left the management of the manor house to me. Step outside with me, and be prepared for at least one surprise.'

As they walked solemnly past the several grave markers that were planted in the grass slope immediately below the shrine, Elinor waved her hand towards a mound of earth that was still fresh. 'That's Elva's grave,' she advised him. 'There can have been very few abbesses buried on top of the man who gave her a child. And next to it, alongside the wife who was by his side for over sixty years, is Grandfather Wilfrid, the former miller's son who made it to knighthood. We owe everything to him. You might at least have been here for the prayers for his soul.'

'You know very well why I could not,' Richard reminded her. 'And as I recall, you were only too eager to make the journey yourself, with only two armed men to guard you. I took your eagerness to depart as a sign that your precious Guy had grown tired of what lay beneath your servant's smock.'

'He pleaded with me to stay,' Elinor smiled as she reminisced, 'but I had other good reasons to depart the Court. Do you wish to cross the river and visit the new priory that Sir Geoffrey has commissioned? It is all but complete, and lacks only the bell tower. There is a small boat moored on this side of the river, to avoid the inconvenience of crossing by the bridge.'

'If I must,' Richard muttered. 'Then may I be fed?'

Ten minutes later, the grey-tonsured but ever boyish-looking Geoffrey de Faverches was welcoming them into the cluster of buildings around the main church.

'As you can see,' he enthused, 'we shall soon have capacity for some twenty brothers, and we already have an Infirmarian and an Almoner. But I imagine that it is the orphanage that you are seeking — Brother Ralph, our Infirmarian, saw your approach across the river, and awaits you inside.'

'The orphanage has become part of the priory,' Elinor explained, 'since Aunt Tilly was appointed abbess by the remaining nuns of her order. They remain back across the river in the old buildings, for reasons which I hope are only too obvious. We cannot have them living in close proximity to the brothers of the priory, once it is completed.'

'Indeed not,' Richard observed icily, 'else they might fall prey to the sort of temptations that beset serving maids when in the chambers of pretty nobles.'

Elinor chose not to reply, simply gesturing for Richard to precede her into the little room with the high windows. Brother Ralph was waiting for them, his hands firmly within the folds of his cassock sleeves as he smiled and indicated two tiny cots off to his right. Elinor slipped past her brother in order to take the lead, then pointed to the two cots, each of which contained a sleeping infant.

'These are our most recent arrivals,' she advised Richard, who nodded politely and looked down. He was not accustomed to viewing babies, with which he was totally unfamiliar, but something about these two seemed to draw his attention. They lay like tiny angels, each with perfect skin and a button nose.

'Very comely,' he remarked. 'If their mothers were forced to abandon them, they must be grieving their loss.'

'They are twins,' Elinor said calmly, 'so they only had one mother, and she did not abandon them. Their names are Alain and William, and they are your nephews.'

Richard was stunned. This latest revelation made matters even worse than he had anticipated. 'Does Guy know?' he enquired breathlessly.

'No, and I'll thank you not to tell him,' Elinor replied as she reached down to gently touch each of her sleeping infants on the cheek. 'I don't want him proposing marriage to me out of either a misdirected sense of duty, or — even worse — pity.'

'But he's entitled to know,' Richard reminded her.

'And I'll advise him when I deem the moment appropriate, even assuming that I agree to return to Court.'

'You have little choice.'

'Because Father insists?'

'No,' Richard replied, 'because the *king* will insist. You are a Lady of the Court now, whether you wish to be or not. God alone knows why the queen chose not to take you with her across to Normandy, but she will surely ask for you upon her return. Have you forgotten that Lady Maude picked you out personally to attend upon her?'

'Only because Father pushed me in her direction,' Elinor countered. 'She's probably forgotten me already.'

'And if she hasn't? The only reason why you have not already received word from the queen to be awaiting her return to Westminster is the fact that no-one other than Father and myself knew where you were. But given that we do, what am I to report back? I have a duty to both Father and King Henry, remember.'

'You will not betray me?' Eleanor pleaded.

Richard gave her a stern look. 'You have already betrayed yourself, in the matter of the greatest importance to any lady. You are no longer a maid, and you are the mother of two boys besides. Which is which, by the way? I cannot tell one from the other.'

'One of them has more hair than the other, and it is already darkening. That one is William. His brother Alain's head would appear to be developing a fine, almost silky, fair head of hair like his father's. But you would surely not force me to abandon two helpless infants?'

'They are not helpless,' Richard argued. 'That is surely the purpose for which an orphanage exists — to ensure the welfare of children without mothers? And given who their mother is, I hardly think it likely that the prior of this establishment would give orders that they be cast out into the winter snows. So why would you hesitate to leave them here?'

Tears began to form in Elinor's eyes as she looked back up at him in supplication. 'Clearly you a not a mother, but if they were yours, could *you* bear to turn your back on them?'

'They *are* mine, in a sense,' Richard reminded her, 'but I regard my duty to the Court to be of a higher priority than cooing over a pair of mewling infants.'

'What duty *is* that, precisely?' Elinor challenged him. 'You hold no position at Court, and Father only took you south with him because you begged him to, and threatened his sanity with your constant demands to be allowed to make your way in life as a knight. Have you yet achieved that, or do you still hang around Father like a dog seeking a bone from the lord's board? You are still plain and simple Richard Walsingham, are you not?'

'The moment has not yet arrived for me to prove myself,' he murmured, less sure of his ground. He then remembered his father's manner towards him during their last meeting. 'But thanks to you I failed in the first task he set me, which was to ensure that Guy de Garlande caused no trouble. True it is that he did not escape on my watch, but the damage he has done to the good name of "Walsingham" does not bear contemplation. If only to restore my own damaged reputation, I intend to return to Westminster with you by my side.'

'And if I refuse?'

'Then Father shall be advised that he has two grandchildren. I imagine that this is a matter that you wish to keep from him also until you "deem the moment appropriate", to use your own words. I would also make it my business to advise the proud father.'

Elinor turned pale and began to tremble as tears rolled down her cheeks. 'Please, Richard — have pity on me!'

Overcome by a rare emotion, he reached out and pulled her to him. 'You are my sister, and I love you dearly, but I cannot sit idly by while you condemn yourself to a life under the veil, as so many women in our family have done. You are beautiful, spirited, and a worthy catch for someone better than a French adventurer. You will return with me to Court, and even though you may curse me for a month or two, the day will dawn when you give thanks for my firmness of purpose, and my genuine desire for your future happiness. Now, may I be supplied with food and drink, or must I impose myself on the charity of these monks?'

XI

If King Henry fondly believed that Louis of France would quietly accept that his protégé William Clito had been deprived of both a bride and the lordship of Maine, he had been deceiving himself. Clito was summoned to the *Île de la Cité* and feted as an honoured ally of France, after he was given the French queen's half-sister Joanna of Montferrat in marriage. He was also granted several estates in what was known as 'the French Vexin', an area of France that lay on the borders of English-dominated Normandy and the Île de France that was the stronghold of Louis of France. From there, Clito was encouraged to conduct guerrilla raids on his English neighbours that barely escalated beyond irritations until he was given the opportunity by Louis to occupy Flanders following the death of its count.

Louis had opened up the door by taking an invasion force into the leaderless province and persuading its minor nobility to accept Clito as the new count. Not to be outmanoeuvred, Henry supplied the necessary finance for a rival claimant, Thierry of neighbouring Alsace, to challenge Clito's rule. The two armies waged war indecisively for over a year before, during the siege of Ghent by Clito at the head of his troops, he received a flesh wound to the arm that proved fatal when it became gangrenous.

One more obstacle to English dominance of Northern France had been removed, but Henry had finally become convinced of the tactical significance of marriage contracts, and set about organising several of his own. First in time was to be that of Stephen of Blois, the man who everyone had regarded as Henry's heir. But that had been while Maude was still Countess of Germany, and Henry had begun to have serious second thoughts. After all, Stephen was a mere nephew, whereas Maude was from Henry's own loins.

Once Maude joined her father in Caen, from where he had been monitoring events in Flanders, they travelled together to Boulogne. Its count, Eustace III, had heard the call of God and wished to take holy orders following a distinguished life on Crusade and patronage of the Knights Templar. This would leave his only child, Matilda, as sole ruler in his absence, and although she was a doughty lady with her father's fighting temperament, she lacked both a husband and a sizeable military force. Boulogne was a crucial seaport of inestimable value to England, given the speed of access which it gave across the Channel from Dover, and Henry could not pass up the opportunity when invited by Eustace to find Matilda a husband.

While she could not in all honesty be described as beautiful, she was only in her early twenties, and possessed a certain magnetism that all but hypnotised men into following her command. She had led a company of knights under the overall control of Stephen into Flanders during its occupation by William Clito, and had been smitten by the noble bearing of her commander in chief. He, in turn, had found his thoughts turning lustful when contemplating what might lie under Matilda's uncompromising battle armour and surcoat. Therefore, when Matilda suggested to her father that she would consent to wed Stephen of Blois and no-one else — and Eustace had tentatively suggested the match to Henry and Maude — Stephen not only raised no objection but in fact insisted that the marriage take place without delay.

It was therefore a contented royal party that disembarked at Dover ahead of the celebration of Christmas at Westminster. Apart from the king and queen, along with the widowed Maude and the happy newlyweds Stephen and Matilda, there was another son of Blois among those taking the tracks to London. He was Stephen's younger brother, Henry, a monk in Benedictine robes that were hastily exchanged for a mitre, stole and pectoral cross when he was appointed Bishop of Winchester, one of the largest and richest sees in the English Church.

Once he had rested after the four-day journey, Henry's first action was to summon Thomas Walsingham for an assurance that the nation lay at peace, and that Westminster Palace was secure for a huge gathering of all the leading barons of the realm. Thomas assured him that it was, and Henry then enquired about their prisoner. 'That impudent young Poitevin brother of de Montfort — he remains confined?'

'Indeed he does, sire,' Thomas confirmed.

'Excellent — see to it that he is permitted to dine in the Great Hall once the barons are assembled. Even when the traditional Christmas celebrations are concluded I wish the barons to remain, in order that I might secure their consent to my succession plans. It is therefore essential that they have no excuse to depart, or to quarrel among themselves, is that understood?'

'Clearly, sire.' Thomas bowed, intent on removing himself from the Audience Chamber before Henry could ask any other awkward questions. He froze when his worst fears were realised.

'That comely daughter of yours,' Henry enquired, 'she is in all ways prepared for her duties as Lady Maude's companion?'

'She — she will be, sire,' Thomas answered evasively. 'She is at present on our former estate at Walsingham, following the death of my father.'

'Sir Wilfrid is dead?' Henry enquired sadly. 'Such a loyal and brave servant of England. He will be sadly mourned, and not just by his own immediate family. When do you anticipate that your daughter will return? What was her name again?'

'Elinor, sire. I have sent my son Richard to ensure her safe return to Westminster, and I expect her by the day.'

Thomas was heartily relieved to learn, two days later, that Richard had returned, with a very discontented-looking Elinor riding alongside him. He lost no time in issuing them both with stern instructions. Elinor was forbidden to even enter that stretch of the first floor hallway in which Guy de Garlande's chamber was located, and Richard was firmly ordered to personally check the identity of every serving maid sent in there with his daily meal.

Matters became more complicated once the Christmas festivities began, and the Anglo-Norman barons who had been summoned to attend occupied five long trestle boards at every meal served in the Great Hall. Guy de Garlande had been allowed out of his chamber to join them, and given that one of Maude's first actions on her return to Westminster had been to call for Elinor to accompany her wherever she went, it was impossible to prevent Elinor and Guy exchanging doleful looks and silently mouthed expressions of affection across the crowded hall.

But only a matter of days after 1125 become 1126, Henry rose slightly unsteadily from his seat at the centre of the high table, and a herald called for silence. Thomas had been briefed in advance, and had installed an extra ring of palace guards around the walls in case a riot followed what the king was about to announce.

'Faithful subjects,' he began, 'I wish to share with you some portentous news that has great significance for the future of my kingdom. As you will recall, the tragic death of my only son William Adelin robbed the nation of its natural heir to the throne. As recent events across the Channel have demonstrated, a nation without an heir is a nation in peril. But today I am delighted to be able to remove that peril, as I ask you all to rise and swear an oath of allegiance to my newly proclaimed heir — the Lady Maude.'

In the stunned silence that followed, the barons exchanged looks of amazement, and began miming silent communications — nods, shakes of the head and gestures of disbelief. Then, one by one, they rose to their feet, until there were only a handful sitting defiantly mute. Finally the last of them was shamed into standing, and in a ragged chorus they repeated the words of the oath of allegiance that Henry proclaimed. Maude sat quietly with her head bowed in what appeared to be humble acquiescence, while Elinor's mouth opened and closed with the realisation that one day she was destined to be Senior Lady and Companion to a Queen of England. Thomas continued to keep a watchful eye on the bemused barons, but was relieved that there appeared to be no sign of either protest or armed uprising. Richard found his gaze drifting towards Guy de Garlande, who was smiling to himself as he in turn looked across the room towards Elinor.

'That seemed to go down reasonably well,' Henry observed later that day during an audience to which Thomas had been summoned. 'I had thought that the barons would resist being ruled by a woman.'

'Not just any woman, sire,' Thomas reminded him. 'A former Holy Roman Empress, and a daughter of the House of Normandy.'

'Indeed,' Henry smiled. 'She has the spirit to rule my nation when I am gone, but I fear that some may seek to take advantage of what they perceive to be her woman's weakness. Little do they know that she has the heart of a hunting dog, and the instincts of a hawk. However, I shall look to you to ensure that none of the barons take to plotting in corners. I wish the palace cleared of guests by the end of the week, and our de Montfort prisoner is to be released and escorted to Dover, where he may take a ship across the water to his homeland. I wish de Montfort to be made aware that there will be no lack of monarch once my days expire.'

'It shall be as you request, sire.'

'The time has perhaps come to make more use of that son of yours, Thomas,' Henry replied with a faint smile. 'He is suitably trained in the knightly skills?'

'He is almost there, sire, but still lacks active fighting experience.'

'But he is capable of supervising men?'

'He probably always has been, sire. What mission did you have in mind for him?'

'First of all, his is to be the escort that accompanies the de Montfort brother-in-law down to Dover, to ensure that he departs without demur. That might otherwise have been a task allocated to you, but I wish you to keep your ear to the ground, and in addition instruct your men to do likewise. I have a suspicion that not all the leading barons were delighted with my choice of heir. And poor Stephen of Blois has already made tearful approaches to me, since he had been expecting to be named instead of Maude. His tears may soon become those of anger rather than disappointment, so I wish you to carefully note the identities of those with whom he communes in the days before he takes his intended departure.'

Thomas battled with his better judgment, and lost. The question was burning a hole in his brain. 'Forgive me, sire, but I will certainly be asked why you chose the Lady Maude to succeed you. I will of course serve her loyally once you are no longer with us, should I outlive you, but it is unprecedented for a woman to rule England.'

'As you already reminded me,' Henry replied testily, 'she is descended from the original Duke William, and before him the Viking warlords who conquered Normandy. Not since the fabled Boudicca, who defied the legions of Rome, has there been such a warrior princess, whereas Stephen of Blois seems to have his father's laziness and indifference over those matters that keep a nation safe. You served alongside his father, the former count, in a Crusade, did you not? Is it true that he deserted when the fighting became too hazardous, and was only shamed into returning when his wife called him a mouse?'

Thomas nodded, albeit reluctantly. 'It's true that we were forced to retreat when the enemy began starving us out and attacking our tents by night, and it's also true that we later returned. But what caused that change of mind on the part of Count Stephen, I have no idea. It was certainly rumoured at the time that his wife — a most formidable lady, by all accounts — urged him back eastwards.'

'That "most formidable lady" was my sister Adela,' Henry smiled, 'and it was from her that I learned of the Count's reluctance to engage in battle. If his son is similarly inclined, then what hope for England?'

'But did he not accompany us when we rode through Flanders and Maine?' Thomas reminded him.

Henry was not to be persuaded. 'You will also recall that we had no real occasion to engage in armed conflict? Everywhere we travelled they surrendered ere a blow was struck. I have yet to be convinced that Stephen is sufficiently warlike, and until I am, the throne will go to Maude. See to your orders.'

Three days later, Richard was closely studying the scared-looking face of a serving maid before granting her entry to Guy's chamber, when a messenger in the livery of Blois appeared. 'My master wishes an audience with you,' he advised.

Stephen occupied a suite of chambers on the next floor up, giving Richard time to collect his thoughts for what he anticipated was coming next. When admitted to Stephen's outer chamber, he found him waiting with a stern expression on his usually jovial face.

'What think you of this latest nonsense, and the king's treachery towards me?' Stephen demanded. When Richard remained silent, Stephen's eyes narrowed. 'You are a son of Blois, remember, and I am your uncle. I do not intend to let this slight go unavenged. I shall go home to Blois and begin raising the necessary forces. When I have succeeded I shall return, and I shall expect you to be waiting here with your own men, ready to support my invasion. You may leave me now.'

XII

'I suppose that this is farewell for the time being,' Guy said sadly as he stood with Richard on the quayside at Dover, next to the vessel that would make the short but choppy journey across the Channel to Boulogne.

The boatswain gave them a meaningful stare as he ordered that the ropes be removed from the bollards. Then, when they appeared not to have noticed, he called out, 'Time ter step aboard, sirs!'

'Not me — just him!' Richard called back as he gestured towards Guy and held out his hand. 'I wish you a safe crossing,' he added.

'A pity,' Guy added as he took Richard's hand and shook it warmly. 'You were a kindly gaoler, but I would have hoped that we might get better acquainted, perhaps through marriage.'

'You have a comely sister?' Richard enquired with a sardonic smile.

Guy smirked back. 'I think we both know the marriage to which I refer, Richard, and perhaps one day I might come back and claim Elinor for my own. I would be eternally grateful if you could put in a good word for me with her. She is the most beautiful woman I have ever set my eyes upon, and with her dark looks she could pass for a lady of my native Poitou. She tells me that her mother came from Aquitaine, which perhaps explains it.'

More than you could ever guess, Richard was tempted to reply. He also had half a mind to advise Guy that Elinor's feelings for him had no doubt deepened after the birth of the twins about which he remained ignorant, but he kept his counsel. To tell him now would only complicate matters, and he realised that his own failure to properly manage the confinement of his prisoner had allowed it all to happen. His father was still barely civil to him, and he had much to live down if he was to progress in the king's service.

As he led the small detachment of the Palace Guard up the chalky tracks on their way back north to London, he was giving considerable thought to his own future. He was still a small cog in his father's powerful wheel. If matters were left as they were, he would end his days in obscurity, dumbly following a daily routine as a minor palace guard, with perhaps a captain's rank, if that. Even his own sister was closer to the throne than he was, comfortably installed as companion to the Lady Maude, now proclaimed by all as their future queen.

Elinor's thoughts, as she sat at her needlework and tried to ignore the constant bad-tempered mutterings of her mistress, took the form of curses against her brother for forcing her back to Westminster. She then cast her mind back to those blissful afternoons in Guy's cramped chamber, writhing with passion on his lumpy single bolster. She hoped that he had safely crossed the Channel, even though it put him beyond her loving arms.

Her thoughts were broken into yet again when Maude enquired, 'What would *you* say if you had only just become a widow, and your father was seeking to have you married off again?'

'I'm afraid I haven't even yet experienced being a wife,' Elinor replied dolefully, and Maude made a noise that sounded like a lamprey dumpling being pierced by a knife.

'Regard yourself as fortunate, my dear, although given your beauty I feel sure that there have been many offers for your hand.'

'None of which I am aware. But to what are you alluding, madame?'

'No more of the "madame", please, Elinor. We are friends, are we not, and not mistress and servant?'

'You are most generous ... my lady?' Elinor ventured.

'Maude,' came the insistent reply, and Elinor smiled with satisfaction.

'It will be my pleasure, but to what are you alluding?'

'My father — who else would be able to treat me like a brood mare at a country market? Not content with marrying me off to a Holy Roman Emperor with whom I argued almost daily regarding his expectations of his "empress", the king now wishes to see me wed to a mere boy.'

'A boy?' Elinor echoed.

'Not just *any* boy, of course — a boy whose estates will blend conveniently with those of England and Normandy. As you may know, the king was virtually at war with that old troublemaker Fulk of Anjou after my brother died, and thereby escaped being married to Fulk's frumpy daughter Matilda. The issue between them was whether or not Maine — which was intended as her dowry — was his to give in the first place, or whether it was already to be counted as part of the estates of Normandy.'

'I was never aware of matters across the Channel,' Elinor confessed, 'since I have never ventured south of London, and my father never considered me to be someone with whom to discuss affairs of national importance. My brother perhaps, but not me. But what has this to do with your prospects for a second marriage?'

'It transpires that the Count of Anjou also has a son, named Geoffrey, who has been installed as Count of Anjou, Touraine and Maine because his father would prefer to risk life and limb on yet another Crusade. He is said to be exceedingly handsome, but he is barely half my age. However, this does not stand in the way of my father insisting that I declare my intention of marrying him. Not for my own happiness, of course, since that would be too much to expect. No, it is in order that the overlordship of Maine in particular may be settled once and for all.'

'When you say that he is "said to be" handsome,' Elinor queried, 'does that mean that you have never met him?'

'When could I have done?' Maude replied with a frown. 'My life thus far — since I was first betrothed at the age of eight — has been in Germany, and even though we travelled widely in the affairs of the Holy Roman Empire, it was mainly south to Rome.'

It fell silent for a long moment, then Maude broached the subject.

'If palace rumour be true for once, you found your own possible husband while he was being held prisoner. A handsome troubadour, no?'

'No!' Elinor denied emphatically, then regretted it when she realised that she would now have to maintain the lie, and in particular could never disclose the birth of her twins. She could never give the burning desire to see her children again as the reason for seeking leave to withdraw from Maude's side from time to time. She caught the disbelieving, probing look from Maude, and partly relented. 'We had occasion to meet, that much is true. But no doubt he has women hanging off both arms wherever he travels, so clearly there was no future for me there. In any case, he has returned home to his sister's estates in Evreux.'

'Why was my father keeping him confined, do you know?' Maude enquired.

'His brother-in-law began causing trouble among the barons in the south of Normandy, who have ever been easy to stir up. Guy was being held as a hostage, but now that peace has broken out again he has been sent back home with a message — perhaps that England will soon have Anjou and Maine as its allies.'

'Only if I submit to my father's plans to marry me off to Geoffrey,' Maude grumbled. 'I am not looking forward to our proposed betrothal ceremony in Rouen.'

The hastily arranged betrothal ceremony was also causing family discord a few floors down in Westminster Palace, where Thomas and Richard were engaged in angry exchanges.

'Why may I not come with you?' Richard demanded, incensed that he was being instructed to remain behind while his father took the Palace Guard with him across the Channel along with the royal party.

'Because you are not yet part of the Palace Guard,' Thomas reminded him, irritated that Richard had not yet faced the reality of his own seeming incompetence.

'Only because you choose not to let me be recruited into it,' Richard pointed out hotly. 'Are you so ashamed of me that you will not let me take my place among those who conduct such important duties protecting our king? How can I expect to attain knight status if you constantly block my progress?'

'May I remind you that when I left you the simple task of supervising the security of a single prisoner, albeit one kept in conditions that were compatible with his noble status, you were not even capable of keeping your own sister from consorting with him? Whether or not she fell from purity at his hand is no doubt destined to remain a dark secret, but he could have held her hostage until released! Did that not even occur to you?'

'I had no idea she was visiting him!' Richard retorted. 'Your men were so slack in reporting back to me that I had no idea what was going on.'

'Which only proves how little respect they had for you as their commander,' Thomas retaliated. 'Why should I have any lingering faith in your ability to lead men in the royal service?'

'So you propose that I sit around Westminster during your absence, whiling away my hours gazing down at the stable yard?'

'No, I propose that you take yourself off back to Walsingham, where you will no doubt still be welcome.'

'And do *what*, precisely?'

'Dear God, must I organise *every* aspect of your life?' Thomas bellowed. 'Take yourself off without delay, in order that I may be satisfied of your departure. And do not think to return here in any great hurry. It was a mistake to yield to your importuning to be trained as a knight — you might wish to consider holy orders. Now, be gone!'

The betrothal ceremony, conducted inside the Abbey of Saint-Étienne during a heavy downpour, was every bit as gloomy as Maude had predicted. The venue had been chosen partly because it was the burial place of Maude's grandparents, William of Normandy and his wife Matilda of Flanders, in order to remind the reluctant bride of her proud lineage, and the need to perpetuate the ruling Norman dynasty of which she was now destined to be a member. As if indicative of his own reluctance to marry a woman reputed to possess the strength of a man and the ferocity of a mountain wildcat, the young Geoffrey of Anjou didn't even put in an appearance, his place being taken by one of his senior nobles who solemnly pledged his master's consent to become Maude's consort.

Geoffrey did, however, attend the following year, when his future father-in-law knighted him. The entire retinue then made their way south to Le Mans, where the boyish Geoffrey stared nervously at the Bishops of Le Mans and Séez as he whispered his way into marriage with the formidable Queen Presumptive of England and its French satellite kingdoms.

As Chief Lady and Companion, Elinor was on hand throughout both ceremonies, and was also with Maude as she climbed into her bridal nightgown and slid between the rose-petal sprinkled sheets to await the arrival of her young husband. An accompanying band of musicians blew and thumped his progress down the long hallway on the main floor of the elegant château overlooking the town.

The following morning, Elinor was waiting discreetly in the Withdrawing Chamber adjoining the bedchamber. When Maude put in an appearance, she smiled wanly at her companion, ordered bread and wine and remarked, 'That could have been worse. I don't believe that it was his first time, but at least he learned what a lady expects.'

When the newlyweds took up residence in Angers, Elinor went with them, while Thomas was required to remain at Caen, where Henry was maintaining his principal Court. The next year or so progressed uneventfully, until the palace staff began to pass on rumblings of a rift developing between Henry and Maude regarding the handing over of certain castles in Normandy that had been designated as her dowry. Henry called Thomas to an audience with him in order to seek his advice.

'Thomas, how strategic are our castles at Domfront, Vernon and Argentan?'

'All castles are strategic, sire, given their capacity to house troops, withstand sieges and act as garrisons from which soldiers may be sent out to lay waste to the surrounding countryside. Might I ask the reason for your enquiry — are any of them under threat?'

'Not in a physical sense, no — at least, not yet,' Henry advised him with a furrowed brow. 'They are all part of my daughter's dowry upon her marriage to Geoffrey of Anjou.'

'So they remain under our control?'

'Certainly, but I am receiving repeated requests from my daughter that they be handed over. They already enjoy the revenues from the surrounding estates, but it would seem that Maude now demands the right to occupy them with troops from Anjou.'

'Would that not accord with our best financial interests, given the expense of maintaining royal garrisons in so many outlying parts of Normandy?'

'Of course it would, but I hesitate to hand them over because I suspect her true motives.'

'Your own daughter?'

'Well, perhaps not her so much as that husband of hers. Or, perhaps more to the point, his father.'

'Count Fulk?'

'Yes, him. As you know, we have long been at odds regarding the lordship of Maine, and he has in the past proved himself to be a veritable fox in his dealings. He let it be known that he was about to take a holy oath as a Knight Templar and join the latest Crusade, but I fear that he is behind his son's insistence that the dowry castles be handed over, thereby creating an Angevin presence inside Normandy.'

'And you wish my advice from a purely military point of view, sire?'

'I hardly need your advice as a father, do I? So — as a soldier — what say you?'

Thomas took his time to frame a suitably diplomatic reply. 'Purely as a soldier, I would not allow a potential enemy to occupy strongholds within my territory. I do not, of course, assert that Geoffrey of Anjou *is* your enemy, and even less do I suggest that your daughter may be plotting against you. But tactically speaking, I would have to advise against allowing Anjou to hide inside Normandy.'

Henry nodded. 'I believe you have given voice to my innermost thoughts. I thank you for your frankness and your loyalty, and I will continue to resist any claims from Anjou to the right to garrison our own fortresses.'

Richard knelt on the damp grass as the now very elderly Prior Geoffrey led the two small boys out of the orphanage door, then released their hands in order that they might stumble uncertainly uphill on their three-year-old legs towards Richard's waiting arms, as instructed. They had no idea who he was, or what the word 'Uncle' meant, but the old man who they both trusted and adored had said that they might do so, so they did. It was nice to be out in the sun again, and their simple lessons were over for the day.

They stood, panting, before Richard, and a lump came to his throat as he enquired, 'Which of you is William?'

'Shmee,' announced the one with the darker hair of the two, while his twin brother replied, 'I Allin.'

'You've done wonderfully with these two delightful boys,' Richard advised Geoffrey through misty eyes. 'Elinor will be *so* proud of them.'

'It is God who gives them health and strength, in His infinite mercy and blessing,' Geoffrey reminded him piously.

Richard's smile broadened as he added, 'Through the hand of his blessed servant Geoffrey de Faverches, who survived a Crusade in order to devote his life to the service of God.'

'Two Crusades, strictly speaking,' Geoffrey reminded him. 'And since you choose to remind me, how fares your father?'

'Middling well, as ever,' Richard replied. 'He wears his years as well as yourself, although his temper shortens with the years left in his life. Regrettably he and I do not always see eye to eye, which is why he has banished me here.'

'For your own welfare, no doubt,' Geoffrey suggested. 'It is a pity he could not release your sister from her duties in order to hug these beautiful boys in the way only a mother can.'

'He is not her master,' Richard advised him, 'and he has no knowledge that he has been a grandfather these past years. But I shall be here for a while, I suspect.'

'You did not find your fortune in arms?'

'Indeed not, but I am still not yet thirty, despite the lines of care that I see whenever I catch my reflection in a glass.'

'I gave up that vanity many years past,' Geoffrey smiled, 'but if you truly wish to thank me for the loving care I have invested in your nephews, you might wish to invite me to dine with you in the manor house. My principal sin these days is gluttony, and our frugal fare in the priory serves as an instant penance.'

Later, as they sat across from each other in the manor hall, Richard sought the answer to a question that had been forming slowly in his head.

'Who is the feudal lord of this manor?'

'The Sheriff of Norfolk, as it ever was. The current sheriff is called Hugh Bigod, and he inherited the role and title when his brother was lost in the same disaster that cost England its heir.'

'And he commands armed men to enforce his rulings?'

'He would not be able to enforce them otherwise. But why do you ask?'

Richard remained silent for a moment, then decided that this wise old man was someone he could trust with his innermost thoughts. 'My father all but expelled me from his side at Westminster with the cruel assertion that I do not have what it takes to become a knight and make my fortune in the world. But there is one overseas who will be relying on my strong sword arm before too many more years have passed. The time has come for me to seek both a second opinion of my fighting abilities, and the means to develop them. I shall try my chances at Norwich Castle.'

XIII

Elinor had rapidly learned that when one was a royal attendant, one became a part of the furnishings. As such, one was assumed to have neither ears nor tongue, so that whatever intimate secrets were being discussed, or sometimes hotly debated, would not be heard or repeated. This, she concluded, was why ladies in attendance on queens were carefully selected for their discretion and silence.

But it could be embarrassing, and the need to maintain a blank face was a torture when one wanted only to laugh out loud, or respond angrily to an insult that was being levelled at one's mistress. This current family squabble between king and daughter was painful to overhear, and Elinor wished that Maude had been left behind in Angers. But her mistress, heavily pregnant with her first child, needed her by her side.

They were back in Westminster, and Count Geoffrey had been left in Anjou. In truth, he had been deserted by the increasingly frustrated Maude, and both her father the king and her brother Robert, now officially the Earl of Gloucester, were attempting to persuade her to return to her husband's side.

'It is the duty of every wife to obey her husband,' Henry reminded his errant daughter, and Elinor winced. She knew her mistress well enough to anticipate the angry response that such a dismissive remark would be guaranteed to generate, and all but ducked her head as from slightly ahead of her Maude spat back her retort.

'Not *this* wife!' she yelled. 'Had you seen fit to marry me off to someone for whom I could at least *attempt* to generate respect, things might have been different. As it is, I am tied in matrimony to a spoiled brat of a boy who believes that one day he will be King of England and Duke of Normandy, as well as Count of Anjou, Tours and Maine. It does not assist matters that you seem to share my opinion of him, refusing to yield so much as a handful of ruined castles to his control. He believes that you are insulting him in the eyes of the whole of Christendom, and he can do nothing but sulk like a child deprived of a favourite toy.'

'There must be some affection between you,' Henry pointed out as he nodded towards her swollen belly, 'given your current condition.'

'Lust is not affection, Father!' she replied bitterly. 'While it is true that he does not lack either regard for, or access to, my body, his main obsession is with becoming the overlord of half the Christian world. As you remind me, I owe him certain wifely duties, but the birth of a child will only make matters worse. If it is a boy, he will no doubt change his complaint to "What do I have that I can bequeath to my heir?" I would have difficulty in answering that question, as matters lie at present.'

'From what you advise us,' Robert interposed in an attempt to find some common ground between them, 'it might assist were your father to yield complete control of the Norman castles currently under your name.'

'It has gone beyond that, I fear,' Maude replied after taking several deep breaths to control her temper. 'Nothing short of a declaration that I am to be the next Queen of England and Duchess of Normandy will convince him that he is not being publicly slighted.'

'I have already declared you to be my heir,' Henry reminded her.

'That was some years ago now, and as you are well aware your barons change their allegiance more regularly than their hose. How do we know that were you to die tomorrow, they would honour the oaths that they took while in their cups here at Westminster?'

'They are even less likely to pledge their allegiance to a woman who cannot even remain by her husband's side when the air between them begins to chill,' Henry responded. 'How, then, could they be sure of your constancy towards their welfare, and the interests of the nation?'

'And how may I be assured of their allegiance to me as their queen as matters stand?' she demanded as her face grew even redder. It fell awkwardly silent until Robert tactfully suggested a way out of the impasse.

'It seems to me that we can find a simple way through this temporary difficulty,' he oozed. 'The first action would be for Maude to go back across the Channel in order to give birth in either Normandy or Anjou — it does not matter which. Once she has delivered her child, then the barons may be asked to once again swear their oath of allegiance to her as the future Queen of England, with hopefully a son to provide the succession.'

'And if it is a girl?' Maude challenged him. 'Will my father marry her off while she is still in her cradle? Remember that I was not even into the second decade of my life before I was condemned to spend my formative years in Germany. At least the women there take no insult from their men, so I learned something of value in return for those years of misery.'

'Will you at least return to your husband?' Henry enquired.

Maude was clearly struggling to shape a respectful response as she nodded and replied, 'I will return to Geoffrey of Blois, anyway, if he would care to compromise by journeying to le Mans in order to be present at my lying-in.'

'That's decided, then,' Robert enthused as he rubbed his hands together and rose from his seat. 'Now, if you will excuse me, I will give orders for your escort to be made ready.'

'And the renewed oath from the barons?' Maude demanded as she glared at her father.

'I will see what can be arranged,' he answered vaguely.

'*Mon Dieu*, you would have killed me!' Eduard de Puys smiled up at Richard from where he lay on the damp grass.

Richard grinned, removed the point of his sword from Eduard's throat and lifted his foot from the man's chest. 'I have learned that one needs only to drop one's guard for a second, and all is lost,' he observed.

He was into his second month of sword training on the grassy slope below the Gatehouse of Norwich Castle. The current occupant, Sheriff Hugh Bigod of Norfolk, had agreed to the request of the earnest young man who had presented himself with a promise to enlist in his service in return for instruction in warfare. Richard had been handed over immediately to the battle-scarred Eduard, the Captain of the Norwich Guard.

Eduard rapidly realised that he was dealing with no starry-eyed amateur, and had grown curious as to why this mature man, who already had a firm sword hand and a good knowledge of how to employ it, was seeking service as a humble man at arms. He had long suspected that Richard had sought out advanced sword training because he wanted to be a deadly rival to anyone who crossed him. Perhaps he had a score to settle with a seasoned fighter who had committed some terrible wrong.

A page in Bigod livery walked down the green and advised Richard that the master wished to speak with him in the hall.

Richard thanked Eduard for his daily tuition and followed the young boy into the main building, where Hugh Bigod was waiting for him. He was kept standing as Bigod looked him up and down appraisingly.

'Eduard speaks highly of your prowess with a sword, and I am curious to learn whence came your skill. You are of the Walsingham estate, are you not?'

When Richard confirmed that this was the case, Bigod frowned.

'I think I begin to understand. My grandfather, in his later years, had dealings with the man who must have been your grandfather. He was constantly defying our authority as sheriffs, and for some time held this castle against us until King William Rufus restored us to our entitlement.'

'For which he was imprisoned for almost two years,' Richard replied sourly. 'That was indeed my grandfather.'

'So, your family have no respect for authority?' Bigod asserted.

Richard bristled. 'You might wish to direct that accusation to his Majesty King Henry, since my father is the Captain of his Palace Guard.'

'And was it he who passed on the family skill with a blade?'

'No. I may well have inherited it, but had my father seen fit to pass his undoubted prowess to me, I would not be seeking tuition from your own captain, who I may say is an excellent teacher.'

'Your father did not wish you to become the next generation of Walsingham fighting men?'

'Obviously not.'

'How is your relationship with your father?' Bigod enquired warily.

'It could be better. To speak frankly, he dismissed me from what I had hoped would be service under him, and suggested that I take holy orders. Most of those on the Walsingham estate have done so.'

'But you prefer to seek your fortune through your sword arm, and you are estranged from your father?'

'That is a correct, if somewhat blunt, summary of my position, certainly. But why might this be of interest to you?'

'Because Eduard has suggested to me that you might be considered as worthy to serve directly under him, as Deputy Captain of the Guard. However, in view of your lineage, I would hesitate to concur. Given the need to protect my estates at Gisors, he is frequently abroad, which places responsibility for the defence of Norwich Castle on the head of whoever serves as his deputy. I would hesitate to entrust that duty to a Walsingham, in view of the history between our two families.'

'Even though my father serves King Henry?'

'*Particularly* since your father serves King Henry. You will be aware that the man is losing his judgement as he enters his declining years, to the extent of naming a woman as his heir?'

'Did you not swear the oath to recognise her right and title, along with the other barons?'

'Naturally, since I wished to retain my office as one of the county sheriffs. But that does not mean that I believe it to be in the nation's best interests. And I am not alone in that.'

'Your meaning?'

'You will perhaps learn soon enough. But high affairs of State are of no concern to mere men of arms such as yourself. You may enter my service as Keeper of the Gate, which requires a man skilled in arms but lacking in ambition. Hopefully this will prevent you from seeking to rise above your place, as did your grandfather, and no doubt your father in his stead. Report back to Eduard and learn of your duties.'

Richard allowed himself a mouthful of curses as he strode angrily back across the Inner Bailey towards the Gatehouse, where he could see Eduard waiting for him. Even without being in his presence, his damned father was standing in the way of his advancement.

Eduard caught the look on Richard's face, and raised both eyebrows. 'It did not go to your liking?'

'No, it did not, but thank you for your recommendation that I become your deputy. Should the occasion present itself, I shall prove that you were right, and that your master was misled.'

Elinor clung to Maude's clenched hand and reminded her to breathe in and out as instructed by the royal midwife. From time to time, she dipped a cloth into the rose-perfumed water bowl and leaned across to mop the sweat from her mistress's brow. The contractions were now coming thick and fast, and with each one Maude would let out a terrified scream and grip Elinor's hand so hard that the fingernails cut into her flesh. The birthing chamber inside the castle of le Mans smelt like a whorehouse, and there was not a breath of fresh air to be had.

It had been like this for many hours. The midwife periodically lifted the sheets to examine what might be taking place, at which times Elinor politely averted her gaze.

'It will be soon,' the midwife advised them respectfully. She moved to the doorway and instructed her young daughter to slip into the outer chamber and request that hot water and fresh towels be left on the other side of the door. No men — not even Count Geoffrey, who was waiting nervously outside with two of his companions — were to be allowed a glimpse inside, or even advised of how matters were progressing. Then she moved back to the bed and asked Maude, 'How go the pains, my lady?'

'They grow no easier,' Maude grunted as she arched her back against another massive contraction, then screamed in pain. 'I think the child is seeking to enter the world!' she cried. 'Please God that is the case, that I might be rid of this torment! I shall never again expose myself to such agony!'

The midwife gave Elinor a knowing smile, then once again lifted the sheets and gave a grunt of satisfaction.

'It is as you believed, my lady, and now you must brace yourself for the worst of the pains.'

Maude began screaming, cursing, writhing against the bolster head, and calling on God for mercy. 'Elinor, have pity on my sufferings,' she pleaded, 'since you know not what it is like! I fear that I am about to die!'

'Be strong, Maude!' Elinor urged her. 'You will not die.'

'And how would you know?' Maude demanded as she gave another scream of agony.

'Because I have been where you lie today, dearest Maude, and I am still alive.'

Thirty minutes or so later, it was all over. Maude lay panting on soaking bedsheets, Elinor was rubbing her lacerated hands in an attempt to restore life to them, and a whimpering red-faced infant had been washed, wrapped in a shawl and placed on Maude's heaving breast.

'Congratulations, and God be praised, my lady,' the midwife smiled. 'You have a son.'

'He is to be called Henry,' Maude croaked, then burst into tears.

XIV

King Henry paced nervously up and down the chamber, muttering angrily to himself and asking rhetorical questions such as, 'How can they be so ungrateful?' and 'Why do they so resent my rule?' Neither Thomas nor Robert of Gloucester, perched nervously on the edges of their benches, felt qualified to answer, but simply awaited the moment when Henry would remember that he had summoned them for a reason.

Eventually the king stopped pacing, threw himself onto the ornate chair positioned between the two benches and invited Robert to speak. 'Tell him what you told me earlier.'

Robert coughed nervously, then explained, 'There are rumours of unrest among the barons to the south of Normandy. This is of course nothing unheard of, but we fear that it may be at the urging of Louis of France, who has much to gain from any rumblings in that region.'

'And you suspect de Montfort again?' Thomas enquired.

Robert nodded. 'He would be the obvious culprit, given his long divided loyalties, arising from his occupation of two large estates on either side of the Vexin border. But my father has another idea.'

'Indeed I do,' Henry fumed as he turned his choleric gaze on Thomas. 'I showed far too much mercy to that ingrate Robert de Bellême after he escaped your men at Tinchebray. He was ever in the pocket of my brother Robert, and I relented after imprisoning him for what was meant to be the rest of his life. Also, in my weakness and unfathomable generosity, I allowed his son William to assume the estate at Ponthieu, which he inherited from his mother's dowry, and which lies just to the

112

south of Boulogne. I have ever suspected him of intriguing with Louis the Fat, and it is reported that, along with several barons to the south, he is now disputing his obligation to pay feudal dues to England, on the spurious grounds that England does not have right and title to Normandy.'

'Does he claim that Normandy belongs to France?' Thomas asked.

'No, that is one of the curious matters that makes me less inclined to suspect him of being behind the current unrest. The other is of course the fact that he has not sought to organise any incursion north into Boulogne.'

'You believe that Boulogne may be the origin of this fresh resistance to English rule?' Thomas ventured tentatively, but both men shook their heads vigorously.

'Stephen of Blois is my nephew, remember, and he owes me everything,' Henry added.

Thomas took a deep breath before replying, 'With the greatest of respect, sire, William of Ponthieu owes you everything, and yet he would still seem to have the ear of Louis of France.'

Henry responded with an ill-tempered grunt, and Thomas was hoping that he had not exceeded the boundaries of courtly politeness when Robert rescued him by suggesting something even worse.

'There is the matter of Angers, of course.'

Thomas restricted his response to raised eyebrows, and Robert expanded on the point.

'Of late, we have been receiving increasing numbers of plaints from the Lady Maude and her husband Geoffrey of Anjou regarding not only the formal handing over of the estates in her dowry, but also his Majesty's delay in having the Norman barons renew their oaths to support her inheritance of England and Normandy. We are now beginning to hear mutterings to the effect that the succession is unclear, and that the Norman barons should no longer have faith in England to ensure peace upon King Henry's death. Put more bluntly, some say that Louis and his heirs can offer more in the way of certainty.'

'I cannot believe that my own daughter could be stirring matters in the manner that you suggest, Robert,' Henry objected as he helped himself to more wine. 'How could you level such accusations against your own sister?'

'I speak only of the known facts,' Robert insisted, 'which is why we summoned Thomas to this audience, is it not?'

'In what way do you believe I could be of assistance?' Thomas enquired, conscious of the fact that *his* daughter was now serving the very lady who was being implicitly accused of stirring insurrection.

Henry smiled for the first time as he explained what he had in mind. 'I wish you and Robert to repeat your tour of the Normandy estates and learn what you can of who may be behind the current unrest. You will recall that on the last occasion that we showed the royal face in those parts, any resistance that might have existed crumbled into nothing. Robert has his informants in many of the households in question, and knows who to single out for what might be termed "persuasive questioning".'

'Torture?' Thomas asked as his stomach threatened to rise in protest.

Henry shrugged. 'The means must be adapted for the ends, must they not? And this undermining of my authority must be nipped in the bud before it becomes open insurrection. Take whatever men you need, but ensure that the security of Westminster is not thereby weakened. Most of my leading barons in Normandy also have large estates here in England, and we know not how far the rot may already have spread.'

Richard suppressed a smile as he rode through the open gates of Walsingham Priory and saw the apprehensive look on Brother Francis's face. He was at the head of a small group of men at arms whose task it was to collect the term rents from all the estates that paid feudal dues to the Sheriff of Norfolk, who in turn would pass a portion of them on to the Royal Treasury. A pack horse with bulging saddlebags was evidence that they were nearing the completion of the routine collection. The sheriff's Comptroller of Accounts would mark off the amount paid by Walsingham in exchange for the tally stick that would serve as proof of payment.

Brother Francis smiled uncertainly as he walked towards where Richard had dismounted, and looked at his livery. 'It is Master Richard, is it not? And you now serve Sheriff Bigod?'

'Correct in both regards,' Richard replied. 'It must be two years since I was last here. How fares Prior Geoffrey?'

Brother Francis nodded towards the south-east corner of the estate. 'The old prior was promoted to glory last year. The new prior is Augustine, and he has the sums due by both the holy house and the estate ready for collection. If you would care to step inside, you and your men will be welcome to share in some humble refreshment.'

'Is Mother Angelica still in life?' Richard enquired anxiously a few minutes later as he partook of the elderflower wine and took a bite of black bread inside the hospitium.

Prior Augustine nodded. 'She may be found in the manor house across the river, but you must make the journey across yourself if you wish to meet with her, since she is currently confined to her bed. You have met before?'

'She is my aunt, and my grandfather once owned this entire estate, before he gave it to Prior Geoffrey of blessed memory.'

The prior thought carefully before enquiring, 'The twin boys?'

'My nephews,' Richard confirmed. 'Born to my sister Elinor, who now serves the Lady Maude who will one day be queen. You know the history of the matter?'

'Only what was confided to me by the former Prior Geoffrey, and what Brother Francis advises me of their progress. I will have them brought in for you to judge for yourself how they thrive.'

The two toddlers who Richard had once embraced with a tear had grown into sturdy young boys, and although their resemblance to their mother was unmistakable, they had grown apart in looks. Alain was the shorter of the two, with a studious countenance and a closely cropped thatch of ginger hair. The taller of the two, William, had a dark mop that matched the dark eyes of his mother.

Richard smiled at each in turn as they stood before him, and advised them, 'I am your uncle. Your mother sends her undying love.'

'We have a mother?' William enquired. 'We were told we were orphans.'

'You have been raised in an orphanage, certainly,' Richard confirmed, 'but your mother still lives, and does important work at the Court of King Henry.'

'And you are a soldier?' William asked.

Richard nodded, adding, 'I serve the Sheriff of Norfolk.'

'Have you ever killed a man?' William enquired eagerly, to the evident discomfort of his brother.

Alain lowered his head and muttered, 'That is a sin before God.'

'I have never yet killed a man,' Richard admitted, 'although I have been trained to do so.'

'I shall send up prayers for your salvation,' Alain promised without raising his eyes.

'When you do kill a man, make it count for something,' William added.

The two boys were ushered back to their classes and told to read, while Brother Francis returned to Richard with a wry smile on his face.

'As you will have deduced,' he said, 'they are as alike as chalk and cheese, even though they were born twins. What can you tell me of their mother?'

'Only that she is my sister, and is currently in the service of the Lady Maude, somewhere overseas. I know not where, I regret to say.'

'If I might make an honest observation,' Brother Francis murmured with downcast eyes, 'yours is not a particularly close family.'

'It once was,' Richard conceded, 'but now there is only Aunt Matilda — Mother Angelica — left, apart from her brother, my father, who serves King Henry as Captain of his Palace Guard. He thought me not fit for the life he had pursued, although as you can see I had other ideas.'

'I mention this,' Brother Francis persevered, 'because the boys are rapidly reaching an age at which our humble orphanage can teach them nothing more. Indeed, they may have progressed beyond that stage. Alain is by far the more spiritual of the two, and mastered his catechism at an age that I have never before known in a boy. As for William, his grasp of the Latin tongue almost places him beyond my capacity to teach, and would that I knew some more Greek. But I was called to serve God in my own way, and not as a fine scholar.'

'What do you suggest?'

'The most natural thing would be to progress them to the abbey school at Ely,' Brother Francis advised. 'There would be no charge, since we are affiliated with that house, and several of our boys have gone on to occupy valued places in the Church, or in the management of estates. All that is required is the consent of a parent — or, in the case of orphans with no parents — some distant relative. Such as an uncle,' he added hopefully.

Richard nodded. 'Please make the necessary arrangements. Should I encounter my sister, and should she recall that she has two sons, then I will advise her accordingly.'

Elinor had every reason to recall her sons as she assisted her mistress through her second labour — a much easier one that resulted in the birth of another boy, named Geoffrey after his father. It was several weeks after that, when the one-year-old Henry and his infant brother had been taken away by the nurse, that Maude recalled something.

'When I was going through that terrible time giving life to Henry, you disclosed that you had been through childbirth yourself, Elinor. I have been meaning to ask for more information ever since, but with all the unrest regarding my father's reluctance to hand over my dowry castles, it keeps slipping my mind. Please tell me — why are they not at Court, and who is their father?'

Elinor sighed and gazed wistfully out of the chamber window. 'As for the father, his identity must remain a secret, else he might be put to death for his actions in breaching the terms of his imprisonment in Westminster. I was the one who took his frugal meals to him, and we fell naturally into lustful temptation. Several times.'

'And your family now have the upbringing of the child?'

'Two boys — twins. The birth was conducted in secret in a convent on my family estate in Norfolk, and only my aunt knew of it. Even now my father knows nothing of their existence, although my brother hopefully looks after their interests, since he returned to Norfolk in disgrace for allowing our meetings to take place. My father had placed him in charge of the man's confinement while he ventured abroad with your father.'

'He is the Captain of the Palace Guard, of course,' Maude recalled. 'Or at least, he was when last I encountered him. Does he still retain that office?'

'So far as I am aware. Since we remain on this side of the Channel, I have not seen him for some time now.'

'It is very sad,' Maude commented. 'You are denied access to your children, and do not even see your father and brother because of your service to me. But can you not marry the father of your twin boys?'

'He was banished from the nation, on the pretext of taking certain information back to Evreux that King Henry wished to reach the ears of King Louis of France.'

'So this man is from the south of Normandy?' Maude enquired as her eyes narrowed. Elinor nodded, and Maude looked round carefully before confiding in her. 'Geoffrey and I are currently seeking the support of the leading barons in that region for our demands that Father hand over my dowry estates and have the Norman barons swear a new oath to recognise me as their queen in the event of his death. Our communications with them have to be circumspect, and from time to time we are visited by one of their number, who brings knowledge of how matters progress. When last we heard, it would seem that the rumblings that we have generated have caused my father to send my brother Robert of Gloucester across the Channel in order to parley with them.'

'Will he be accompanied by my father?' Elinor asked nervously. 'If so, he must not learn of the existence of my children. You must honour my confidences, my lady!'

'I will not honour them as your mistress,' Maude smiled, 'but I *will* honour them as your dear friend and protector.'

'God bless you, madam!' Elinor murmured as she wiped a tear from her eye.

Maude paused for a moment, choosing her words carefully. 'You have known no man since the birth of your sons?'

'No, certainly not!' Elinor replied, almost insulted by the suggestion. 'In truth there can be no other man for me, after the bliss I experienced at his hands. It has, I regret to say, spoiled me for any other, and of late I feel the fire of that youthful passion to have dimmed somewhat.'

'So you have no understandings, or liaisons, here at my Court?'

'Did I not just confirm that to be the case?'

'Yes, forgive me, but I have a reason for enquiring. Your beauty is famed throughout the Court, even though you are no longer a young maid. I had to be certain that there would be no complication were I to set you the simple task of acting as hostess and companion at table to a very important visitor who will shortly be arriving here at Angers. He comes as a secret messenger from those whose murmurings will hopefully bring my father to the bargaining table, and I wish him to be made welcome. I do not suggest anything carnal, you understand? Simply sit with him at banquet and be so agreeable that he will speak well of our assembly, and be eager to return.'

'I would be delighted to perform such a service,' Elinor murmured, with a slightly embarrassed downcast gaze, 'and thank you for your generous words regarding my fading looks.'

For the next few days, the Castle at Angers was alive with nervous energy. Guest chambers were aired, fresh rushes were strewn on the floors of all public rooms, and tradesmen's carts began rumbling into the kitchen yard loaded with sides of meat, fresh fruit and sacks of flour. An air of expectant gaiety hung over the Court, and Elinor laid out her best gowns.

Early one afternoon she heard the unmistakable sound of a group of horsemen clattering in towards the stables, and men giving orders for their horses to be rubbed down. Then just as the sun was beginning to sink towards the western horizon, she was summoned into Lady Maude's presence in her Withdrawing Chamber, in order to see to her mistress's toilet and attire.

Maude gazed appreciatively at Elinor's best dark blue gown. 'I fear you will put me to shade for beauty, but this is perhaps as well. We wish our valued visitor to be seduced by your allure. Let us go through to the Audience Chamber to receive him, before we crease our gowns too much.'

They took their seats in the adjoining chamber, Maude alongside her husband Geoffrey, with Elinor slightly behind her mistress and partly hidden from view. The usher was instructed to open the doors, and three men walked in, one in the lead and the others in attendance upon him.

'Welcome to Angers,' Geoffrey smiled warmly as he rose, further blocking Elinor's view of proceedings. 'We have prepared a banquet in your honour, and later you must impart the latest news from your part of Normandy. You will of course recognise my wife, the Lady Maude, from the many images of her that are now to be seen in Anjou and Maine, through which you have travelled to be with us. It now simply remains for me to introduce the lady who will be at your side during the banquet, and hopefully for most of your brief stay with us. She is named Elinor of Walsingham. Step forward please, Elinor.'

Elinor did so with a broad smile, then her eyes lit upon the honoured guest whose attentions she was instructed to capture. As she did so, the colour drained from her face and she fell gracefully to the rushes in a dead swoon.

XV

When Elinor opened her eyes there was a sea of faces swimming before them, peering down at her. Maude was yelling for a physician to be summoned, while Geoffrey was calling for wine to be administered.

'I must apologise,' Elinor croaked faintly. 'I must have been too excited. I will rise to my feet, if someone could assist me.'

A hand reached down towards her, and she almost swooned again as she caught sight of the face that had remained in her memory for so many years.

'Guy!' she whispered.

'So it *is* you, and I have not dreamed this reunion,' he beamed. 'We have much to talk about.'

'More than you know,' she replied, wondering how he would react when he knew that he was the father of twin boys.

'Once Elinor is back to herself,' Maude instructed Geoffrey, 'we must leave these two to speak privately. Elinor, is this the man you spoke to me about, from your days in London?'

Elinor nodded, then looked back up at Guy. 'It has been ten years,' she reminded him.

'You remembered me fondly, I hope?'

She held back her tears as she replied, 'How could I forget? You left me with so much to remember you by.'

'I think that we need have no fear that Elinor will not make him welcome,' Maude whispered tersely in Geoffrey's ear. Then she called to several of the attendants who had been looking on, bemused at this departure from normal Court behaviour. 'Have Elinor Walsingham conveyed to my Withdrawing Chamber, where she may recover her senses.

Perhaps our honoured guest would sit with her until she is fully composed?'

'In your Withdrawing Chamber?' Guy enquired in disbelief. 'That is hardly seemly Court practice.'

'It would not be the first time, however, would it?' Maude smiled enigmatically, and Guy chose not to pursue the point.

Seated in a padded chair in the adjoining chamber, Elinor was forcing herself to draw deep breaths as she smiled invitingly up at Guy. He stood awkwardly in the centre of the room, twisting his bonnet.

'I had not thought that we would ever meet again,' said Elinor, 'least of all in circumstances such as these. You come with a secret message from your sister's husband?'

'I do, but it is only for the ears of your mistress and her husband the Count.'

'But you still reside on the estate at Evreux?' she persisted.

'In truth, I now manage it, along with my … that is, my sister.'

'And no doubt your wife?'

'You knew?'

'I guessed. A man as handsome and courtly as yourself would not long be allowed to remain single. No doubt you chose wisely, and now have a wealthy and somewhat dame-like lady awaiting you back on the estate, with children hanging at her skirts?'

'One child only — a daughter aged seven. As for my wife, I chose with my heart, and she is the daughter of a minor estate within our own. Her name is Loisette, and if it is any consolation, I chose her because she reminded me of you. What of yourself? With your beauty, you are no doubt now a Countess.'

'I remain unmarried, despite being the mother of twin boys — at least one of whom reminds me of his father with his fair hair and his angelic features.' She saw the question written across his face, and took pity on him. 'And yes, they are yours, and are now some ten years of age.'

'They are here at Angers?' he asked eagerly.

'No,' she said sadly, 'they remain on the family estate in Norfolk, where they were born in conditions of such secrecy that not even their grandfather knows of their existence.'

'The man who imprisoned me?'

'The very same.'

'And the brother whose laxity made it possible for us to tryst in my chamber?'

'He was dismissed by my father for his slackness, and retired to our Norfolk estate with very bad grace. I hope he has since looked to the welfare of our sons, because I have not set eyes on them since they were old enough to be fed by a local wet nurse.'

'So they may not even be alive, for all that you are aware?'

Elinor shot him a resentful look. 'If that was meant to be critical of my actions, do you imagine that I do not take myself to task every day for my desertion? My only way forward in this world is in service to the Lady Maude, and in her service I am many miles from them. I have not even seen my brother since he was dismissed. Apart from the birth of two sons, our few brief times together have brought no-one any good — although they will always be nurtured in my memory as the happiest times I have ever known. And now you come seeking to stir up trouble within the realm.'

'What has your mistress told you of my mission?' Guy instinctively looked towards the closed door.

'Merely that it is intended to sow discord among the Norman barons who owe allegiance to King Henry. Do you plot to overthrow him and install Maude as queen?'

Guy smiled and shook his head. 'No, we are merely intent on ensuring that the barons confirm their loyalty to her. Due to Henry's stubborn refusal to have the matter clarified, we are obliging him to come back across to Normandy, where he may be forced to the point.'

'Surely he would be only too eager to ensure that when he dies, there will be an heir to continue the business of government?'

'For someone so beautiful, you seem to have filled your head with serious matters that are best left to those in a position to handle them. Come, take my arm, if you have fully recovered. We must not risk being accused of having resumed our former frolics, must we?'

The Countess Matilda of Boulogne, Blois and a good few places besides jumped down from the saddle and handed the glistening horse's reins to a groom with a dismissive snort. 'You are feeding him too much — he grows fat and windy,' she complained.

She turned on her heel and marched through the scullery door and the length of the castle kitchens, causing half a dozen sweating servants to pause and bow their heads. She stopped briefly to sniff at a dish of lampreys, gave a nod of approval and continued up the serving stairs into the Great Hall of her palace in Boulogne, where she strode silently up to the serving table and helped herself to a large mug of wine. She burped several times, and only then thought fit to turn and smile at their visitor.

'Count William, it must be at least a week since we last fed you. What brings you to our humble hearth this time — searching for your lost dignity, perhaps?'

Her husband Stephen of Blois chuckled nervously and sneaked a sideways glance at their visitor, but as usual he seemed not be offended by Matilda's customary sharp tongue.

'I shall not be staying for supper, you will be delighted to learn,' William of Ponthieu replied, 'since my innards are still rebelling from the last time. I am sure that I heard the allegedly roast lamb still bleating as I cut slices from it.'

'William calls to advise us that his forces are in readiness,' Stephen told his wife. 'Once the current unrest to the south is sufficiently concerning, and old Henry deserts London in order to deal with it, we may slip across the Channel and visit our many English estates, most notably those in Kent. We'll spend a few weeks marching through the orchards, reminding the English that they might prefer a man on the throne.'

'How go things in the south?' Matilda asked as she poured herself more wine and perched indelicately on the edge of the large centre trestle table, swinging one riding boot from side to side.

William grinned. 'De Montfort needed no encouragement from anyone to set the hare running, and was probably urged into it by Louis of France. Gisors in particular has been diligent in sending despatches to Henry of England that are perilously close to being treasonous, and it is rumoured that no feudal dues have been forthcoming from there for several quarter days in succession.'

'And you have put it abroad that the source of the trouble is my cousin Maude?' Stephen enquired.

William nodded. 'As we agreed. Your sailors here in Boulogne, and mine in Saint-Valery, have been fed the same false information, to the effect that Maude wishes to be queen without delay, and will depose her father if necessary. It should bring him over here quickly. Then we'll slip in behind him, perhaps even employing the same vessels from which he disembarks.'

'This is comforting news, William,' Stephen beamed. 'Are you sure you will not stay for supper? The same maid to whom you seemed to show considerable attention on your last visit is still in service here.'

'And she is no doubt as flea-ridden as last time,' William grimaced. 'My wife blamed the laundress when I could not otherwise account for the state of my hose. I will, if you will excuse me, decline your dubious offer.'

'I feel as if my behind is on fire, if you will pardon my crudity,' Robert complained as they dismounted outside the inn at Montreuil-Juigné, on the northern outskirts of Angers. 'I grow tired of all these days spent in the saddle, and all these evenings listening to false protestations of allegiance to Maude and loyalty to England. But at least we have learned that there is someone stirring the mud around the fishpond, and that he is currently just down the road.'

'Your network of "advisers" has certainly proved effective,' Thomas agreed. 'Do you have any in Angers?'

'Two,' Robert replied. 'One in the kitchen and the other engaged as a server at table. I sent word for them to meet us here this evening, and so if we survive the pigswill that passes for supper, we may be well placed to apprehend the rat before we trot into Angers to bring fatherly greetings to the Lady Maude. Were she my daughter, I would thrash her for her ingratitude and impatience, but then she is only my half-sister, so I cannot. We can only hope that the man we seek has not met with a warm welcome here.'

Later that evening, as they attempted to digest one of the worst suppers they had ever encountered, Thomas and Robert were visited by a furtive little man wearing a long riding cloak and a wide-brimmed hat to conceal his identity. He was handed a small bag of coins after advising them that Maude had been entertaining visitors wearing an unfamiliar livery. There were three of them, he told his paymasters, and they were planning to leave on the morrow. Their leader was described as very tall, with a noble bearing, answering to the name of 'Guy', and readily identifiable by his long fair hair.

Thomas blasphemed and turned to Robert. 'If he be who I believe him to be, I shall enjoy ordering his imprisonment and torture. Not only did he play the king false when he undertook to spread despondency at the Court of King Louis — who has no doubt sent him here to divert Lady Maude from the path of loyalty to her unsuspecting father — but he also took the honour of my daughter Elinor, thanks to the stupidity of my witless son.'

'How do you propose that we ensnare him?' Robert asked.

Thomas grimaced. 'We ride with four men at arms, which makes us a party of six in all. There are, we are advised, only three of them, so we ambush them on the road, then take them back to Caen as our prisoners.'

'You do not propose that I wield a sword?' Robert replied, aghast.

Thomas smiled and shook his head. 'You simply wave one around and look fierce.'

'If we do as you suggest,' Robert pointed out, 'then we shall foreswear the opportunity to visit Angers itself. You will not be reunited with your daughter, and I will not see my sister.'

'A sister who is almost certainly playing you and your father false, and hatching dark schemes with our ages-old enemy of France,' Thomas reminded him. 'Once we have Guy de Garlande in chains, and this time held in far less luxurious accommodation than was afforded him in London, we may learn the whole sorry tale. We owe our first duty to your father, and my king.'

It went as planned. Two hours' ride east of Angers, as Guy and his two companions trotted along the narrow track through the wood, Thomas and Robert stepped out from where they had been hidden, awaiting their approach. The group of three halted on a command from Guy de Garlande, who turned in his saddle to look behind him, then ordered his men to offer no resistance as four heavily armed men at arms walked their horses out from the trees behind them.

Thomas smiled sadistically as he took Guy's offered sword, and gave an order to everyone to ride on.

'Where are you taking us?' Guy asked.

Thomas took great delight in advising him, 'To the dungeons under the *Château de Caen*, which you will find far less comfortable than the last chamber that you occupied whilst my prisoner. And on this occasion, your food — should you receive any — will be served by a verminous gaoler who smells worse than the goat whose overripe meat he will be serving you.'

It took them four miserable days, riding hard by day and subjecting themselves to the rigours of wayside inns each evening, before they saw the spires of Caen up ahead. There had been virtually no conversation during those four days, and Guy had been granted ample opportunity to invent a reason for his journey to Angers. Thomas led him at sword point down into the lower keep to the door of the dungeon corridor, and hammered on it with his sword hilt in order to command its opening. Guy treated him to a sarcastic smile.

'Am I being punished merely because I was visiting the beautiful woman who captured my heart ten years ago in your Palace of Westminster?'

'No, you are being detained until you tell us the true reason for your visit to the Lady Maude and her husband at Angers. You may do so of your own free will, or if not we might have an opportunity to try one of the instruments of persuasion that was brought back from the last Crusade.'

'You would torture the father of your two grandchildren?' Guy enquired mockingly, just as the door opened. The gaoler grabbed his prisoner by the shoulder of his jerkin and hauled him inside, and Thomas stood looking like a man dealt a mortal blow.

Back in Angers, it took several weeks before the news was received that Guy had been taken prisoner by men in the service of King Henry. When it was, Maude was white with fury and apprehension, and sat with Geoffrey discussing how they should respond. Elinor sat behind her mistress, sniffling her grief into a cloth.

Finally, Maude had made up her mind. 'We have nothing to lose, now that our part in the unrest will have been revealed to my father. We ride east with all speed, to mobilise those barons loyal to our cause.'

'And then?' Geoffrey enquired languidly.

'And then we set sail for England. The barons loyal to us here on this side of the Channel have estates over there. It is time that they had a new monarch — and this time a woman!'

XVI

Robert looked askance at Thomas, and Thomas stared back at him in disbelief, as King Henry yet again refused to march against Maude. He was back in Caen and convinced that the unrest of the southern barons was the work of Louis of France.

'He has ever disputed my right to Normandy,' Henry insisted, 'and the quarrel goes back to my great-grandfather's day, when Duke Robert asserted his title, and his grandson claimed England.'

'But sire,' Thomas tried again, 'we captured the man who travelled to Angers in order to conspire further with the Lady Maude to create unrest.'

'How do you know that he was not *sent* to Angers by Louis?' Henry argued, refusing to believe such treachery of his beloved daughter. 'It was a de Montfort who was entrusted with the business, was it not? The man you have in the dungeons beneath where we sit?'

'He is merely a de Montfort in-law,' Thomas reminded him. 'His sister is married to the de Montfort of Evreux.'

'The same de Montfort with estates in the Vexin, where he is pledged to the service of Louis!' Henry insisted as his countenance grew redder. 'There is one obvious way in which to learn whether or not this prisoner of yours was sent by Louis or summoned by Maude. You must order that he be tortured!'

Thomas blanched and swallowed hard. Although he had no regard for Guy de Garlande, he was the man beloved of his daughter. Elinor would never forgive him if he had Guy maimed, blinded or crippled for life. There would also be two children bereft of a father if the process resulted in the man's death. Robert could tell at a glance that Thomas was shrinking from the prospect, perhaps because he shared his abhorrence of such barbarity in a Christian society. He therefore came to Thomas's rescue.

'Perhaps we could march south to the border with Vexin in a great show of military strength?' he argued, banking on his father's vanity when it came to armed pomp.

Henry appeared indecisive as he stared into his wine goblet, then looked up at Thomas. 'We have tried that before, have we not? All we achieved was a series of snivelling assurances of fidelity. As soon as we led our men off their estates, they were at it again, scheming for Louis and seeking to put the blame on Maude.'

'Perhaps if we were to take hostages this time?' Thomas ventured. 'If each of the barons had a wife or child confined here at Caen, or perhaps transferred by ship across the Channel to Westminster, they might think twice before allowing their loyalties to be swayed. You might even make them swear the oath to Maude in return for a promise that their hostages will be treated with kindness?'

'What say you, Robert?' Henry enquired, seemingly unconvinced.

Robert nodded. 'Thomas here has far greater knowledge of military tactics than I,' he reasoned, by implication making the point that Henry possessed even less. 'We have a large force of men eating Caen out of provisions for as long as they remain here. Once on the road south, we may impose on the reluctant hospitality of your subjects.'

'Very well,' Henry agreed grudgingly. 'Let us seek a very clear renunciation of the foul lie that your sister is behind all this. As for the man in the dungeons, he should at least be *threatened* with torture. See to it all, Thomas. In the meantime, I wish you both to kneel and swear an oath before God that you will support the claim of Maude to my crown when I am gone.'

Later that day Thomas sought admission to the dungeons, where he diverted his attention from the foul stench of fear, and worse, by contemplating what he was committed to. Other men might swear oaths before God that they had no intention of honouring, but Thomas had been raised in the shadow of a shrine to the Holy Mother, in which several of those dear to him had devoted their lives to Christ.

He recalled his solemn pledge before the altar at the shrine on the day that God had granted his plea to allow him to spend his remaining years with the beautiful Emma of Blois. She had been taken from him many years since, but there remained the daughter who reminded him of her every time he allowed himself to gaze lovingly into her dark eyes, and watch her long, dark hair swirl around the collar of her gown. Her interests were those of the lady she served, the lady to whose service he had just sworn an oath. And now he had grandchildren to think of.

The heavy wooden door grated open against the dirt floor, and Guy rose defensively as Thomas entered. He smirked bravely and asked, 'Is it the day of my torture?'

'Shut up and listen carefully,' Thomas instructed him. 'The king ordered that you be given agony until you reveal who was the instigator of the plot against his throne. I defied him, not because of any love for your miserable carcass, but because you and Elinor have children. Two, as I believe you revealed when we first brought you here. I wish for more information regarding them, and in particular where they may be found. In return, I will allow King Henry to continue in his belief that

Louis of France is behind your treachery, whether it be true or not.'

'I know only what Elinor has revealed to me,' Guy replied with a relieved smile. 'I knew nothing of their existence until I ventured to Angers, but Elinor advises me that they are twin boys, and that they are lodged on your estate in Norfolk.'

'It is no longer my estate,' Thomas replied with a frown, 'but there is a priory there now, to which they may have been consigned with the blessing of its prior. They would now be some ten years old, yes?'

'Yes, but are you saying that you are no longer welcome where they may be found?'

'I have no idea, since I have not been back there for that entire time, given my duties ensuring the personal safety of King Henry. You have spoken recently with Elinor, who I have also not seen for that same period. Did she seem to be in good health?'

Guy gave him a look that mingled disbelief with pity. 'What sort of family are you, where father and daughter have not met for ten years?'

'None of your business,' Thomas retorted, 'and bear in mind that thanks to me you will not be tortured. I don't suppose you are prepared to satisfy my curiosity? Was your journey to Angers at the request of Lady Maude, or at the instigation of Louis of France?'

'Since I owe you a great deal,' Guy replied, 'I will simply advise you that Elinor is well, and that my journey to Angers would not displease the French King. I shall see to it that your mercy towards me is suitably rewarded when I am in a position to do so.'

'Which may be never, should your treachery become more fully exposed,' Thomas advised him curtly. He turned and hammered on the door for the gaoler to let him out.

A month later, there were wagonloads of hostages making their way along the ice-rutted roads north to Caen. In the main they were first-born sons and daughters of Norman barons who had failed to wax enthusiastic when asked to swear an oath of allegiance to Maude. There were some who were wives and mothers, and Thomas had long since hardened his heart to the pitiful screams of infants and women wailing for their husbands.

King Henry's men eventually arrived at the château at Gisors, one of the southernmost estates that was notionally under the feudality of England, but whose proximity to the border of the Vexin made the loyalties of its lord suspect. It was one of the Norman estates owned by Hugh Bigod, Sheriff of Norfolk, and Henry had long suspected him of being under the influence of his southern neighbour. However, given that most of his time was spent in Norwich, he had never been openly challenged regarding his loyalty.

In his absence the fine château that was the centre of the estate — and had been heavily fortified by Henry himself before he'd granted it to the Bigod family — had become a byword for fine living. Rich tapestries kept out any inclement draughts, fine galleries overlooked its great hall, and a fortune in statuary could be found along the walls of all the public rooms. It was under the daily management of a steward, and the current holder of the office, Raymond Bartelier, was obviously not accustomed to having his authority challenged.

When Henry's men began removing tapestries and marble images of the saints, Bartelier made such a nuisance of himself by complaining that the items belonged to his master, that Henry was called in to remind the man of who was the ultimate owner of the château and its contents. When Bartelier gave Henry his opinion on the impertinence of English pretensions over land that rightly belonged within the province of France, he joined the others in the wagon train destined for Caen. The men at arms were then given permission to loot at will.

In high spirits, Henry took himself and his inner circle back north to the luxurious former castle and hunting base favoured by his father at Lyons-la-Forêt. The area was famous for its wooded lakes, and the cook kept a fine lamprey pond that she was ordered to pillage for a magnificent banquet to celebrate the end of their campaign. All the leading Norman barons had given up at least one close relative as a hostage to their future good behaviour.

Thomas excused himself early from the feast. He was quietly seated in front of the banked fire in his chamber, when the furtive arrival of Robert of Gloucester was announced by the usher who had been guarding the door. Robert took a seat by the fire, and accepted a goblet of the local *vin du pays*.

'I really should not, since I have had more than enough already,' he admitted, 'although it would seem that we are celebrating. At least, my father is. He never could resist lampreys, although they are known to give him a gripe. He is already as drunk as a dog, so we may be here for several days until he recovers.'

'Get all your men together, tell them to pack everything they will need for at least three months of fighting on the move, and assemble them on the front green within the hour,' Hugh Bigod ordered Richard as he stormed into the armoury, where

Richard had been supervising the sharpening of his sword.

As almost two hundred men in various forms of military attire stood to attention on the lower slope of Norwich Castle Green, Bigod stepped forward and yelled as loudly as he could against the prevailing wind.

'I have today received word that my estate of Gisors — that's in Normandy — was recently plundered by men under the command of King Henry. Property of considerable value was carried off, women servants were violated and my steward has been taken in chains and thrown into the dungeons at Caen. It will come as no surprise that I do not intend to sit idly by and ignore such an insult. We march to Caen in order that I may register my protest, and if I do not receive satisfaction, we shall be proceeding against the forces of our so-called king. I say "so-called" because no king worthy of that name would behave so ill against a loyal subject. He must therefore experience the wrath of a *disloyal* subject. That is all — prepare to move out within the hour.'

As they trod south along tracks rutted with frozen slush, Richard reflected with sad irony on the uncertainty of life. He was now part of an armed force travelling across the Channel to confront the king to whom he had sworn allegiance all those years ago. Thomas Walsingham would no doubt be in charge of the defensive ring that would encircle King Henry should it come to armed rebellion. Having been deemed unfit to defend the king, Richard would now be taking up arms against his own father, demonstrating how badly he had been misjudged when it came to a fight to the death.

On the final day of a two-week march, they were called to a halt on the long slope that led down to the harbourside at Dover. Richard was in the front rank, as befitted his status as a captain, and could clearly see the chaos below them. The harbour seemed to be filled with vessels in the process of coming alongside the jetty and disembarking both men and their horses, while lower down the slope a large contingent of armed men was marching towards them.

'Who in God's name are they, and why are they marching inland?' Hugh Bigod roared.

'Some of them are wearing the livery of Blois,' Richard replied.

'How would you know, since you assure me that you have never been involved in affairs across the Channel?' Bigod demanded.

Richard thought quickly before answering. 'Stephen of Blois was a regular visitor to Westminster during my days in service with my father, and that bright blue shield is easy to remember.'

'Then the other livery being worn by some of those in the front line must be that of Boulogne,' said Bigod. 'From this distance, it looks as if a beast with three red eyes is advancing towards us. We had best order our men to the side of the track.'

Richard gave the command, and the men of Norfolk parted down the centre as the incoming party approached. Their leader came into closer focus, and Richard gave a slight gasp as he recognised the features under the battle helm. It had been over ten years since their last meeting, and he turned his face to the ground in the hope that he would not be so recognisable. His eyes averted, he heard the arrogant exchange between the two leaders.

'Where might you and your men be headed?' Stephen of Blois demanded.

'To avenge the sacking of my estate at Gisors by a king who is not worthy of his subjects' loyalty,' Bigod replied. 'Even if he takes my head for it, I shall avenge the insult to my lineage.'

'I believe that we may share that sentiment, whoever you are, but the word has obviously not yet reached you that my uncle King Henry is dead. The old fool ate more than was good for him, as usual, and expired some weeks ago. I am Stephen of Blois, and I ride to London to claim the crown of England and Normandy. You may settle your petty disputes later. In the meantime, have your men drawn up behind mine as we march north.'

Without thinking, Richard stepped forward and gave the instruction, 'Do as he says — my men to the ranks immediately behind those who are already on the road.'

Bigod turned on him with a face red with anger. 'Who are you to be ordering my men around without my leave? You are merely a captain in my service!'

Stephen gave a long, slow smile as he recognised Richard, now leaner in the face and more lined. The family resemblance was still unmistakable.

'He may be your captain, but he is also my nephew, and he will ride alongside me as we travel to Westminster. You have a new king, and you will obey my command.'

XVII

Thomas and Robert were exhausted. They had loyally seen to the immediate matters necessitated by the unexpected and undignified death of King Henry, and they had been in the process of having his embalmed remains transferred to England when they received news that Stephen of Blois and Boulogne had crossed the Channel to claim the English crown.

'We must release all our hostages if we are to have any hope of maintaining the loyalty of the Norman barons,' Thomas insisted as they sat sharing a jug of wine in the royal apartments overlooking the town.

Robert posed the question that they had each been struggling with privately. 'Loyalty to *which* of the claimants, do you suggest?'

Thomas gave him an admonishing stare. 'You may break the oath that you swore so recently, but to me a solemn vow can only be dishonoured if one is prepared to answer to God for doing so. We swore allegiance to Maude, did we not?'

Robert nodded reluctantly. 'Were we wise to do so?'

'In the circumstances that then obtained, yes we were. And the Lady Maude — Queen Maude, in my eyes — now has sore need of that allegiance.'

'Though she be my sister,' Robert confessed, 'I fear her cause to be greatly weakened by recent events. She claims through her father, whose name probably stinks more in Normandy than his corpse did, after what he recently inflicted on those of his leading barons who he suspected of treachery. Can we now expect them to rally around his daughter? A *Queen* of England, never before known?'

'Every momentous event must occur for the first time,' Thomas argued philosophically. 'Whether her path to the throne will be strewn with posies of flowers, or littered with the corpses of her enemies, I am sworn to uphold her claim, and I intend to do so. Should you not be so inclined, then we part company today on terms of amicable friendship. Look to your conscience, is all I ask.'

'My conscience bids one thing, my common sense another,' Robert replied gloomily. 'But I cannot be seen to desert my own flesh and blood at the first sign of difficulty.'

The reference to flesh and blood drove a dagger of guilt straight into Thomas's heart as he recalled who was still, so far as he knew, seated alongside Maude and serving her in a more humble capacity. 'We must at least travel to Angers and seek further counsel as to what our new queen needs of us. And I must ensure that my daughter remains safe, should there be any threat of an uprising in Anjou or Maine. But first, as I already counselled, we must arrange for our hostages to be freed before all the barons here in Normandy, and those who may travel from England, stage their own rebellion.'

Robert put down his wine goblet and rose to his feet. 'I shall give appropriate instruction to those of our household who will travel with us, and see to the release of the prisoners and the gathering of the men at arms who will guarantee us a safe journey west.'

A week later, Thomas stood with his heart in his mouth outside the heavy oak doors that gave access to Maude's Audience Chamber in the Castle of Angers. Robert had already entered, to advise Maude of their arrival and to pledge their renewed loyalty, but Thomas had sought leave to remain outside, on the grounds that he did not wish to intrude on a family reunion. The truth was that he was seeking to avoid one of his own. His every nerve was twitching at the prospect of the bitter reception he deserved from the daughter he had all but abandoned after having the man she loved expelled from her arms. He had not then known about the twins she'd been carrying, but he doubted if his actions would have been any different if he had.

In his fevered anxiety he began pacing up and down the hallway. As he turned at the end of his latest journey, the chamber doors flew open and a distant memory rushed towards him.

'Father! Dearest Father!' Elinor gasped as she threw her arms around him. 'It has been *so* long, and I have *so* much to impart! But just to see you again, well, it … it's so...' Whatever she might have said next was lost to choking tears as she clung to him and bawled like a child.

Through the waterfall of his own tears, he looked over her shoulder and saw a smiling Robert waiting by the open door.

'If the family reunion might be postponed for but a short while, Queen Maude wishes audience with us both.'

'I cannot be expected to hazard the life of my unborn child in order to don armour and march at the head of an army in the manner of Boudicca defying the legions of Rome,' Maude protested as they sat sharing wine and wafers. Pages laid the small trestle in the centre of the chamber and serving maids brought in trenchers and goblets. Supper was not long away, and Thomas had suddenly regained his appetite.

'The time is not meet for that, my — Your Majesty,' he advised. 'The first task will be to determine the strength of your support in Normandy. We must be sure of that before we contemplate any return across the Channel.'

'Will that not give the usurper Stephen further opportunity to strengthen his hand on the crown?' Geoffrey argued.

Robert nodded. 'It will also give him ample opportunity to reveal his true colours, once the initial enthusiasm has died down. If there *is* any, of course. We do not know how he will be received by the English barons.'

'Many of whom are also the Norman barons, of course,' Maude reminded him. 'My child is due at mid-summer, or so my physicians advise me, so would the next six months be enough time to determine our best course of action?'

'Almost certainly,' Robert confirmed. 'Might I suggest that you summon all your Norman barons to some convenient place within Normandy itself, in order that we may assess who is with us, and who — by their absence — is seemingly not?'

After a brief consultation between Maude and Geoffrey, the castle at Argentan was selected, partly for its location a convenient two to three days' ride from Caen and partly because of the luxuriousness of its accommodation. It was agreed that Thomas would ride north in advance, taking Elinor with him, in order to ensure that the castle garrison was adequately manned, that everyone knew what was expected of them, and that the household staff were properly instructed in the preparation of the guest chambers.

Over supper, Maude had another matter to raise with Robert. 'Are you aware of the likely reaction of the Pope to any attempts to repudiate the solemn oaths of allegiance to me that the barons swore? I realise that you are not a clergyman, but surely a solemn oath invites punishment from God if broken?'

'We shall none of us know until we are no longer able to return and warn others similarly inclined,' Thomas grinned as he sliced roast lamb, 'but as I had occasion to remark to Robert, I for one would not be prepared to take the risk.'

'I hope I have your support for reasons *other* than your fear of Hellfire,' Maude replied.

'Of course. It was what your father wanted, and I owe him everything.'

Two days later, as father and daughter rode side by side, surrounded on all sides by men at arms in the livery of Anjou, Elinor enquired after her twin sons. Thomas shook his head.

'I only learned of their existence when I took Guy de Garlande prisoner as he left Angers, and I have not been back in England since. I take it that you left them with Prior Geoffrey?'

'I did, but I doubt if he remains alive after all this time,' she murmured dolefully. 'Hopefully Mother Angelica has seen to their welfare if there has been a change of prior, but I yearn to return to Walsingham in order to learn how they have fared. I will have to harden my spirit to the fact that they will not know me.'

'I harboured similar fears when I came to Angers,' Thomas admitted. 'Thank God that you were prepared to be so forgiving, after the callous manner in which I abandoned you, never once journeying to enquire about your welfare. If it is any consolation, I have seen nothing of your brother Richard either these many years. Perhaps he is back at Walsingham, caring for your sons.'

At that moment, Richard was at Westminster, offering apologies of his own to Stephen of Blois for his failure to keep him advised of how matters had been progressing at the English court during the intervening years.

Stephen replied with an expansive wave of his hand. 'There was nothing you could have told me that was not faithfully reported back by my several spies within the royal palaces.'

'Robert of Gloucester employs similar informants,' Richard advised him. 'I'm sure there are those in his pay concealed about us even here at Westminster, reporting your every word and action to Lady Maude, who is no doubt attended by both my father and her half-brother.'

'I am aware, not only of their existence, but also of their identities,' Stephen assured him. 'I make it my business to ensure that Robert only hears what I want him to hear. But to judge by your choices in recent years, you have abandoned the world of diplomacy for the battlefields. Are you much of a horseman, or do you prefer fighting on foot?'

'Even mounted knights find it advantageous to dismount from their steeds and fight on foot on many occasions,' Richard replied, 'and if one can arrive at the arena of battle on horseback, one is more refreshed for the challenge ahead.'

'So you esteem the value of horses?'

'Yes I do,' Richard replied.

Stephen clapped him on the shoulder and announced, 'You are hereby appointed my Master of Horse.'

Richard's mouth dropped open in surprise. 'You do me a great honour — sire.'

'Then see that you discharge your duties with the utmost loyalty and attention to detail. Now, for when I make the announcement, what is your precise title?'

'The one you just gave me, surely — "Master of the King's Horse"?' Richard replied.

'You misunderstand me. Where is your estate?'

Richard shrugged. 'I was born and raised on the estate of Walsingham, which my grandfather then owned. But he gave it away to the Church, and since then I have lived wherever I have served, which in the main has been Norwich.'

'So you have no estate of your own? This will not do. I cannot have a nephew of mine without an estate, because without an estate I cannot give you a title. But all is not lost. Come back to me in an hour. I will introduce you to the man who knows all about estates, given that he owns several already, largely thanks to his ability to flatter and wheedle.'

An hour later Richard was being presented to a man of approximately his own age, although to judge by his rich dress he was a nobleman of high esteem.

'This is my good friend and ally Waleran de Beaumont,' Stephen advised him. 'His father was Robert, Earl of Leicester, which is one of the few estates that he cannot hope to enjoy, given that he has an older brother. He and his brother were wards of King Henry, who was most generous towards them both. Waleran is already Earl of Worcester, and Henry displayed his fatal weakness towards those close to him when on the death of their father the estates were divided in such a way that his brother inherited Leicester while Waleran acquired Meulan, an estate that lies within the Vexin. If you have any knowledge of the lands across the Channel, you will know that the Vexin stands as a defensive buffer between Normandy and the stronghold of the French kings on the Île de France.'

'I will strive to absorb all this,' Richard replied, bemused by all the detail.

'See that you do,' Stephen smiled as he continued. 'Waleran proved to be particularly irksome to the late King Henry, and particularly useful to my interests, when he conspired with Count Amaury de Montfort, whose Normandy estate lies in Evreux, to support the cause of William Clito.'

'Evreux I *have* heard of,' Richard assured him as he remembered the handsome adventurer who had seduced his sister and left her with twin sons. 'What is more, I have visited it.'

'This is good,' Stephen smiled, 'since you and Waleran will be working closely together. Shortly before Henry died, Waleran seemed to have been forgiven his treachery, and was present at the deathbed, where he assures me that he overheard Henry absolving his barons from their oath of allegiance to the pretender Maude. This reinstates the original oaths sworn in my favour and gives me clear right and title to both England and Normandy. In return for his sworn allegiance to me, Waleran is confirmed in all his existing estates, with more to come if he fulfils his promise as a leader of armed men. Armed men that will include you, of course.'

'I shall be honoured to serve under him,' Richard announced with a slight bow in the man's direction.

'*Alongside* me, not *under* me,' Waleran replied as his first contribution to the conversation. 'You will command my cavalry. But before that may occur, Stephen here advises me that we need to find you an estate.'

Richard opted to remain silent, and Waleran warmed to the theme.

'There are basically two ways to acquire an estate. The first is to prevail upon the king to bestow one upon you, but Stephen feels that on this occasion it might not be wise to commence his reign by elevating a hitherto totally unknown minor relative. The other method is more subtle, and potentially more pleasing. You remain unmarried — why is that?'

'I have never met a woman who I wished to wed,' Richard advised him, 'given that my life thus far has been around stables, barracks, fighting men and castle defences.'

'But you do not prefer men?' Waleran demanded.

Richard blushed as he replied, 'Most certainly not! But neither do I favour camp women and palace serving maids.'

'So your tastes would run to a plump widow whose estate you could inherit?'

'Probably, but you should know that I am no great lover, so far as I am aware.'

'You have remained pure?' Waleran enquired with eyebrows raised in disbelief, and when Richard nodded his questioner gave a hollow chuckle. 'This will be easier than I thought. Leave matters in my hands.'

Westminster Abbey was crowded to capacity three days before Christmas Day, 1135, when Archbishop of Canterbury William de Corbeil anointed Stephen with the crown of England and Normandy. The rousing cheers of the attending barons echoed around the high vaulted ceiling. The coronation procession snaked out of the abbey and across the courtyard to the royal palace on the far side, where the nobility of England, in company with its leading prelates, slid their outer garments of rank into the waiting hands of their servants and made their way into the Great Hall for the banquet. As he moved towards his designated seat at the table reserved for senior officers of State, Richard felt someone tugging at his sleeve. He turned, and there stood Waleran. Beside him was a woman in her late thirties, somewhat pink of countenance and undoubtedly well fed. She smiled uncertainly at Richard, then looked him up and down somewhat artlessly as Waleran effected the introductions.

'Richard, please allow me to introduce Agnes, Dowager Countess of Chalfont. She will be pleased to become your wife whenever the time is appropriate, but we thought perhaps sometime after Easter.'

XVIII

Maude gave birth to her third son, William, in July of 1136, at Argentan, by which time the vast majority of the Norman barons had, with varying degrees of enthusiasm, pledged their loyalty to her cause. Content that there were to be no local uprisings, Robert and Thomas made plans for a proposed invasion of England in order that Maude could remind the leading barons there of their oaths to her father, acknowledging her as their queen. Late one afternoon, once Maude was back on her feet, baby William was consigned to his wet nurse, and Count Geoffrey had returned from his annual tour of Anjou and Maine, they gathered in the Audience Chamber to discuss what Robert had in mind.

'My extensive estates in Kent are secure for the moment,' he advised them, 'and I have sufficient men at arms installed in each of them to stage an uprising. I am in regular contact with them all, and they have been instructed simply to await my word. While Stephen is busy putting down outbreaks of rebellion south of London he will not notice our arrival in, say, Portsmouth, with the full force of our troops from Normandy, Anjou and Maine. Stephen has isolated himself from his potential support on this side of the Channel. If we strike quickly once the Kent uprisings begin, he will have insufficient forces to fight on several fronts at the same time.'

'Assuming that you are in Kent when we land in Portsmouth, is it your intention that I should lead the main force?' Thomas asked.

Robert shook his head. 'First of all, I shall not be in Kent in person. I have sufficient faith in my men at arms — and, more to the point, those who lead them — to be able to remain over here. When we cross the Channel in force, it is, I would suggest, appropriate that Count Geoffrey be at the head of our army, since a substantial number of our combined force will be sporting the liveries of Anjou and Maine. You, I suggest, will act as his second in command.'

'Since the invasion of England is in Maude's name, would it not be more symbolic for her to ride at its head?' Geoffrey queried.

Maude snorted. 'The mother of three infants? Have some sense! By all means allow me to be there wearing my crown — assuming that one may be made for me here in this country town — but surely not in the front rank?'

'These are matters of detail that can be hammered out later,' Robert intervened. 'What is needed now is broad agreement to my recommended strategy.'

'I see no reason not to agree,' Maude smiled, 'and I am fortunate to have a brother who is so gifted in the matter of military strategy.'

'And I am fortunate to have Thomas here as my strong sword-arm.' Robert nodded in his direction. 'But this is about to become a family struggle without precedent, at least in England. Brother fighting alongside sister, and two cousins waging warfare over a single crown.'

And father fighting against son, Thomas reflected ruefully as he prayed that Richard had put aside his original military ambitions and settled quietly on the estate at Walsingham.

'I suppose you were ordered by our new king to occupy this seat alongside me,' Agnes Chalfont muttered as she helped herself to a very generous portion of pigeon pie.

Richard took another swallow of wine as he framed a suitable reply. 'I was under the impression that the seating allocations at these functions are the province of the Chamberlain,' he responded coolly, 'but no doubt he had his instructions.'

'There'll be no carnal nonsense, by the way,' Agnes announced tersely.

Richard opted to milk the humour of the situation. 'You're too busy eating anyway, I observe.'

'I meant once we are married,' Agnes replied huffily. 'I gave that sort of thing up many months before my late husband decided to depart this life. I have no intention of reviving it, particularly not with a new husband who is not of my choosing.'

'Is it the strenuous exercise that you fear, or the prospect of lying with a younger man who may damage the bolster in his enthusiasm?'

'You are mightily offensive for someone seated next to his intended,' Agnes replied as she suppressed a wry smile. This one was a worthy opponent in a verbal contest, if nothing else, unlike her milk pudding of a late husband, who usually bolted for the chamber door when her barbed wit got too much for him.

'You must forgive me, but I never was very respectful towards my elders.'

'Just how old do you take me to be, you insolent young puppy?' she demanded as she turned sideways to glare at him.

Richard thought for a moment, remembered something he had once been advised by Elinor regarding the vanity of older women, and replied, 'I am not used to assessing the age of ladies, high-born or otherwise, but I would hazard a guess at thirty-two or thereabouts.'

'And you would be incorrect,' the thirty-eight-year-old widow advised him with a broad smile. 'However, you were incorrect in the right direction. So what age are you?'

'I believe myself to be thirty-four years old,' he replied mysteriously. 'My father advises me that I was born in 1102, and although I was there at the time I was not recording the event on a calendar.'

Agnes giggled despite herself and placed a hand on his arm. 'I believe that we shall get along well enough, even though we shall occupy different bedchambers.'

'I thank you for *both* reassurances,' Richard smiled into his salmon pastry.

As the weeks rolled by, and winter prepared to take its bow in favour of spring, Richard made regular visits to the estate he was about to acquire through marriage, along with the title that came with it. Chalfont lay a day's easy ride to the north-west of London, among the chalk slopes of the ancient County of Buckingham, and the estate itself was one of those that ran through a verdant valley between two ranges of hills. It boasted some of the most fertile land in Southern England, and the rent roll was such that whoever owned the estate need never lift a finger.

The previous earl had died childless, and Agnes considered herself too old for childbirth, even had she entertained any lingering desire for a man in her bed. The entire gift from newly crowned King Stephen was therefore a most generous one, and when Richard made his first appearance as a guest of 'the mistress', the servants rightly deduced that the tall young man who had suddenly come into their presence must be someone highly valued by their new ruler. They bowed, scraped and smiled to his face, then giggled behind his back and nudged each other in the ribs as they concluded that he might perhaps have been intended as a prize for Agnes herself in the days of her fading beauty. Several of the female servants would have gladly welcomed the elegant and self-assured dark-haired warrior into their own beds, and silently cursed what wealth could buy a grumpy old widow.

Richard was totally unaware of the stir that had been generated by his sudden arrival. He occupied his waking hours in a frank assessment of the fighting potential of the idle layabouts who passed for men at arms, notionally defending an estate that required no defence. He soon had them parading before him at daybreak, then working on their overall fitness by dint of long runs through the valley, followed by ritual exercises with tree branches that would be replaced with swords when he deemed them fit and ready to be entrusted with them.

Finally Easter arrived, and the Court assembled as summoned at Westminster. The recently installed Bishop of London, Anselm the former Abbot of Bury St Edmunds, was reminded that he owed his preferment to King Stephen and ordered to conduct a wedding ceremony in the king's chapel.

'You might at least *pretend* to be pleased to be here,' Agnes muttered to Richard as they stood side by side to take their wedding vows. 'I would have expected the bishop to look bored, but your face resembles that of a man facing an execution.'

'I was wondering what to tell the servants regarding our wedding night,' Richard whispered back, and she chuckled.

'We shall occupy the same bed, perhaps for the last time, if only to set tongues wagging. Do you snore?'

'How would I know? I have only ever shared sleeping accommodation with my horse. I can only hope that you smell better.'

'King Stephen was right about one thing,' she grunted. 'You are no romantic poet. Now, pay attention — this is the point at which you and I become conjoined in holy warfare.'

Later that night, with a pale moon casting faint beams into the chamber in which they lay, Agnes turned over in half slumber and realised that she was lying groin to groin with her new husband, who could now call himself the Earl of Chalfont. Old memories came flooding back, and she began to seriously question whether her threat of marital chastity would survive the coming summer. At least it might until he rode north on some business or other that the king deemed important.

The newly created Earl of Chalfont raised his buttocks from the saddle in order to ease the pressure on his thighs after so many days spent on the forced march north. He turned to pass on to his mounted division the instruction he had just received from William of Aumale, the battle-hardened Norman knight who had been chosen as the actual commander of the ten thousand or so men who had travelled north to halt the southern encroachment of King David of Scotland. Waleran de Beaumont would no doubt ensure that he enjoyed the rewards that would flow from any suppression of the Scots threat, but Richard was relieved that his first taste of battle would be under the command of someone who actually knew how these matters were best conducted.

'We dismount here, and prepare to fight on foot!' Richard yelled to the thousand or so mounted knights who made up his battle wing. They had just passed through the village of Northallerton, and their forward scouts had reported that the Scots force had recently crossed the River Tees, on its way to sack York in the same manner that it had already sacked

Berwick. Most of Northumberland now lay under the Scottish king's command, and he was no doubt eager to push forward in order to extend the Scottish Borders further south. He also had an official reason for marching against King Stephen, given that Maude was his niece, but no-one doubted that his greater motivation was territorial.

The original force sent north by Stephen had been well under half its present size, but had been considerably enlarged when Archbishop Thurstan of York had recruited God into the business of defending the north against the reputed heathens across the border. His cross of office held high in the air, he had preached a virtual Crusade from town to town and village to village, proclaiming to the unimaginative men of Yorkshire that to hold back the forces from the north — who, rumour had it, were cannibals — was the work of God, for which they would be rewarded with eternal life.

In consequence, although the majority of the infantry were more skilled with a plough than a broadsword, they both looked and sounded fierce as they yelled the indignities they intended to inflict on any invader. Even more inspirational was the unusual weapon that Thurstan had trundled into the centre of the English ranks — a cart on which was mounted a mast bearing a pyx that in turn contained 'the consecrated host', around which were flying the consecrated banners of the minsters of Durham, York, Beverley and Ripon.

When the approaching Scots came within sight of the defenders and their curious icon, they halted and formed four lines abreast. The spearmen and archers were called to the front, and launched a barrage of missiles that threatened to turn the sky black with their density. On a command from Richard and those in charge of the infantry, shields were raised in defence, and the lethal metallic rain fell harmlessly on the jeering English ranks. Many of their shields resembled pincushions by the time the Scots realised that they were running out of missiles, and had long since squandered any hope they might have had of resembling a formidable foe.

Embarrassed and enraged, King David's son Henry sought permission to lead a cavalry attack, and Richard hastily ordered his men back into the saddle. The two lines met each other in a sickening cacophony of clashing metal and shrieking horses, and Richard experienced his first taste of real combat. Two hours later, as he sat in a pool of blood-soaked mud, breathing hard and listening to his heart pumping blood through his head, he had little memory of what had transpired other than the terrifying need to hack down the howling lunatics who appeared before him with raised axes and swords.

'Thank God you're still alive,' Waleran grinned as he reached down to pull Richard to his feet. 'Are you wounded?'

'I don't believe so,' Richard croaked back, then stared in alarm at the blood that all but obscured the livery of Waleran's battle tunic.

Waleran guffawed. 'All this blood was donated by those who came at our infantry ranks while you were slugging it out on horseback. They are in full retreat, and William has ordered that we chase them back to their hovels across the border.'

The pursuit was short-lived, mainly because a sizeable number of the English forces desired nothing more than to return to their local homes with plunder from the corpses. King David reformed the remainder of his troops behind the walls of Carlisle, from which he threatened to break out again if any English force came near him. The desertion of the locally recruited militia had left the English with insufficient men to engage in a siege, and the eventual peace treaty negotiated by a visiting Cardinal of Rome left David with

Carlisle, Northumberland and Cumberland under his sovereignty in exchange for an undertaking to venture no further south.

Five weeks later, the first of the returning troops clattered through the gates of Westminster to a rousing heroes' welcome. Crowds lined the narrow cobbled passage towards the stable block to one side, and Richard acknowledged the cheers with several waves as, behind him, men dismounted in order to be hugged joyfully.

He led his horse through the throng to the stables. His eyes on the uneven ground, and weary from the final stage of the journey from Barnet, he looked up as he saw a pair of riding boots blocking his way. Expecting to find some palace official demanding his attention, he was amazed to see Agnes standing before him, a wry smile on her face.

'I thought I'd confirm that my investment in a new husband had not gone awry,' she advised him awkwardly. 'I was informed that you were among the living, but given the confusion that surrounds such events I deemed it appropriate to see it with my own eyes.'

'Don't pretend that you missed me,' Richard grinned.

'That might be stretching the matter *too* far,' she smirked. 'It's just that it would be very irksome to be widowed again so soon. To celebrate your return you may embrace me, provided that you smell better than your horse.'

Richard did as instructed and detected a slight trembling of the ample waist with which his arms made contact. And when he broke the embrace and stood back slightly, Agnes quickly dropped her head in an attempt to conceal the tears that were sliding down her cheeks.

XIX

The mood inside the Audience Chamber at Angers was one of despondency and frustration. Geoffrey was doing his best to raise Maude's spirits, but as usual he was only making things worse with his false bonhomie. Robert and Thomas sat, embarrassed, as Maude's petulance spilled over into her husband's perceived failings on the domestic front. Not even the fact that little Henry, now a chubby five-year-old who seemed to possess limitless energy, was racing up and down with a make-believe toy horse seemed to lighten her mood.

'Stephen and Matilda's forces cannot remain in Dover forever,' Robert announced. 'Matilda will need to guard her home port of Boulogne should we launch an attack on it.'

'And you are seriously proposing that we march all the way across a hostile Normandy in order to achieve that?' Maude sniped, and Robert regretted his words as he hung his head without reply.

His attempted uprisings in Kent had been badly timed, allowing King Stephen to mop up each one as it arose with only a small handful of mounted knights led by a newly emerged military commander named 'the Earl of Chalfont'. Robert had never heard of him. 'Stephen has given titles to a considerable number of his hangers-on, and this one only succeeded because the idiots I was relying on clearly didn't see fit to ensure that they all rose up at the same time,' he told the company.

'None of them would be capable of relieving the blockade of Dover, I suppose?' Thomas enquired gloomily.

Robert shook his head. 'That can only be lifted by sea, and we'll need all our vessels to transport our troops when we invade.'

'You mean *if* we invade, do you not?' Maude fired back sourly, and again Robert had no answer. He hadn't anticipated that as well as sending land troops south from Westminster to put down the sporadic outbreaks in Kent, Stephen would also conclude that the invasion from Anjou would come by way of Dover. He'd therefore called upon his formidable wife Matilda of Boulogne — who had remained at home in order to guard their back door — to send a flotilla of vessels across the Channel to block the approaches to the most obvious of entry points into his newly claimed kingdom. As yet there was no news that Portsmouth was blocked to them, but it was much further west from London. Any invasion force would need to march for four additional days before laying siege to Westminster — more than enough time for Stephen to organise its defence.

As if that were not enough justification for Maude's ill temper, there was also the rejection of her appeal to the Pope to annul Stephen's coronation, news of which had reached them that morning. As if to rub her nose in moral slime as well as vindicating Stephen's claim, the reason given by Pope Innocent for denying Maude her birthright was the old, but frequently denied, assertion that her mother Matilda of Scotland had broken her holy vows as a nun in order to marry her father Henry. His Holiness had been clutching at straws, but clearly it suited Rome to have King Stephen on the English throne rather than Queen Maude.

'There is also word of fresh outbreaks of rebellion in the south of Normandy, and through the Vexin,' Geoffrey added.

Maude snorted. 'I knew I could rely on you to lift my spirits with stale news! If you have nothing more encouraging to add, at least make some effort to stop your son breaking any more vases as he careers around the chamber like a drunken ferret!' She turned to Robert, red-faced. 'Which shall we confront first, brother? The uprisings in Normandy or the wicked usurpation of my crown by a cousin spawned by a whore of France?'

Tactfully refraining from reminding her that the 'whore' in question had been her aunt, and a daughter of William of Normandy, Robert tentatively unveiled his proposals. 'There are rumours that the barons on the Welsh borders are using the contested crown as an excuse for one of their regular uprisings. While Stephen's looking north again, I propose to land our army along the south coast somewhere. Portsmouth is too far away from London to my mind, and Dover is blocked to us, but somewhere between the two — perhaps Pevensey — we should be able to find a suitable beach on which to disembark. After all, that's where Duke William landed, and if it was good enough for our grandfather...'

'That was almost a hundred years ago,' Maude interrupted him sullenly. 'There must be somewhere better than that, surely?'

'We won't know until we carry out our own reconnaissance,' Robert asserted, 'which is why I propose that I take a ship from Barfleur with just a handful of men and sail up the south coast looking for a safe harbour where a hundred vessels can be safely moored.'

'Then you propose to come back and find a hundred vessels?' Maude replied sarcastically. 'And in the meantime, while you go sailing, you'll leave me and my babies without protection?'

'You need little additional protection, here in your homeland of Anjou,' Robert reminded her. 'And in any case, I propose that Thomas remains here in command of the Palace Guard. That was his office under your father, and he can spend his idle time training up new recruits who are arriving here by the day, hopeful of plunder overseas.'

When Maude announced that she was tired and intended to retire to her chamber before supper, Elinor rose to follow her. Maude turned and said, 'I think you have heard enough of my ungrateful noises for the time being, my dear. Remain here with your father while Geoffrey takes little Henry back to his nurse. It is a fit time for families to be reminded of the love that binds them, and you see little enough of your father.'

'At least you won't be leaving us to venture back across to England with Robert,' Elinor smiled sadly once she was alone with Thomas. 'Maude was right about family. It breaks my heart when I see dear little Henry growing up surrounded by love, while I don't even know where my two may be found, or how they fare. Do you really think that Richard will be seeing to their welfare, and that they are still at Walsingham?'

Thomas sighed and shook his head. 'Maude's words were like a knife to my heart, when I reflect on my own neglect of you and your brother. You and I have been reunited, but I fear for Richard, if he is back in that cauldron of intrigue and back-stabbing that passes for an English court. If he has become ensnared in Stephen's pretence at being the lawful King of England, then we may be destined to cross swords. Father against son — have you any idea how the fear of that chills my soul?'

Thomas's worst fears would have been confirmed had he been able to eavesdrop on the terse words being exchanged in the armoury behind the river wall of Westminster Palace. Richard had called in to collect the sword that had required more edge to its blade after its frequent employment in the suppression of the recent rebellions in Kent. Two hours earlier, he had dined with King Stephen and Waleran de Beaumont in order to discuss their immediate future strategy, and both men had left feeling undervalued and cheated. They were rapidly becoming jealous of each other, and each, for different reasons, resented the outcomes of their recent joint meeting with the king.

For Waleran, it was the praise that had been lavished on this handsome young devil for his part in holding back the invasion from Scotland. It had been Waleran himself who had lifted Richard from the ground where he sat, exhausted and seemingly half-dead, and others — including himself — had fought just as bravely. The mere fact that he was a nephew of the king did not make his fighting prowess any greater. Waleran would also have welcomed the gift of the estate at Chalfont, and the comely widow who came with it, rather than betrothal to the infant daughter of King Stephen and Queen Matilda.

Richard, for his part, was anxious to build upon his early reputation as a military commander. He was therefore aghast when Waleran was appointed the king's lieutenant in Normandy, where he was being sent with an army in order to reinforce his strategic estate of Meulan and enlist the support of the de Montforts and King Louis of France for unrest among the confused and leaderless barons of Normandy. This, it was calculated, would divert the attention of Maude and Geoffrey sufficiently to defer any invasion plans they might have. If Waleran succeeded in all this, he would clearly be receiving further titles, and general acclaim as England's leading warrior. Richard had no interest in any further title, merely military glory. He would have loved to return from Normandy bearing plunder and hostages like a Roman emperor.

Instead, he was being consigned to a lowly visit to Ely, whose bishop, Nigel, was suspected of rallying support for Maude's cause, and had fled to Devizes in Wiltshire. Richard was instructed to seize the abbey in Stephen's name, plunder it of all items of value and enlist such armed forces as the bishop might have recruited. He was then to move on to Lincoln and do the same, largely because its bishop, Alexander, was, like Nigel of Ely, another nephew of the all-powerful Roger, Bishop of Salisbury. Roger had been the head of royal administration under the late King Henry, and although he continued in that role Stephen was suspicious of his loyalty, and wished to test it when his two nephews were thrown out of their sees.

This posed a massive dilemma for Richard. He had no reason to believe that Stephen was aware that Ely Abbey was currently providing a home and a fine education for his two nephews, or that their mother Elinor was still in service across the Channel in Maude's court at Angers. But if he *was* so aware, then this latest mission could be a test of his loyalty — would Richard be prepared to see his own family uprooted from a comfortable life in order to carry out a royal command? And how was he to explain, to two young men who hardly knew him anyway, that he really *was* mindful of their welfare when he rode into the abbey precincts with orders to loot?

'I don't think you'll be needing that sword in the immediate future,' Waleran gloated as he handed his own to the armourer for its hilt to be re-gilded. 'You don't need steel to defend yourself against swinging incense.'

Richard took several deep breaths before replying coldly, 'Diplomacy can be equally as important to a king as the mere slicing off of arms and heads. It takes a tongue as gilded as your sword hilt to ease bishops from their positions of authority over men.'

'Or a lack of fear of Hellfire?' Waleran prodded, hopeful of weakening Richard's resolve, but he had a ready answer for that.

'We dice with the fires of Hell whenever we take human life, if we are to believe the drivelling cant of those who shave their heads and hide behind dusty parchments. If that be so, then you may not live to enjoy the pleasures of the marital bed, should God reclaim his debt on the field of battle.'

'Which you are about forsake in order to strike terror into the hearts of monks?'

'And sorrow into the heart of my wife. We each have our burdens to assume, and our ways of displaying loyalty to the throne.'

As the grounds of Ely Cathedral came into sight, Richard was reflecting on his final words to Waleran, intended to make him jealous of his married state. He was well aware, from the looks that Agnes received from courtiers whenever they attended banquets or other celebrations, that lusty men with normal appetites were peeling off her gown with their eyes and fantasising about what lay underneath. Richard was not about to admit that he was no more familiar with that than they were. His wife had maintained her insistence on separate bedchambers, to the considerable prurient speculation of the servants. Several of the serving maids had hinted to Richard that they might not reject any frustrated attempts on his part to besmirch their honour, but he had kept the pledge within his heart to be a true and faithful husband. As a result, he had yet to experience any carnal delights.

But this time he thought he'd detected a reluctance on Agnes's part to see him ride away on yet another mission for King Stephen. Had he mistaken the wistful, almost sad look in her eyes as she'd wished him 'God Speed' as usual, then added 'Come back safely to us'? If she was beginning to warm towards him, then perhaps he should prepare himself for a new experience.

The clergyman who came to the hospitium door on Richard's approach was unfamiliar to him, and he looked fearfully out at the twenty or so armed men whose horses were being walked in circles around the green. Richard dismounted and announced his business.

'I am the Earl of Chalfont, and I come on the king's business.'

'I am Brother Ralph. In the absence of the bishop from the adjoining abbey I am honoured to welcome you to our humble house, although whether we can accommodate such a large number is somewhat of a quandary. Perhaps we might revive the tradition of the loaves and fishes.'

'We shall not require accommodation,' Richard advised him, to the man's obvious relief. 'But it is the absence of Bishop Nigel that is the nature of my business.'

There was no reply, so Richard got to the point.

'I am instructed by his Majesty to assume command of the abbey and its associated offices, and remove therefrom anything that is not strictly required for your religious observances.'

'You have come looting, you mean,' Brother Ralph replied coldly. 'I shall of course not stand in your way, nor will any of the brothers. But I would ask that you go about your shameful duty with the minimum of violence, or display of blasphemy. There are novitiates and scholars at their studies and devotions here in the abbey school, and it is too early in their innocent lives for them to be made aware of the wickedness of those in positions of power without accompanying spiritual grace.'

Richard moved closer to the monk and lowered his voice. 'I shall personally supervise my men in what they have to do, and ensure that there is not even a raised voice. In return, I should deem it a favour if you could advise me if you have two boys here whose names are Alain and William. They would now be some twelve or thirteen years of age, and they come originally from the estate at Walsingham. They are my nephews.'

'The Walsingham estate was owned by a most pious man of my acquaintance from our younger days,' the monk replied suspiciously. 'His name was Geoffrey de Faverches, and he had no brothers of whom I was aware.'

'But the estate was gifted to him by my grandfather,' Richard replied with a smile. 'I was not always the Earl of Chalfont.'

'Then who were you prior to such elevation?'

'Richard Walsingham, son of Sir Thomas Walsingham, and grandson of Sir Wilfrid Walsingham. I have a sister named Elinor, whose sons may now be under your care here at Ely. As I already advised you, their names are Alain and William.'

'We have two boys of those names, certainly,' Brother Ralph conceded, 'but I have never heard either of them speak of an uncle — even less a mother.'

A few moments later, inside the sparse dormitory in which Richard was perched uncomfortably on the edge of a low bench, he felt a lump come to his throat as two young boys, dressed in plain white garments that extended all the way down to their rudimentary footwear, were brought into the room and told to stand in respectful silence. Richard didn't need to ask which was which, since the shorter of the two boys had hair the colour of straw, while his taller twin was the image of his mother.

'Have you been told who I am?' Richard began.

Alain responded with a nod. 'The Earl of somewhere or other, we were told.'

'Yes. My story is a complicated one,' Richard explained. 'Are you allowed to sit down? I feel awkward seated here while you both stand.'

'We are accustomed to standing for hours at our work or our devotionals,' Alain explained, 'but we shall sit if it will make your task easier.'

In unison, the two boys assumed cross-legged positions in the rushes, and Richard was reminded of his days in the schoolroom run by his Aunt Tilly in the orphanage. When they appeared to be comfortably arranged, he began to explain.

'The world outside this cathedral is in turmoil. The king known as Henry died several years ago, and he wished his daughter Maude — the lady who your mother serves — to inherit his throne. But he had previously promised that same throne to a nephew called Stephen of Blois, which again is a place across the sea, and he has travelled over here to claim it. I am in his service, and that is why I am here today.'

'So this Stephen, and this Maude, have agreed to share the throne?' William enquired.

'Would that this were so, but they are likely to go to war.'

'And you will fight for Stephen, while this woman you say is our mother will be on the side of this Maude?' William probed.

Richard dropped his glance to the ground. 'Regrettably, that is the case. Hopefully we shall meet again in happier times.'

'So you have not come from her?' William persisted. 'If not, then how do you know if she is still alive?'

'In all truth, I do not,' Richard replied, 'and it was not she who sent me here.'

'No — the king you serve sent you,' said William. 'You already told us that. Are we to become your prisoners?'

Richard tried not to laugh. 'No,' he assured them both. 'I had to come to Ely on the king's business, and I took this opportunity to enquire about your welfare, and to meet with you again.'

'Again?' Alain echoed. 'Have we met before?'

'Only a couple of times,' Richard admitted, shamefaced, 'and that was when you were small boys back in Walsingham.'

'Has our mother ever met us?' Alain asked.

The naivety of the question left Richard breathless with grief. 'Not since you were born, so far as I am aware.'

'It was kindly of you to enquire after our welfare,' Alain suddenly announced, 'but it will shortly be time for the Sext bell to be rung, and I have copying work to complete for Brother Dominic, while William must take cabbages to the refectory. So if we might be excused?'

As Richard sat staring blankly at the empty doorway through which the boys had politely made their exit, his spirits sank. They were his nephews, and they had spoken to him like polite young men entertaining a respected visitor. His heart went out to Elinor, should she ever find herself face to face with her sons.

After several weeks in both Ely and Lincoln, then the return journey along the dry, dusty tracks of late summer escorting wagonloads of wealth towards London, Richard opted to leave the procession at St Albans and thunder west to Chalfont. He was barely off his horse before Agnes appeared at the front door to the manor house, only her twisting hands revealing the emotional turmoil that his unexpected return had provoked.

'You were missed,' she said as she squeezed harder than she ever had before.

'Surely not?' Richard reached round to see if she would allow him to fondle her bottom.

Agnes knocked his hand away. 'Not by me, you coarse oaf — the king. He has sent messengers here twice, seeking news of your return. They left instructions that you are to lose no time in riding to Westminster to collect your men and journey south. It would seem that Maude and her Angevins have landed somewhere along the coast.'

The war had begun.

XX

'It was most generous of you to allow us sanctuary here, so close to London,' Maude enthused as she grasped her stepmother Adeliza's hand, then took the seat next to her in the Great Hall of Arundel Castle. Elinor stood dutifully behind her as usual.

Adeliza smiled sadly. 'It's the least I can do, since it was your dear father's wish that the crown go to you, and you were always most gracious towards me. Both you *and* Robert here, although I was not your birth mother. As for that upstart Stephen of Blois, he hung around the Court like a badly drained privy, always seeking an opportunity to ingratiate himself with your father. I never did warm to him, and I told your father so, which I believe was one of the reasons why he tried so hard to persuade his leading barons to support your cause and swear fealty to you. He did not, of course, know that he would die when he did, but his eating habits finally caught up with him.'

They were safely disembarked after a smooth crossing, and Maude's ten ships were securely moored in the river that ran through the town of Arundel, having disembarked the one hundred and forty knights who made up their spearhead invasion force. Robert was confident that others would rally to their cause once he marched west, and the only remaining point of dispute was how many men should be left to defend Arundel under Thomas's command. He constantly assured Robert that the castle had been so craftily constructed by a cousin of William of Normandy against direct attack that its existing garrison would require only a modest augmentation from his own men.

This would allow the majority of those who had journeyed across the Channel with them to move westwards, to where it was hoped that they would be joined by Miles of Gloucester, the former Constable of England under Henry. He had yet to be formally confirmed in his office, and he was known to be apprehensive of being replaced by Waleran de Beaumont, Stephen's favourite.

Eventually Robert relented, principally because he wanted to strike west before news of the landing reached Westminster. A week later, he was being welcomed into Gloucester and advised that he could also rely upon strong support from across the Welsh border once he established a military base in Bristol. He lost no time in doing so, and in company with a large contingent of Welsh bowmen and Angevin knights he returned to Arundel to invite Maude to establish her alternative court in Gloucester.

In his absence, there had been a brief scouting visit from some of Stephen's armed forces, who had held a brief council of war before deciding that Arundel Castle was too well constructed to be stormed, and probably too well provisioned for a siege to have any effect. But the event had been an unnerving one for Thomas, as he stood on the north-facing battlements surveying the 'royal' troops milling around on horseback, conducting a preliminary reconnaissance of the castle's perimeter.

At the forefront of Stephen's almost token force, clearly visible from over forty feet above, was an enthusiastic knight wearing the distinctive livery of Blois, who had removed his battle helm in order to issue instructions to his men. Thomas's blood froze as his worst fears were realised, and he ordered that no-one on the ramparts was to attack the intruders. He thought it best not to give his reason for that, because he was both too horrified and too embarrassed to disclose that the enemy were being led by his own son.

He remained tight-lipped on the same matter when Robert returned with a vastly increased force that had been supplemented with men supplied by Welsh Marcher barons. They relied upon the English throne being in a state of disarray in order to continue their practice of plundering the estates of their neighbours and claiming that they were doing so in order to free Wales from a foreign yoke. Robert knew that he could not rely on such men in the longer term, once Maude was safely installed at Westminster with all competing claims suppressed, but for the time being they were invaluable. His first priority would be to take Maude back west with him, behind a secure if invisible border.

But there needed to be more action if she was to reclaim her rightful crown. It was one thing to be on the defensive, hiding behind high castle walls a week's ride from Westminster, and another to strike eastwards towards London. This was the task allocated to Thomas and the army now at their disposal.

'The key is the castle at Wallingford,' Robert explained. 'When you hold Wallingford you are at London's back door, and can block any move westward by forces coming out of Westminster. At the same time, you can make it your base for any attack of your own on the royal palaces to the east.'

'I'm well aware of the strategic significance of Wallingford,' Thomas reminded him grumpily. 'You forget that from time to time I led the Palace Guard at Windsor. Would you not regard it as just as significant in military terms?'

'No,' Robert replied firmly, 'if only for one reason. Wallingford is located in one of the few places in which the

173

mighty Thames can be forded. It was the way by which my grandfather William made his eventual entry into London in order to stamp out any Saxon resistance.'

'With *my* father by his side, enabling him to speak with those he was terrorising into submission,' Thomas reminded him.

'The family histories can be exchanged later,' Maude interjected tersely as she pierced the crust of a songbird pie with her dagger, 'but what we need now is a plan of action with dates attached.'

'I propose that by no later than Monday coming, after we have sought God's blessing in the chapel next door, we send Thomas eastwards to secure Wallingford,' Robert replied with a defiant glare at Thomas. 'I might add that I am a little nonplussed at his apparent reluctance.'

'There is no reluctance on my part,' Thomas insisted sharply, 'merely concern that we have the right target.'

'There could be none better,' Robert insisted. 'Not only will we have London's western entry and exit secured, but we will have safe passage across the Thames, *and* we are providing a perfect distraction while I hasten Maude safely westwards to Gloucester.'

'I am no military strategist,' Geoffrey chimed in as he reached for the wine jug, 'but it makes eminent sense to me.'

'No, you are not,' Maude reminded him, 'which is why you will be travelling with me, as a reminder that "Queen Maude" has a husband with wide estates across the Channel and three sons who can guarantee a strong succession. My only regret is that I will not be seen at the head of my loyal troops.'

'We do not wish you to resemble another Boudicca,' Robert grinned. 'The people will more readily accept your femininity if it is not also warlike. You are the wife and mother of the nation, not its warrior chief.'

A week later, Wallingford was being held in the name of 'Queen Maude'. There had been very little effort required, and virtually no clashing of arms. Thomas had led several hundred heavily armed men in a ring formation around the castle at the dead of night, then at daybreak he had sent a messenger in to the garrison commander with a stark choice — surrender or be starved out. During the following week, the surrounding countryside was stripped of any provisions that might be required in order to withstand any further siege. Then, after dispatching messengers west to convey the news to Gloucester that the road into London was wide open, they sat and waited.

'I'll hang the cowardly bastard from the castle walls!' Stephen thundered as he sat, quivering with rage, at the news that Wallingford had surrendered so easily. It followed hard on the news that the treacherous Miles, Earl of Gloucester, had pledged his allegiance to Maude and her bastard half-brother Robert and sacked the Worcester stronghold of his Court rival Waleran de Beaumont. Waleran was back at Westminster after securing the support of enough Norman barons to ensure that Maude and Geoffrey could expect no reinforcements from that quarter, and now he was seeking leave to exact a bloody revenge.

'Give me a week and I'll drag him back in chains on my way east!' Waleran promised.

Richard allowed himself a smirk. 'On your way back from regaining your own estates, you mean?'

'Nobody asked you, pretty boy!' Waleran snarled, and Richard's hand was almost on his sword hilt before he remembered where he was. In the event, it was Stephen who put Waleran in his place.

'That is no way to speak to a royal nephew, Waleran. You forget your place, and you forget why you are summoned here this morning. Is it your proposal to travel to Worcester, make the royal presence felt, then come back by way of Wallingford?'

'Yes, sire,' Waleran muttered as his ire subsided and he began thinking strategically. 'I should be able to accomplish this in little more than a week, if I march my men at twice the normal pace.'

'Thereby exhausting them, and rendering them unfit for battle when you get there,' Richard pointed out with another smirk.

Stephen nodded. 'He has a point, Waleran — you will need two weeks at least if you are to achieve both objectives, and you forget that we have news of Bishop Nigel sneaking back into Ely while our backs have been turned.'

'Richard was supposed to have silenced Ely,' Waleran reminded them.

'And so he did, most effectively. The money that funds your army has come in part from the sale of the booty from Richard's successful sally north, but it would seem that the slimy prelate will not take no for an answer. Ely must be occupied in my name on a more permanent basis — and who better than Richard, since he is already familiar with both the town and its cathedral?'

'And why may I not head west and put down this treachery before it has time to spread?' Waleran demanded.

Stephen frowned. 'Leaving me to defend London with what few armed men you choose to leave at my disposal? You will remain here, while Richard reminds the Bishop of Ely where his loyalties lie.'

'You wish him brought back alive?' Richard enquired, hoping for an affirmative answer.

Stephen raised his eyebrows. 'If you would take the life of a holy man such as he, then you clearly have no fear of the fires of Hell. Of *course* bring him back alive, but that does not mean that you make his journey back down here a comfortable one. Nor does it mean that the citizens of Ely should be left with the false impression that we are kind to rebels. I feel sure that you know how to handle matters.'

At least the first part of Richard's mission played out predictably. At the first sign of the approach of a royal force, all the gates that gave access through the Ely town walls were locked against them. It was only by threatening several monks in the adjoining abbey with a slow, painful and ignominious death that Richard learned that Bishop Nigel had fled to a small monastic cell that he used as a retreat on a remote island in the middle of the inaccessible fens.

Undeterred, Richard made good use of one of the tales that had been recounted countless times around the fireside in his youth, when grandfather William told of the strategy he had adopted in order to flush a renegade called Hereward from a similar sanctuary. Knowing that the local rush cutters earned their daily living by venturing across treacherous marshes on specially made flat boards, Richard ordered his men to raid every cottage within a ten-mile radius of Ely, and once they had sufficient boards for a select handful of men to slide across the swamp, they made short work of roping Bishop Nigel and bringing him back into the town. There he was locked in the dungeon that he himself had extended when recently fortifying the castle in the hope of defying King Stephen. The town surrendered to Richard almost immediately.

Since he was in Ely anyway, Richard made the somewhat reluctant decision to visit his two nephews, if only to be able to assure Elinor, should their paths cross, that they remained well. He got as far as the main door of the cathedral school, where an angry Brother Bartholomew, who claimed to be the magister in charge of studies, advised him curtly that the two boys had no wish to meet with him, in view of the treatment meted out to the town, the cathedral and its bishop. There seemed little point in arguing, so after securing an assurance that both Alain and William were in good health, and prospering in their studies, Richard rode sadly back to his temporary base in the castle.

In London, Stephen was once again in a foul temper when he was advised of the treachery of one of the leading nobles in the land, Ranulf of Chester. This wily, powerful but volatile baron, whose estates traditionally stretched from Leicestershire all the way through Lancashire and Cumberland to the Scottish border at Carlisle, had several reasons to be discontented with his lot since Stephen had claimed the crown of England.

First had been the grant of the Earldom of Leicester to the de Beaumonts, one of whom — Waleran — was now enjoying such favour at Court. The de Beaumonts had long been squabbling with Ranulf's forebears over which family had the greater historical claim to Warwick Castle, its principal fortress. While Ranulf might have been content to sit and await the moment when, like all royal favourites, Waleran overreached himself, he could not sit idly by after Stephen granted Cumberland and Lancashire to David of Scotland as part of their peace treaty. Since he was married to Maude, daughter of Robert of Gloucester, Ranulf had a further reason for throwing in his lot with the other contender for the English throne, and when he learned of the fate of Nigel of Ely he marched east and took Lincoln, to which he laid an ancient and somewhat spurious claim.

Royal messengers thundered north to Ely from Westminster, ordering Richard and his men to remain where they were, and await an additional force led by Stephen himself, with Waleran following in his train like a lapdog on a long leash. By the time that the combined royal force was in a position to move north on Lincoln, it had been heavily refortified by Ranulf, and the city gates were closed in preparation for a siege.

It could have lasted indefinitely, so well had Ranulf provisioned the ancient town and the castle that dominated its centre, but once it became known that Stephen was moving on it messengers had been sent across the country to Maude at Worcester. Robert conducted a hasty recruitment drive in the West Country, and within a week there were over ten thousand armed men, a significant number of them mounted, and many of them Welsh bowmen who sang for every mile as they marched to the relief of Lincoln, with Thomas at their head.

When word was brought to Stephen and his besieging forces outside the west wall of Lincoln that a mighty army was marching towards them from the direction of Leicester, Richard and Waleran ordered their men to turn, ready to give battle. Night fell, and the watches were ordered to keep the fires burning in their pots to a minimum level, so as not to betray their precise position. In consequence the invading force from the west came, through a freezing fog, much closer to their target than they were aware. At dawn on the second of February 1141, the leaders of both sides found themselves staring at each other over a frost-encrusted plain, with barely a quarter of a mile separating them.

Richard was hastily summoned from his tent by a messenger sent by Waleran. As he struggled into his armour with the assistance of a young squire, and looked to the east, he realised that the battle to come was destined to be a family affair on several levels.

Thomas, for his part, called out to Robert as he squinted through the lingering mist at a figure that looked all too familiar. Robert came to his side. 'Did you call me over merely to advise me that they are badly outnumbered?' he enquired. 'Any fool could have told me that.'

'Well, this fool is enquiring as to the identity of that tall man at arms wearing the livery of Blois. He's staring across at me as if marking me down as his own personal adversary.'

Robert followed his gaze, then gave a slight start as he replied. 'I have not seen him for some years, but from his position in the vanguard I believe that he is now calling himself the Earl of Chalfont, and is one of Stephen's leading commanders in the field. Order the cavalry into the centre while I raise infantry on either flank. You may, in the circumstances, wish to remain to the rear, since this promises to be a one-sided slaughter. I can see by the colour of your countenance that you share my opinion, and that you have made the awful connection, so let us begin without delay.'

Thomas stood for a moment more, his face drained of all colour and his heart as heavy as lead, asking himself two questions. The first was whether the man who was staring at him across what was about to become a charnel house was aware of *his* identity. And the second was how his only son had become the Earl of Chalfont.

XXI

Thomas and Robert ordered their mounted knights onto horseback before Stephen's infantry could mount any attack on the deep ranks of Welsh bowmen, who were ordered to loose as many shafts as they could into Stephen's cavalry ranks before Thomas ordered the charge. The royal forces were barely into their saddles, delayed by the incoming assault, before the Angevin horsemen were upon them, and the familiar cacophony of shrieking horses, cursing men and clashing metal replaced the sound of pounding hooves.

As the vastly outnumbered royal cavalry were rapidly overtaken, many of the barons who had turned out for Stephen broke ranks and fled. Richard stood desperately on foot, having wisely decided not to mount his battle charger. As swords and axes flashed all around him, he concentrated on one man at a time, thrusting here, slashing there and mentally counting off the number he had brought down. He was not to know that his little knot of defenders was rapidly diminishing in size.

Soon the infantry brought under the Angevin banner by Ranulf of Chester waded into what was left of the dismounted royal cavalry, and Richard realised to his horror that the enemy were behind him as well as to the front and the sides. He fought bravely, like a human windmill, swirling and slashing at everything that came within his line of vision, but it was not long before he felt the familiar fatigue in his upper arms, and his resistance rapidly faded. There were simply too many of them, and his own centre line had collapsed too early in the encounter.

Sweat began to obscure his vision, and for the first time in his life he felt that a horrible death was not long away. Then a man twice his size reared up out of nowhere and with a mighty sideways sweep knocked the sword from his weakening grasp. The force of the impact also knocked him sideways, and as he rose to his knees he saw only the massive broadsword blade levelled at his throat.

Thomas had hung back from the melee for several reasons. The first, and justifiable, one was that as a commander in the field it was his priority to assess how the fighting was progressing and to order men into position accordingly. The second reason was the one that had led him to the spot under the castle wall where Richard was about to be despatched by William de Keynes, a mountain of a man who had been recruited in Normandy by Robert and allocated to Thomas's infantry division as a lieutenant.

Thomas raced over and placed himself between William and the fallen Richard, calling, 'Hold your hand! This man is my prisoner and will fetch a fine ransom. Harm him at your peril!'

William was not about to argue with his field commander, and in any case he had spotted an even more important quarry. 'The man is yours, sir — I see the pretended king about to flee the field!'

As he lumbered off towards the small knot of men who were falling like autumn leaves in a gale as they vainly fought to protect the retreating Stephen, Thomas reached out a hand and hauled Richard to his feet.

'I was not jesting — you are my prisoner, so disport yourself accordingly. You will leave the field with me, and you will submit to being taken into secure custody tied behind my horse. The fact that you are my son will not preserve your neck if you attempt to escape. You know the custom, I assume — as long as I claim you as my prisoner, no-one else may set about you. If not — well, take a look around and you will quickly learn how foolish was your choice of sides in this ill-favoured family dispute. Now, can you walk?'

When Richard nodded, speechless at the turn of events, Thomas led him by the arm across the open space between the remains of the one-sided slaughter and the Angevin camp. He tied his hands into a halter that was then fixed to the rear harness of his destrier.

'Remain there until I can summon a wagon,' he instructed Richard, then disappeared briefly from sight.

Two hours later, Richard looked through the spars of the hay cart that his father had commandeered at that portion of the victorious procession that was wending its way west, leaving at least half the original force to secure Lincoln against any possible counter-attack by the defeated royal forces. Ahead of his swaying conveyance was a similar one, but this second one had four mounted knights riding alongside it, two down each side, and he was to learn later that it contained Stephen himself, captured and ransomed on the insistence of Robert of Gloucester, who had resisted all suggestions that the pretended king be hanged from the walls of Lincoln.

'He is royal, when all is said and done,' Robert had reminded William de Keynes, who had taken him prisoner, 'and one sets a very poor example if one hangs a member of the extended Norman family. He may be only my cousin, but he is also a cousin of Lady Maude, and I would shrink from the task of advising her that I had him done to death.'

'Why did you not advise me that I was a grandfather?' Thomas demanded as he brought Richard's only meal of the day into the cell that he was occupying in the dungeons of Bristol

Castle, to which he had been transferred after a few days in Gloucester.

'Why did you not advise me that I was of the royal House of Blois?' Richard countered defiantly as he pretended to ignore the food. 'King Stephen is my uncle, as you well knew, and my mother was no mere lady in attendance on Lady Emma. She *was* Lady Emma, was she not?'

Thomas nodded, but was not distracted from what he had to say. 'You have betrayed both me and your sister, and dragged the family name into dishonour! Maude was bequeathed the crown by the king whose cause you were sworn to uphold, and you sold out for a paltry title. "The Earl of Chalfont"? Was that worth the calumny of betraying your oath? And does Chalfont even exist?'

'It does indeed,' Richard grimaced, 'although I doubt I shall see it again. It lies in rich pasture a single day's ride from London, and it will shortly be managed by a woman widowed for a second time, if your Gorgon of a mistress has her way. I take it I am to be executed in due course, as a warning to others?'

'That will depend upon how you choose your future loyalties,' Thomas advised him. 'Lady Maude holds much by family loyalty, and she has three sons who will one day inherit the throne of England. She is also very fond of your sister, and if both she and I plead with her for your life, she will spare you. We would welcome another experienced knight into our forces, albeit one who has fought on a losing side. Perhaps *because* of that, if you can give us information of value regarding the identities of those who are likely to cling to a lost cause.'

'You expect me to desert my appointed mission, and betray the oath that I swore to King Stephen? You underestimate my sense of duty and honour, as usual.'

'Don't talk such nonsense!' Thomas yelled. 'You have already demonstrated your capacity for breaking an oath by joining the ranks of a usurper in exchange for a bauble. I merely suggest that you break another, and pledge your allegiance to she who was bequeathed the crown in the first place. The one already served by your sister, who has at least remained true to her oath of service.'

'But not to her duty of chastity,' Richard reminded him. 'How do you think you became a grandfather, and I an uncle? That was no immaculate conception, Father. The one who took her honour is also no doubt serving another of England's enemies as we speak. So do not preach to me about family honour!'

'You have seen your nephews?' Thomas seemed to weaken slightly in his resolve to persuade Richard to change sides. 'They are thriving?'

'I have seen them only a few times,' Richard replied with a smile of remembrance, 'and you will be proud of them. Alain is fair of complexion, and appears to have taken naturally to the air of religious fervour by which he is surrounded. The other one, William, is markedly taller and darker of countenance, like myself, Elinor, and our mother — whose true identity you kept so quiet all those years.'

'The circumstances were hardly appropriate,' Thomas replied dismissively. 'But before you wax too critical of me, how have you and your sister been any different? Elinor kept the birth of two grandsons from me for ten years or more, while you skulked away and joined the enemy!'

'We probably inherited that talent for secrecy from you.' Richard was confident that he held the moral high ground. 'But in these uncertain times, who is to know which claimant for the throne of England to follow?'

'The one to whom you first swore a solemn oath,' said Thomas, 'which, if my memory serves me correctly, was King Henry.'

'The King Henry who is now dead,' Richard countered. 'And before that even occurred I was dismissed from his service — by *you*, if you recall, because of my failure to prevent events that yielded you two grandchildren. I swore no oath to Maude. The second oath I swore was to Stephen — would you urge that I break that also?'

'That depends upon how much you value your life. I am here to offer you your life, and the confirmation of your estate, in return for an oath of allegiance to Maude.'

'You have already condemned me as a breaker of oaths,' Richard replied, 'so why would you place your faith in any further oath I might swear?'

'I am concerned solely for your continued life,' Thomas admitted as he weakened further. 'I am, first and foremost, your father.'

'And I am, first and foremost, a soldier in the service of King Stephen — my uncle, may I remind you? An uncle who has displayed more faith in me than you ever did as my father.'

Thomas gave a noise of disgust and frustration and walked back to the cell door, on which he hammered to be released. When the door was opened, he turned one last time with a look of desperation.

'Think of the mother who bore you, Richard. What would she think of your wanton throwing away of your life?'

'She was of the House of Blois, of course,' Richard reminded him bitterly. 'I now serve her half-brother — perhaps I display a degree of family loyalty that you find uncomfortable.'

'The Bishop of Winchester, Your Highness,' the usher

announced, as Henry of Blois swept into Maude's presence in his full ecclesiastical regalia and removed his mitre before making a deep bow.

Maude frowned. 'A word of advice, my Lord Bishop. Before you replace your somewhat ridiculous hat, be cautioned that the mere fact that you purport to be a man of God will be of no assistance to you here on this occasion. Your brother languishes in the cells below us, where he will remain until he renounces all claim to the kingdom bequeathed to me by my father. You may now speak.'

'I do not seek my brother's release, My Lady…'

'Your *Highness*!' she yelled, but Henry merely blinked as he continued.

'Not yet, with respect, but that day may come.'

'Tomorrow?'

'Little more than that, if my proposal meets with your approval.'

Maude glanced sideways at Robert, who fixed Henry with a glare as he picked up the point.

'Your terms?'

'In these uncertain times I have taken counsel of my fellow prelates, and I speak for all but the Archbishop of Canterbury, since Theobald remains uncertain as to where God would direct his efforts. But I speak for the remainder of the Church, and as Treasurer of England, when I declare that we all wish to see an end to the chaos in which the realm finds itself.'

'Your terms?' Robert repeated, more ominously this time.

Henry finally came to the point. 'If the Church were granted independence of the Crown in the conduct of God's mission here in England, we would pledge our support for your coronation as Queen of England. If God is pledged to your cause, then the vast majority of the barons would fall into line.'

'The vast majority of the barons currently have little choice,' Maude reminded him coldly, 'since the usurper who some of them misguidedly followed is currently unavailable to lead them further astray. There is but one authority in this nation, Henry of Blois, and it is mine.'

'Yours under God, shall we say?' Henry suggested, to an outraged bellow from Maude.

'Mine and mine alone, you snivelling priest! You are here solely to preserve your stupid brother's unsightly carcass, are you not? Let there be no talk of God in all this!'

Robert caught her arm urgently, and she leaned down to listen. Elinor, seated as always immediately behind Maude, was able to hear the whispered conversation, which took the form of stern advice from Robert not to appear either blasphemous or too arrogant in victory. Maude nodded and took several deep breaths as Robert took the initiative.

'What do you offer us wearing your Treasurer's hat?'

'The contents of the Treasury, clearly,' Henry smiled back affably, 'although these days it might need only one moderately sized bullock cart to empty it.'

'And your brother? You seek his release?'

'I seek only that he remain unharmed,' Henry assured them. 'In due course it might prove advantageous to have him release the barons loyal to his cause from their oaths to him, in order that they might swear oaths of allegiance to their new queen.'

'Accept with as much grace as you can summon,' Robert whispered hoarsely in Maude's ear, and she forced a smile to her lips as she nodded towards Henry.

'I think that we may be *ad idem*, my Lord Bishop. The Church is yours to manage as you deem appropriate, while I shall make appropriate arrangements to travel to London, there to be crowned. In the meantime, let it be known that I am to be addressed as "Lady of England and Normandy".'

Henry bowed from the presence, and Maude turned to Thomas.

'Do we still hold Wallingford?'

'Indeed we do, Your Highness,' he assured her.

'Then that is where we shall proceed without delay. The prisoners may remain securely locked down in Bristol while we are away.'

'Would it not be a kind gesture to have them released?' Robert suggested tactfully, but Maude turned on him with a blazing glare of defiance.

'I am almost your queen, and it shall be as I say!'

With that she rose and swept from the Audience Chamber, followed by a pale-faced Elinor, leaving Robert looking humbled, and Thomas with a worried frown.

If Maude and her supporters were under the impression that the coronation was only days away, they had reckoned without the guile and determination of Matilda of Boulogne, the coldly determined wife of the imprisoned Stephen. She was not accustomed to being bested, and she was scheming.

'She accepted your reason for being there, and was prepared to relinquish control over the entire English Church simply in order to get the crown on her head?' Matilda asked of Henry of Blois when he returned to the Westminster Court to report on the meeting in Bristol. 'Said she aught of releasing your brother?'

'No, Your Majesty,' Henry conceded. 'She was most adamant on that point, but I see a way of securing her downfall.'

'Pray tell.'

'I took the opportunity to gain the confidence of several of her servants, in my capacity as Bishop of Winchester, and with the pretence of absolving their sins.'

'And?'

'And it would seem that as the prospect of her becoming queen comes closer to fruition, she grows arrogant and overbearing. Even her own immediate counsellors seem reluctant to cross her, and it is my belief that we can work this to our advantage. She believes that she has relinquished control over the Church as a condition of my loyalty, but that is not yet known to Archbishop Theobald of Canterbury, who of course would be the one required to place the crown upon her head. A few lying words in his ear regarding her alleged plans to wrench all control of episcopal matters from his control, and I believe that the old fool will refuse to have anything to do with her coronation.'

'She does not suspect your double-dealing?'

'Of course not. I left her with the distinct impression that my true motive — poorly concealed — was the release of my brother.'

'So what are her immediate plans?'

'To move closer to London ahead of her coronation. Perhaps into London itself.'

'Was it wise to encourage her that far?'

'Think of how we might use that to our advantage, Your Majesty. We have her closer to our own army, which she believes she has routed, so that capturing her person would not require a long march west. She would be forsaking the sanctuary of those parts of the realm where she enjoys the greatest support, and we allow the citizens and merchants of London to believe that her intended reign would bring them no good.'

Matilda smiled. 'I take it that you have other devious schemes under your soutane?'

'Just one should be sufficient, I think. We let it be known that she plans a massive coronation ceremony, the like of which the city has never seen. Processions, banquets, streets festooned with garlands, and the like. In order to finance that — given that the Royal Treasury is depleted from the cost of resisting her invasion — she intends to impose a tithing on every citizen, free man and merchant in London.'

Matilda allowed herself a peal of laughter as she threw her head back, then locked eyes with Henry. 'When I married into the House of Blois, I little knew that it was capable of so much deviousness. However, it works in my favour, so I am not displeased. But do not lose sight of the fact that I want my husband back, alive and unmaimed.'

'I may proceed in the manner that I indicated?'

'You may indeed, and as soon as possible. The arrogance of the woman will be the worst weapon we could ever hope to wield against her.'

XXII

'What did the old misery give as his pathetic excuse?' Maude demanded angrily when the news was brought to her in Wallingford Castle that Archbishop Theobald was refusing to preside over her coronation. 'And if he won't do it, why can't we find a bishop who will? Henry of Blois, for example?'

Robert looked nervously across at Thomas, who grimaced back at him. Robert cleared his throat. 'There was a time, of course, when the monarch could tell the Church what to do, but…'

'But *what?*' Maude demanded testily.

'Well, for one thing, you are not yet queen — and the other consideration is that you recently relinquished control over the governance of the Church.'

'On *your* recommendation, let me remind you!' Maude sniped back. 'Do you now tell me that your advice was ill-conceived?'

'If I might make a point…' Thomas began, only to be silenced by a glare from Maude.

'When I require advice on the disposition of my armed forces, then you may. But this is a matter of diplomacy, so keep your point under your bonnet. It's not as if you fared well when you announced my coronation to the people of London.'

Thomas needed little reminder of the humiliation and indignity of having his men pelted with offal and overripe fruit when he'd attempted to proclaim from the steps of the ancient cathedral on Ludgate Hill that England was about to receive a new monarch. The temptation to remove heads from shoulders had been strong, and his men had begged for the order to retaliate. Instead he'd ordered them to retreat, and was still burning with the embarrassment of the mere memory.

'I am at a loss to understand their response,' he muttered, 'unless they … that is, they…' He hesitated, and shot a helpless look towards Elinor, seated behind Maude and shaking her head in silent warning.

'Unless they prefer Stephen, you mean?' Maude demanded angrily. 'I hardly think that likely, since even his own brother has rallied to my cause. Although I wonder when he will deliver the Treasury, as he promised. We shall need its contents for my coronation. Has there been any further word from him?'

'No, Your Highness,' Robert advised her in a soft voice that all but betrayed his distaste at being obliged to speak so deferentially towards his own half-sister. 'Perhaps we might consider proceeding to Winchester in person, to enforce our point?'

'What say you, Thomas?' Maude enquired.

Thomas shrugged, suddenly unwilling to give more than the minimum amount of advice to such an ungrateful and unsympathetic mistress. 'Since the Treasury is housed at Winchester, it would seem logical to seek it there, rather than venture back to London in the belief that Henry of Blois has already removed it to Westminster to await collection by us. This hardly seems likely, since my latest information is that Matilda of Boulogne is still in residence there.'

'Not for much longer,' Maude muttered. 'Robert might best spend the days before our departure to Winchester enquiring after a suitable convent in which to house the Flemish whore once I am seated where she now sits.'

'So we proceed to Winchester?' Robert asked, bowing his head.

'Did I not say so? Have you added deafness to your failing wits? And where is our dinner? Elinor, dear, could you enquire? And tell the cooks that they will be roasted on their own spits if it is not served within the hour.'

On a hot day in July of 1141, Maude's army encircled Winchester Castle, the traditional repository of the Treasury since the former days in which Wessex had been the seat of Saxon government. There had been several demands made of the guards on the main gate to open up 'in the name of your queen', which had received several offensive responses to the effect that the only queen they recognised was the one back in London.

Now they were looking for the weakest part of the outer walls to which to draw the siege engines, or perhaps to begin burrowing under the stonework. If Winchester would not open its gates voluntarily, then it was Maude's uncompromising order that they take it by force, and hang a few of the leading Treasury officials from its outer walls.

As a consequence they were spread thinly around the wide perimeter, most of them dismounted and examining either stonework or the earth beneath their feet, when a shout went up from a man at arms closest to the track from London. A seemingly endless line of mounted knights was picking up speed as they galloped towards the besieging forces under Thomas's command.

Recognising their leader as William of Ypres, and realising that he had seriously underestimated the size of the ongoing baronial support for Stephen, Thomas yelled for Robert to take a sizeable escort and ensure the safe escape of Maude and her retinue, while he would fight a rearguard action. Not having time to argue, Robert did as instructed, and Maude and her several ladies, including Elinor, were hastily surrounded by armed knights and escorted as quickly as could be achieved around the western side of Winchester's outer walls.

Thomas turned his men to face the onslaught, and those who possessed mounts hastily leapt into the saddle. But instead of the anticipated clatter and crunch of collision, there came the sound of horses skidding to a halt on wet ground as William of Ypres raised his hand fifty yards from the opposing forces, then reined in his horse before nudging it forward to where Thomas was waiting with a drawn sword.

'I do not come to engage in battle, should you and your men agree to withdraw,' William advised him haughtily. 'It would gain us little glory to take on a host so lacking in numbers. We seek only to protect the Treasury, and to ensure that no harm comes to those within the walls of Winchester.'

'As an experienced warrior, I concur in your assessment of the odds,' Thomas replied, 'and I thank you for your chivalry.' The two men were still exchanging smiles of mutual respect when a yell came from the top of the wall, where the face of a man at arms appeared from nowhere.

'There's some of 'em escaped the back way, whoever yer are! It were that woman what reckons she's queen, along wiv soldiers!'

'After them!' William called to one of his seconds in command, before turning back hastily to glare at Thomas. 'You will remain where you are, along with your men, or I'll have you all cut down!'

Feeling helpless, but recognising the futility of any attempt to race after Maude, Robert and their small party, Thomas ordered his men to remain where they were. He and William sat glowering at each other as they awaited the outcome of the pursuit that had commenced.

A mile and a half down the track, and conscious of their relatively slow progress, Robert turned in the saddle and saw the dust cloud behind them that betrayed the fact that they were being followed at speed. He yelled an instruction for the remainder to increase their pace and seek the shelter of any woodland that they might encounter on the track back north to Oxford, the Angevin stronghold from which they had launched their ill-fated bid to seize the Treasury. Then he wheeled his horse and sat, with two chosen men at arms, awaiting the pursuers.

'Say nothing of the others,' he instructed his companions as the group of eight mounted knights came into view through the dust, then reined in their mounts to form a circle around them.

'Who might you be, and where might you have been heading in such a hurry? Where's your supposed queen?' demanded the man who appeared to be their leader.

'On the road to Portsmouth, which is heavily guarded by men loyal to her who will ensure her safe crossing of the Channel,' Robert replied. 'She was met by an escort of fifty of her finest men at arms, and you would clearly be outnumbered were you to give chase.'

'But she left you behind? Why was that, and who are you?'

'I am Robert of Gloucester, her half-brother, and your prisoner, it would seem. I hope that she will pay my ransom, although given that we failed to acquire the Treasury on our way back to Anjou, that remains to be seen. I offered to remain here in order that she might make good her escape.'

'They can't be far ahead of us,' one of the other men commented. 'This man is surely just a decoy, and we'll gain far more reward if we can lay our hands on the whore.'

'Decoy or not, if he is indeed Robert of Gloucester, then he will fetch a pretty ransom. And he may have been lying about the fifty soldiers guarding her, but are you prepared to face those odds if he was not?'

There were no more suggestions that they continue the chase. Three days later Robert was thrust rudely to the floor of a dusty cell inside the main tower of the fortress that his grandfather had commissioned further down the riverbank to the east of Westminster. He was unharmed, but very despondent as to what the future might hold were any harm to be inflicted on Stephen in Bristol. His wife Matilda had a reputation for vindictiveness and spiteful revenge.

'You did nothing to prevent his capture?' Maude demanded of Thomas, white-faced, when word reached Oxford that Robert was now a prisoner in the infamous Tower of London. 'He turned to meet our pursuers in a brave attempt to ensure our escape, and in many ways, he might be better off dead. Whatever tortures are inflicted on him will be visited on you!'

Elinor gave a sharp cry and her hand flew to her mouth.

'Silence!' Maude commanded, and Elinor bit hard on her knuckles as her eyes widened in fear.

Thomas smiled reassuringly across at her, then transferred his steady gaze back to Maude. 'I have no immediate fear of that, Your Highness, since we still hold Stephen in Bristol, and Matilda will no doubt expect you to exact any revenge on him, rather than a devoted servant such as myself. I do not mean that in any way disrespectfully, but consider the matter as I have done these several days, and you will appreciate the logic of what I suggest. There is also the not inconsiderable point that I am now your only military commander, and that you are as needful of my fighting ability as am I.'

Maude's expression softened. 'Forgive me, but the events of this past year have left me less peaceful in my mind than at any time before in my life. I meant no threat to you, of course, and would be grateful for your advice as to how we might secure the safe return of my brother.'

'An exchange of prisoners, perhaps?' her husband Geoffrey suggested, to an irritated tut from Maude.

Thomas nodded. 'That would be the obvious way forward, Your Highness, but the only one of sufficient rank and importance that we could offer would be Stephen himself. There is also the consideration that should Stephen succumb to his current conditions, Matilda would not scruple against taking Robert's life in revenge. If your principal concern is for the safe return of your brother, then an exchange would be the perfect solution.'

'While I take my revenge on Stephen's estates in Normandy,' Geoffrey offered enthusiastically. Thomas raised his eyebrows, while Maude snorted derisively.

'On your own? Or do you propose further diminishing our already depleted forces in a vain show of pomp and bluster?'

'I merely point out the obvious,' Geoffrey argued, 'which is that many of those who have rallied to Matilda's side since the capture of Robert have been the Norman barons who hold estates under the English crown. They act in supposed support of the man crowned as their next king, whether that crowning be just or not. Even the Pope seems to regard Stephen as the rightful King of England, remember.'

'Thomas?' Maude enquired with a cynical expression, but Thomas couldn't argue.

'There is merit in what he says, Your Highness. Were we to swing all of Normandy behind us, then those English barons who are currently swaying in their loyalties might well fall in

198

line. It is not so much a matter of who is crowned, or who is the rightful monarch — it is more a question of who commands the power.'

Maude sighed. 'It is all so complicated, is it not? Little did my father appreciate the uncertainty and bloodshed that he was unleashing when he wavered between myself and Stephen. Had I ceased to be Empress of Germany earlier than I did, this would never have happened.'

'We must deal with the dice as they fall, not as we would wish them to fall. I propose that I visit Henry of Winchester, who may still have the ear of Matilda, and suggest an exchange of prisoners. This will in one sense set back our cause, but with Robert back among us we would be well placed to move forward again, particularly if certain Norman noses can be tweaked back into line.'

'Please do so, Thomas, and soon. If possible, secure an assurance of the continued welfare of my dear brother. Apart from my concerns for his safety, there would be little point in negotiating the release of Stephen if Robert is beyond saving.'

Several anxious weeks later, a solemn group formed immediately outside the castle at Oxford, to which Stephen had recently been transferred from the dungeon in Bristol that had held him for the best part of a year. King Stephen himself was in the centre, surrounded by men at arms, and if he was happily contemplating his long delayed release, it hardly showed in his face. He was shivering, and occasionally sneezing, but it *was* November, and he wasn't the only one suffering from the late autumn chill.

Across the frosty ground immediately before the Barbican trotted a small contingent of armed men in the distinctive livery of Blois. Between them, on horseback but with his hands tied discreetly to the saddle pommel, was a relieved-looking Robert of Gloucester. The advancing group halted, words were exchanged between the leaders of each escort, and then the horses bearing the prisoners who were being exchanged moved slowly forward. As King Stephen reached the party sent to collect him, a heavy mantle was draped across his shivering shoulders, and the leader of his party turned the escort back across the green, through the city gates and onto the London track.

Inside the Great Hall of the castle, Maude threw her arms around her half-brother, and a tear of relief rolled down her cheek. 'Thank God!' she whispered. 'Without you we were lost, and now you must rest and restore yourself to full health. Were you mistreated in any way?'

'No,' Robert reassured her. 'I was fed regularly, and thank God a fire was always kept burning in my Tower chamber. But with this terrible winter that is upon us, I was beginning to fear that they might leave me to freeze to death. By the look of Stephen, he was less fortunate.'

'We treated him exactly as you describe your own treatment,' Thomas advised him, 'but of late his own bodily infirmity seems to have overcome him. Perhaps we should have kept him longer in Bristol, to let him die naturally.'

'Then we would not have got Robert back when we did,' Maude reproved him. 'Once he is recovered from his ordeal, we must decide how best to take advantage of Stephen's current weakness.'

The following year was one of mixed fortunes for Maude and her supporters. No sooner was Stephen back in London than his sharp-tongued wife Matilda all but shamed Archbishop Theobald of Canterbury into conducting a fresh coronation ceremony for herself and Stephen, which was followed by a series of lavish banquets to which all the barons loyal to him were invited. Maude retaliated by building new castles at Cirencester, Bampton and Wareham that strengthened her authority to the west of London, heartened by rumours that King Stephen was either very ill, or dead, as the result of the ague with which he had left Oxford.

Those rumours were swiftly dispelled when Stephen's army headed west and began either destroying or occupying Maude's new castles. Maude, Thomas and Robert were still considering how best to respond to this when disaster struck.

The guards on the eastern walls of Oxford Castle alerted those inside that a large host of armed men had waded across the River Isis and were streaming through the town towards the castle. Word was hastily sent to close the gates, and as Stephen's men clattered to a halt before the Barbican main gate they realised that they were too late to take the castle itself and its noble residents.

'What do we do now?' Maude enquired nervously as she gazed down at the heavily armed mob that was milling around outside, hurling vile obscenities.

'This castle is well built,' Thomas assured her, 'and we are well provisioned for at least a week.'

'Then what?' Maude demanded.

Thomas shrugged. 'Then we starve, unless the siege can be broken. They hold the town, but not the castle. I propose that I lead a party of men to break out of here, escape the town and bring reinforcements to attack Stephen's forces from behind.

This was how we won Lincoln, by attacking the besiegers from the rear. It was successful then, and can be successful again.'

'And we are to remain here, at the mercy of those oafs below?' Maude queried anxiously.

'I will leave you with enough of my men to guard against any intrusion. It is starvation and bad water you should fear, not Stephen's fighting men. Once I return with reinforcements, you will be freed without delay.'

'Have you no better plan?' Maude demanded. 'If we lose you in a suicidal attempt to break out of here, then we might perhaps consider surrender, otherwise all will be lost.'

As the cold, wintery night began to fall at its usual early hour, Thomas made plans for the breakout. He was fortunate to have retained the services of his former lieutenant, John Loverseed. As the two men stood outside the stables, having their battle armour adjusted by their squires, Thomas announced his intentions.

'It will be a full-on charge, heads down and horses at full gallop, John. Our objective is not to lift the siege, or even to kill the enemy, but to escape the town and head back towards Gloucester, where we may seek reinforcements. We need to have this siege lifted, certainly, but I propose that we adopt the same strategy that won us Lincoln. So when I give the word, the barbican gates will be flung open, and we go out at full tilt, hoping to reach the eastern town gate alive. We are agreed?'

John nodded, pale of face and far from convinced. But he had never yet failed to be at Thomas's side, and was not about to set any precedent. The fifty or so men who had been carefully selected for the breakout were gathered in a tight bunch as the word was given to open the barbican with all speed, and even before it was fully open Thomas dug the spurs into the flanks of his destrier, which gave a shriek and leapt forward through the gap. The few drowsy royal soldiers seated on the frozen ground in front of the barbican either scrambled to their feet or were mown down by flailing hooves as the escape party pounded across the open space, then turned and galloped down empty streets.

They had almost made it to the eastern postern when someone shouted an order for it to be closed against them. There was just a faint hope that they could urge their mounts through the rapidly narrowing gap, and Thomas yelled for John to go first. John was safely through as Thomas gave his mount one final jab with the spurs and lowered his head to cling on for grim death as it squeezed through the opening. He emerged on the other side onto the track that led east, and was trying to recall where it joined the track they needed to follow west when he felt a sickening blow to his left shoulder. His last conscious memory was of sliding from the saddle and offering prayers to God for his salvation.

XXIII

The pain was almost unbearable, and it hit Thomas even before his eyes opened. When they did, he found an anxious-looking John Loverseed gazing down at him. Someone slipped furtively away from his line of sight, carrying something in a dish.

'You were badly injured, and it is necessary to bathe your wound with honey and other balms,' John advised him. 'I believe, from your cries just now, that it hurts badly?'

'It does,' Thomas assured him, 'but at least I am still alive. May I thank you for that?'

John nodded. 'Not just me alone, however. There were five of us who escaped through that gate, including you and I. The other three had to fight their way out, and when they rode up the track and found you lying in the snow, with me pulling the bolt from your shoulder, they stood guard and helped to tie you to your horse.'

'The remaining men are dead?' Thomas asked fearfully.

John shrugged. 'I cannot be certain, but they did not manage to get through the gate, so they probably fell.'

'And this chamber? Which castle are we in?'

'It is no castle, but it is somewhere where the enemy will never think to look. Now you must rest, according to the monk who has been tending to your wound. It must be dressed regularly if it is to avoid becoming poisoned. I only hope that I got you here before any poison could set in.'

'I owe you my life, John, and I will never forget that.'

'Consider it a debt,' John grinned. 'When the appropriate day comes, you can preserve mine. Now rest.'

Time seemed to lose all relevance as Thomas passed in and out of restless slumber, the pain ebbing and flowing according to whether or not the bumbling old monk was gentle with the application of the dressings. From time to time he could be heard muttering in a low voice to John, and some middle-aged woman standing alongside him who Thomas took to be a serving wench, or perhaps a cook. After what felt like several days, when he began to shiver with cold even though there was a fire burning in the corner of the room, he opened his eyes again as he felt an additional covering being laid gently over his existing bedding. John was there again.

'How long have I been here?' Thomas asked.

'Four days now,' John replied.

'It is too long,' Thomas complained. He attempted to sit upright, then screamed as the pain in his shoulder reminded him of why he was lying there. 'How far west have we travelled? Where is the nearest castle from here? We must summon help for Queen Maude and her attendants, including my daughter.'

John appeared uncomfortable. 'In truth, we have travelled east. The track we were on promised more in the way of a manor house or castle where I could seek assistance for your wounds, and this is the first estate I came to once the sun rose and the snow ceased for a brief while.'

'So where are we?'

'An estate near London, or so I am told. It is owned by a woman whose husband is fighting for Stephen, but she has pledged not to betray us. Given that we have been here for so long without capture, I have reason to trust her. She has also been supervising those dishes that you have managed to consume, so in due course you owe a deep debt of gratitude to the Countess of Chalfont.'

'Chalfont?' Thomas echoed. 'Is her man the Earl of Chalfont?'

'We have to assume so,' John confirmed, 'since she is the countess. Do you know her man?'

'I believe I do, and if I am correct he is the man to whom you gave early sword training. You remember my son Richard, who we captured at Lincoln, and who lies captive in Bristol?'

'I was too engaged in mopping up the fleeing enemy at Lincoln,' John replied, 'but I remember Richard well enough, since I never had a better pupil. He has gone over to King Stephen's side?'

'So he confirmed to me, when he also proudly announced that he was now the Earl of Chalfont. The lady to whom you refer must be the widow he married in order to acquire the title. Is she comely?'

'Certainly, if you like them plump and past their simpering youth,' John smiled. 'Do you wish me to call her up here?'

'Later,' Thomas replied. 'I must rest again, and decide how best we can serve the Lady Maude. We either have to break that siege or we have to somehow get her past those who blockade the castle.'

The next time that Thomas opened his eyes, they lit upon the friendly, smiling face of a woman much as described by John, and he smiled back up at her.

'I must thank you most profusely for all you have done for me, and in particular for your unstinted hospitality. But then, if the truth were known, I have reason to believe that we are family.'

'How can that be?' Agnes enquired in a voice that confirmed her place among the ranks of the nobility. 'My first husband was an only child, and my second one has told me little of any family he may have.'

'Did he say aught about his upbringing?'

'Very little, other than that it was somewhere in Norfolk, alongside some sort of shrine. His mother was from somewhere in France, and his father was in the service of the late king. But they were estranged because his father regarded him as unworthy to follow him into knightly service, so he set out to prove him wrong. As I believe he did, if you know him.'

'Indeed I do,' Thomas confirmed, 'since it was I who misjudged him.'

'You are the father of whom he spoke with such regret?'

'Yes I am, and believe me when I confess that his regret is nothing compared with mine. I am your father-in-law, it would seem, and your husband's name is — or, rather was — Richard Walsingham.'

'It is true then what they say, that Fate moves in a curious fashion. I pray to God that you are not about to tell me that Richard is dead.'

'No, he is imprisoned in Bristol. By me. I fight for Lady Maude, who would be queen, while he has remained loyal to the House of Blois into which he was born through his mother. He was captured at Lincoln a year or so ago.'

'You imprisoned your own son?' Agnes recoiled slightly from the bedside. 'Perhaps I now regret hiding you here — I should have let you die out there in the snow.'

'Imprisoning him was better than letting him be slaughtered on the battlefield. I have since pleaded with him several times to come over to the side of Lady Maude, but he has a stubborn and misplaced sense of loyalty, it would seem.'

'So you would release him, were he to pledge allegiance to Lady Maude?'

'Willingly! And indeed, were he to agree I might be able to employ him in such a way that she would be forever in his debt. She is currently in a prison of her own, besieged in Oxford Castle, and my daughter — Richard's sister — is similarly placed, since she is one of the queen's ladies.'

'I have so far managed to stay clear of all involvement in those matters that are currently ravaging the nation,' Agnes advised him as she shook her head sadly, 'and if my husband is currently a prisoner because of his unwise alliance with one side, then perhaps it was a wise move on my part. However, being married to one side, and granting sanctuary to the other, is not perhaps the most comfortable position to be in.'

'Do you think you might persuade him to change sides in order to regain his freedom?' Thomas asked tentatively.

Agnes gave him a hard stare. 'He is in Bristol, you say, and it is the depths of winter. How might I achieve that — by messenger?'

'No, in person,' Thomas replied as the idea began to take firmer root in his mind. 'I can provide you with a very experienced man at arms for your escort, and no-one would think to question a lady such as yourself travelling from estate to estate. In fact, given the weather, there are very few armies on the move at present. I would also supply you with a letter to the gaoler of Bristol Castle authorising Richard's release.'

'And if you have been unable to persuade him to change sides, how might I, do you imagine?' Agnes challenged him.

'While he might have little regard for me, he may still retain affection for the sister he has not seen these many years. But tell him that she is imprisoned inside Oxford Castle along with her mistress, and that there is a man currently residing here on the estate who can give him instruction regarding its design, and the location of its entrances, and he might be persuaded. But do not tell him that the man to whom you refer is his father, else he will be likely to respond very rudely.'

'It is clearly not just princes who cannot maintain sufficient love between them,' Agnes nodded sadly, 'but if it means the return of my husband, and the reuniting of father and son, then I will do as you ask. And in the meantime, you must take your rest. Brother James advises me that there is no sign of your wound healing, and he fears that poison may have set in, in which case you will be greeting your son with only one arm to your name.'

Richard looked up languidly as the cell door opened. It was not the customary hour for his daily meal, and he was hoping that the surly wretch in charge of his cell was bringing more firewood. His eyes flew wide open as he saw a man and a woman being admitted, and he feared that he might be hallucinating as two memories from the past approached him. He leapt to his feet defensively and called out, 'No further, I beg you! I smell worse than my horse!'

'But you possess less sense than it,' John Loverseed muttered, 'to have allowed yourself to fall to this level. I would seem to have wasted my time when I taught you how to fight.'

'At least I remain alive,' Richard smirked back at him. 'As do you, obviously, although I assume that you have been fighting alongside my father during the intervening years?'

'I have,' John confirmed, 'and my loyalty to him seems to have been stronger than yours.'

'Had I remained with him, I would not now be the lord of a wealthy estate, with the woman beside you as my wife. And I did not desert him — he dismissed me from service at Westminster because my sister gave herself to a French adventurer.'

Agnes broke her silence. 'If you cannot express any delight at seeing me again after all this time, then at least be advised that your sister is now in mortal danger. Her name is Elinor, is it not?'

'Yes, it is. But what speak you of danger? Has she fallen into such sin that she is to be burned as a witch?'

'We are wasting our time here, madam,' John said angrily as he turned to leave. 'The coward cannot even contemplate leaving the comfort of these surroundings in order to save the life of his own sister. I have no time for such as he — even dogs fight to preserve their young.'

'I am no coward!' Richard bellowed. 'And if you would care to spend but a day in this dismal chamber, you would soon learn that it lacks all "comfort", as you call it.'

'So why have you refused all offers to have yourself released?' Agnes asked.

Richard's eyes hardened. 'Speak only of matters that you understand, wife! The condition of my release would be that I desert he to whom I have pledged allegiance. Despite what may be said of me by others, I am a man of honour.'

'And such a man would pledge his sword to protect a woman and her children,' John reminded him. 'Are you therefore such a man?'

Richard nodded. 'If there were no pressing reason against it, of course I would.'

'Your sister is currently held under siege in Oxford Castle, along with Lady Maude,' John replied coldly, 'and they are likely to die of starvation unless they are rescued.'

'That is surely my father's duty,' Richard replied dismissively.

'He lies wounded in another place, and Stephen's men have the castle surrounded, starving out those who have taken refuge inside it. You may not regard yourself as having any remaining duty towards your sister, but what of her two sons?

Do they not have the right to grow up knowing a mother's love?'

'They have managed well enough without it thus far,' Richard said bitterly. 'But who told you of their existence? It was meant to be kept a secret known only to myself and my father.'

'You have answered your own question,' John replied. 'Now, answer me this one — are we to leave here in the sad knowledge that you did not lift a finger to save Elinor from dying a miserable death? If so, then I will gladly go, for I will not breathe the same air as a wretch such as you.'

'And if you are ever released,' Agnes added, 'you may seek a warm hearth and a generous cook somewhere other than Chalfont.'

'I am the Earl of Chalfont,' Richard protested, 'so how can that be?'

'That is easily explained,' Agnes retorted. 'To be able to claim the lordship of Chalfont, you need to prove inheritance through marriage, do you not? If you do not leave here with me today, I shall seek to have our pretend marriage annulled for want of consummation.'

John looked askance at the pair of them, unable to believe that a fit and lusty man such as Richard could have failed to bed such a well-endowed lady, but the shame in Richard's eyes betrayed the truth.

'And if I leave with you?' he enquired.

'Then,' Agnes replied, 'we shall take steps to secure your hold upon the Chalfont estate, *after* you have given your word to seek to rescue your sister. We have a man currently residing on the estate who can advise you as to how the castle at Oxford is laid out, and no doubt John here will act as your companion.'

Richard thought only briefly before treating them both to a reluctant shrug. 'I must own that this chamber ceased to inspire me the day after I was admitted to it. I yearn for some more action, if only to storm a castle single-handed. Or will the brave John Loverseed here join me in that?'

'The *wise* John Loverseed will do his best to preserve your rash neck,' John agreed. 'Before that, I shall be delighted to escort you back to Chalfont — but only after you have washed.'

XXIV

'This man who knows how Oxford Castle is laid out,' Richard began as they trudged the final few miles through snow that covered their horses' hooves well above their iron shoes, 'from whence comes his knowledge? Is he a former servant there?'

'In a sense,' John replied. 'You will find out shortly. The building we just passed was the monastery attached to Missenden Abbey. Brother James from that place has been attending to the wounds of your — of your guide to Oxford Castle.'

They were met at the manor house door by a defeated-looking Brother James. John hustled him to one side, safely out of earshot of the others as he asked, 'How goes he?'

The monk shook his head sadly. 'The poison spreads too fast, but he will not let me take the arm.'

'He is a fighting man, remember,' John replied as he held back a tear.

Brother James nodded. 'He will be no man at all if he insists on retaining that arm.'

'Let us lose no time in meeting this man with the knowledge of Oxford Castle,' Richard called out eagerly. 'Then I may set about my task without further delay.'

John looked helplessly across at Agnes. She took Richard's arm gently and steered him into the house, to the foot of the staircase. 'He lies in the guest chamber, but he is weak from poison that entered his body with the wound that he sustained as he fled from Oxford. Deal with him gently.'

Richard mounted the staircase and entered a chamber that was stiflingly hot, although to judge by the movement under the bedding piled high over the sleeping man, he was still shivering from the cold.

'I am told that you can advise me regarding the disposition of Oxford Castle,' he breezed as he drew closer to the bed, then froze in dismay.

'I can if you are prepared to listen to your father for once,' the sick man croaked as he opened his eyes.

Richard stared down, horror-stricken, at the wad of stained, crumpled and creased cloth that covered the whole of his father's left shoulder, oozing blood and puss. His gorge rose at the stench that it was giving off, but he tried not to betray his revulsion. 'What happened?'

'An unlucky crossbow bolt from one of those besieging Oxford Castle, from which I escaped in company with John, and in which your sister is likely to be starved to death if you don't do something.'

'I am advised that you ordered my release solely in order that I might achieve her escape, along with Lady Maude's,' Richard replied as he diverted his eyes from the mess. 'What precisely had you in mind?'

Thomas whimpered with pain as he turned his head. 'Over there, on that table. I've drawn a chart of the way in which the castle is laid out. You can use it to work out how best to get them out of there.'

'And why should I assist Lady Maude, when I am sworn to serve King Stephen?' Richard demanded.

'This is no time to be taking sides,' Thomas reminded him. 'Your own sister, for God's sake — the mother of two children!'

'And what of Maude's army? Can they not break the siege?'

'The main body are over in Normandy, with Geoffrey, Robert and the three boys, seeking to raise support among the local barons. They left before the siege was laid, and we are hopeful that they will return with a fresh army, but the remainder of their English forces are spread all over the West Country in disarray, while the tracks are deep in snow. It was a miracle that you were able to reach here from Bristol, but an army on the march would have little chance. Pass me that parchment from the table, and I will show you your best course.' Thomas groaned as he levered himself more upright and pointed at the rough drawing he had made. 'This is the eastern side of the castle, where the moat has been created from the original Mill Stream. It is shallow, and when last I was there it was frozen over such that a man might walk across it. Here is the door that gives entry to the kitchen, through which the other rooms in the castle may be accessed. You understand me thus far?'

'I am not without some intelligence,' Richard muttered. 'Sorry, but you were ever critical of my wits.'

'This is no time to renew that particular grievance,' his father insisted. 'In any case, you have proved me wrong in that. Now you must prove me wrong regarding your courage against all odds.'

'The odds in question being that this door to the kitchen will be heavily guarded?'

'Precisely, but guarded by simple foot soldiers, who you will know from your own experience are easily distracted, but will follow orders from a man seemingly in command. Your release will not yet be widely announced, and you may claim to have escaped. You were once known to be a senior commander in Stephen's army, and there is a good chance that those who have been left to guard the castle against escape will not be drawn from among his best men. They are required to mount guard for every hour of every day, in the freezing depths of winter, and they will be far from content with their lot. They will also welcome any opportunity to be relieved of their duties. You follow my drift?'

'I follow it, but do not see how I might distract them, short of taking a bevy of whores to their guard post.'

'That is where you must prove your skill and daring. I say merely that once through that door, you have access to where Maude and Elinor are lodged. You must then also devise some scheme to sneak them out of there.'

'You do not ask a great deal, do you?' Richard muttered with heavy sarcasm.

Suddenly, Thomas's hand shot from under the bed covers to grip Richard's wrist. Both of them winced from the pain as Thomas spoke. 'When I escaped, there was little more than a week's supply of food left to them, and the water was already beginning to smell. That was well over a week ago now, so their only hope of escaping a horrible, slow death by starvation is for you to employ your wits to their advantage. Bear that in mind when you go downstairs for your supper.'

Those parting words echoed through Richard's conscience an hour later as he dipped his bread into the lamb stew and looked at the roaring fire. John Loverseed stared at him with eyebrows raised in an unspoken question, and Richard dropped his glance to the table as he muttered, 'My father has some hare-brained scheme for me to enter the castle across the Mill Stream and sneak Lady Maude and my sister out of there.'

'Do you have any alternative scheme?' John asked.

Richard shook his head. 'The easy part would no doubt be crossing the stream, since it is frozen over. But then how do I distract the guard? And assuming that I succeed in that, how do I get the ladies across the stream without their being seen?'

They were still contemplating both tasks in silence when Brother James came down the stairs, shaking his head morosely. Both men looked up enquiringly, but it was Agnes who summed up the expression on the monk's face. 'There has been no improvement?' she asked.

'It gets worse, and my heart sinks to watch a man expire in such fashion. We might consider joining in prayer, then I must depart in order to return to several starving wretches who sought Christian sanctuary in our hospitium earlier today. This foul weather has left many of the local folk in sore distress, and they say that these blizzards are set to endure for another week. I can barely see my hand before my face when I make my way back and forth from here to the abbey house.'

Richard looked up sharply as an idea flashed into his head. 'Brother James, does your holy house have a sister house?'

'It does, why?'

'And have you any novices?'

'We currently have three, but what might be your interest in them?'

'When I was at Walsingham, the novices wore white — is it the same in your order?'

'Yes, but where is this leading?'

'To the possible escape of two ladies, one of whom is my sister. When you return on the morrow, could you bring with you two novices' outer garments?'

The following evening, while the blizzard continued to obscure everything beyond the immediate ground before them, Richard and John led two spare horses on halters behind their own down the narrow Mill Stream path that overlooked the high walls of Oxford Castle. A faint light across the water betrayed the presence of guards grouped around a brazier, although nothing could be seen of them through the wall of white.

'Wait here, and if the cry goes up, make what effort you can to escape and tell my father that I did my best,' Richard instructed John. He dismounted and lifted the heavy sack that had been tied behind his saddle onto his back. Then he slid down the steep bank of the stream and gingerly tested the ice that lay on the surface of the narrow stretch of water. Satisfied that it could bear his weight, he began to move slowly across it towards the castle side, half walking and half sliding, praying that he would not fall and either crash through the ice or betray his position. It took only a few minutes before he was edging up the far bank, from which he could make out, through the heavily swirling snow, the fuzzy outlines of three men at arms warming their hands before their brazier. Now came the most hazardous part of the whole lunatic enterprise.

Dressed in his Blois livery, Richard drew himself to his full height and strode as carefully as the rutted icy path permitted towards the three guards, who had their backs turned to him.

'Call yourselves guards?' he bellowed, wielding his sword. 'I could lead a herd of cattle through here and you wouldn't notice!'

The men turned, and one of them spat disrespectfully. The phlegm was already freezing on his unkempt beard as he demanded, 'Who might you be?'

'The Earl of Chalfont, no less!' Richard yelled. 'Sent here by King Stephen to inspect the guard on our valuable prisoners. Assuming that they are not yet dead of starvation, they might have sung and danced their way past you sorry lot, for all the attention you were paying to your duties. Report to the gate guard immediately, and tell them that the Earl of Chalfont wishes you charged with dereliction of duty. If you do so at the double, I'll recommend that you not be hanged. Now go!'

'Who'll guard this door?' another man demanded.

Richard spat as he let fly a mouthful of oaths. 'What do you take me for? I'll mount guard until your replacements arrive. Now, move — that's a direct order from King Stephen's Master of Horse!'

The men scuttled as best they could towards the gatehouse, and Richard put his shoulder to the kitchen door. It failed to yield, so he stood back and drew his sword before hacking at its hinges in an effort to detach it. On his third unsuccessful attempt the kitchen door was unlocked from the inside, and a sleepy head appeared through the narrowed opening.

'Whaddya want at this hour?' a fat woman demanded. 'If it's food, then I'll let yer 'ave me back there on the straw if yer give me first go at it.'

'Out of my way, or I'll run you through,' Richard whispered hoarsely as he looked anxiously behind him. 'I'm here to rescue your mistress, then you can safely surrender the castle and you'll all be able to eat properly again. Where's the kitchen?'

'Dahn there,' she advised him, pointing. 'Yer turns left at the end there, then there's anovver door. Good luck ter yer.'

After scuttling hurriedly through a cold, dark and empty kitchen, he located the serving stairs that led into the Great Hall, which he found in total darkness. He called Elinor's name loudly, adding, 'It's Richard — where are you?' A door opened at the far end, towards which he blundered, colliding with the edge of a heavy oak table with a loud oath.

'Well, that sounds like my brother anyway!' came a hoarse chuckle from the open doorway. 'In here!' Elinor called. She threw her arms around him as they made contact in the doorway. 'It's been so long! Where have you come from?' Tears began to well in her eyes, but then she pushed him gently away. 'The pretended King Stephen sent you, didn't he? Well, tell him to shove his surrender terms down his hose — we'd prefer to starve!'

'I'm here to rescue you, you stupid woman!' Richard half laughed. 'Where's your pompous mistress?'

'She's in here,' called a voice from inside the chamber, 'and I'll have your head for that.'

Elinor led him gleefully into the chamber, where a fire was burning low in the grate. 'It's my brother, Richard,' she announced to the woman huddled over the sparse warmth that was coming from the dying flames. 'He claims that he's come to rescue us. We have to trust him, even though he was last heard of fighting for King Stephen.'

'He's no king,' Maude muttered. 'He only claims to be. And how do we know that we can trust a man whose livery shows him to be a servant of Blois?'

'I needed that to get past the guards on the kitchen door,' Richard explained, 'and now I need you both to enter holy orders.'

He swung the bag from his back, opened it and spread the contents across the bare floorboards. They consisted of two white shifts as worn by convent novices, and the stunned silence was broken only by a nervous giggle from Elinor. 'Do we have to take vows of chastity as well? Poverty we already know, but as for obedience…'

'Shut up and listen,' Richard demanded, 'if you want to get out of here.'

'How *dare* you speak to my companion like that!' Maude exploded.

'That includes you,' Richard informed her, far from overawed. 'You will forgive me if I don't bow and scrape, but right at this moment I require you both to do as you're told.'

Elinor looked fearfully across at Maude, who nodded. 'Since this impudent rogue is offering to escort us to freedom, we might at least play his silly game, since we have nothing else to amuse us. But why the white rags?'

'It's snowing hard out there,' Richard reminded them, 'and my plan is that once you slip into the night, you'll both be damned near invisible. But you need to hurry, since the distraction I worked on the guards will only last for a few minutes more. Put these garments over your gowns, cover your heads, and come with me. Wear sensible footwear, because you'll be walking across the frozen Mill Stream. Now, come on!'

He led the way back down the service stairs, through the kitchen and down to the entrance door, where he raised a hand to hold them back, whispered for them to remain silent, then peered carefully through the door as he opened it a crack. There appeared to be no-one on guard, so he gestured to the stream and told them to make their way carefully across it. 'There will be a man with horses, waiting to take you to the safety of Wallingford. Off you go, while you have the chance!'

As the two women disappeared into the swirling snowstorm and rapidly became lost from sight, he carefully closed the kitchen door. Then he heard the unmistakable sound of boots crunching through crisp snow, and four men at arms hove into view, led by a man who had a captain's insignia on his surcoat. In the split second available for rational thought, Richard opted to remain behind and bluff it out. He drew himself up to his full height and was the first to speak.

'I hope that these four are better than the last lot, who couldn't stop a commotion at a village fair.'

'Who are you, to be ordering my men about?' the captain demanded.

Richard sneered. 'Clearly my fame has diminished during my imprisonment. When I see how badly King Stephen's orders are now carried out by men who were once under my command, I regret making such an effort to escape. I am Earl Richard de Chalfont, Master of Horse to King Stephen, and I was sent to test the efficiency of the guard you are mounting here at Oxford. Thus far, I weep at what I have discovered.'

'We weren't told to expect you,' the captain complained suspiciously.

Richard smiled. 'It would hardly have been a true test of your alertness to have been forewarned of my arrival, would it? You were taken unawares, clearly, and now I should appreciate some hospitality before I return to Westminster with my findings. Or must I report adversely on that also?'

A short while later, he was supping ale and enjoying bread and cheese inside the alehouse that Stephen's forces had commandeered, and was lying fluently regarding his daring escape from custody in Bristol. Halfway down his second pot, he looked across at the captain. 'Is the midden out at the back?' he asked.

Once outside, where the rank smell from the pit in the centre of the open ground gave clear warning that it was to be avoided, Richard scaled a low wall and found himself in a main thoroughfare. Being totally unfamiliar with the layout of Oxford, and with the blizzard obscuring any distant landmarks, he wandered uphill in the belief that the castle, like all others he had ever encountered, would have been constructed on the highest part of the available land. His instincts were rewarded when he saw the outer walls of the castle looming up through the driving flakes, and he took the track to the right. From his brief study of his father's drawing, he seemed to recall that this would lead him to the eastern pathway alongside the Mill Stream.

He was just congratulating himself on his presence of mind, and gazing down at the frozen moat as he picked his way carefully across and around the track's icy ridges, when he saw the outline of a horse ahead of him, tied to a tree. Giving silent thanks to the foresight and loyalty of John Loverseed, he climbed into the saddle and nudged it forward.

XXV

The snow had begun to abate slightly, and a very pale dawn added a pink tinge to the flakes that drifted past Richard's nose. He patted his horse's flanks encouragingly once the Chalfont manor house came into sight between the lines of yew hedge. Rush lights were already glowing brightly in the main hall as he kicked the snow from his boots and strode in to the delicious aroma of freshly baked bread.

Agnes looked up from her seat before the fire, smiled, then rose to greet him. 'God be praised that you at least are safe — what of those you sought to rescue?'

'They escaped Oxford Castle,' Richard advised her as he stood before the fire and kicked off his boots. 'Hopefully John has escorted them safely to Wallingford. I take it that he has not returned here?'

Agnes shook her head, then looked up as tears began to form in her eyes. 'Your father was asking by the hour whether or not you had returned, and was resisting all efforts to get him to sleep. Perhaps you should give him the good news before retiring. I've had a fire lit in your chamber, and extra covers put on the bolster.'

Richard did as suggested, and he had barely made the top step of the staircase that led to the sick room before he heard his father's voice.

'You were ever heavy-footed, and there is no mistaking your clumsy gait even without your riding boots. How went matters?'

'Lady Maude and Elinor were extracted from Oxford Castle under the very noses of their captors, employing a ruse that required them to dress as nuns,' Richard advised him with a proud smile. 'They crossed by way of the frozen Mill Stream, as you proposed, and I would expect them now to be behind the walls of Wallingford. John has yet to return, but I have no reason to apprehend that any ill fortune befell him. Now, perhaps you will deign to sleep.'

Thomas sighed. 'I will if the pain will allow. Brother James has given me a potion to ease the pain and encourage sleep, but I dared not take it until I knew that you were safe. It is in that mug on the side table, if you would be so good as to pass it to me.'

Richard handed him the potion.

'I take back the unkind words that I spoke to you during the years of your youth. You have proved yourself worthy of the name of "Walsingham", although you no doubt think of yourself as a "Chalfont" these days. Either way, I am proud of you.'

A tear rolled down Richard's cheek as he nodded, too choked to reply. He urged his father to drink the full measure of the potion and give himself up to sleep.

When he walked back downstairs, there was a table groaning with food awaiting him. A serving maid stood with a pitcher of red wine, while Agnes was already seated at the board.

'No doubt you are tired and hungry after your exploits, so eat and drink your fill. Then you have one more task to accomplish before you can take your ease.'

'Have I omitted something important?'

'For the past ten years or more, regrettably. You are not yet the Earl of Chalfont, you may recall. The time has come for you to repair that oversight.'

Richard looked up with apprehension at her eager face. 'You know that I have had no experience in that ... that matter in all my forty-three years?'

'Nor have I for the past twenty-odd years, so your teacher will be accordingly unpractised. But the process has not changed since the dawn of mankind, so I imagine that it will all come back to me. Now, eat your breakfast, because my loins advise me that you will require all your energy.'

They were awoken by the sound of a man shouting for attention, and sat bolt upright in unison. Agnes tutted, then turned to Richard.

'Whoever that might be, he has spoiled the plans that I had for you when you awoke. But at least you can now answer the summons as the Earl of Chalfont. Off you go, but remember to put some clothes on first.'

Downstairs sat a tall man at arms, being shamelessly fussed around by Lucy, one of their serving maids. He looked up as he heard Richard descending the narrow staircase, and enquired, 'You are the Earl of Chalfont?'

'I would hope so,' Richard jested, 'since I have recently had connection with his wife. What brings you here — a message from Wallingford, I hope?'

'The very same,' the man replied. 'You are invited to supper this evening by Queen Maude.'

'How goes the weather?'

'The blizzard has eased, my lord, and there is now only intermittent snowfall. The track to Wallingford is passable if you have a sturdy horse.'

'I have both a sturdy horse and a sturdy appetite,' Richard assured him, 'so advise both ladies that I would be delighted to accept their invitation. At the risk of overstepping my mark, please also advise the cook that my favourite dish on a cold winter's night is venison.'

Richard was just donning his riding boots when Brother James entered the hall, with a gourd attached to the rope belt of his cassock. He caught Richard's eye and shook his head sadly. Richard's heart was in his mouth as he asked, 'How goes my father?'

Brother James gave a sigh and sat on the bench next to him. He reached for the rosary inside his cassock and began fingering it nervously. 'He is needing more and more of the mandrake that I keep in my cell back at the abbey for the easing of pain. The pains are spreading throughout his body, and are caused, I believe, by the progress of the poison from the original wound. As a man of charity, I cannot turn my back on your father's suffering, but as a man of God I fear for my soul should I increase the dosage any further. The same properties of the mandrake that take away the pain can also deprive a man of life.'

'You are to be thanked for your humanity and courage,' Richard reassured him. 'God will surely not punish one who shows such mercy to a fellow human being. When do you believe that my father will die?'

Brother James shrugged. 'It is not possible to tell. He is very strong, and has great courage, but the poison has now reached those parts in which death can come rapidly. You should make your peace with him before much longer, should there still be any ill humour between you. There is also a woman called "Elinor", is there not? He calls for her often in his delirium — as well as a woman called "Emma".'

'Emma was my mother, dead these many years,' Richard explained. 'Elinor is my sister, and she attends Queen Maude. I shall be taking supper with them at the end of the journey on which I am about to embark — do you wish me to bring Elinor to my father's bedside?'

'If you wish them to have one final meeting on this side of the veil of death, then I would advise it.'

Saddened beyond words, but anxious in case the experienced elderly monk's forebodings might be accurate, Richard mounted the stairs and looked down at his sleeping father.

Thomas stirred faintly and appeared to be rambling in his sleep, until he said clearly, 'Take what steps you can to be on the winning side, and ask yourself where the crown would best lie in the next generation.' Then he lapsed back into slumber, and Richard descended the stairs deep in thought.

When Richard's entry to the Hall of Wallingford Castle was announced, Elinor rose from her chair next to Maude with a squeal of delight and threw her arms around him. 'Thank you *so* much for what you did, Richard. We would have starved within days had you not rescued us!'

Maude allowed herself a smile as she added, 'Although it is customary for me to have the first word at any audience, I can only add my thanks. I will even forgive your impertinence at the time.'

'There was, as I recall, little time available to us, and it was important that we moved with all speed,' Richard reminded her. 'I take it that John Loverseed is safely installed somewhere here at Wallingford?'

'He is indeed,' Maude confirmed, 'and we hope that you also will agree to be our guest for a day or two — at least until this dreadful weather has abated. Then we must decide how best to employ your talents.'

It fell awkwardly silent for a moment, until Richard spoke hesitantly. 'You have no doubt been informed that I was, at least until yesterday, in the service of Stephen of Blois?'

Maude smiled and nodded. 'At least you did not refer to him as your king. But given that you announced your identity in order to bluff our way out of Oxford, you are presumably no longer welcome to serve him?'

'Only on the end of a rope, perhaps,' Richard confirmed.

'In which case, consider yourself in my service. But not here in England.'

'My Lady?' said Richard, then he reddened as he hastened to add, 'Or should I address you as "Your Highness" or "Your Majesty"?'

'Either will suffice, if you wish to avoid a hanging closer to home than Westminster. What I had in mind is that you join my husband Geoffrey, who has journeyed back to Anjou to raise an army that will enforce our authority over the Norman barons, while Robert awaits his return back at Bristol. I am of course the Duchess of Normandy by virtue of my father's bequest, as well as the rightful Queen of England. But I am hopeful that Geoffrey will return with the glad tidings that the Norman barons have accepted my suzerainty over them, which will in turn convince those English barons with estates in Normandy where their best interests lie.'

'I would be happy to fight alongside your husband, Your Highness,' Richard agreed, 'since I would seem to have little in the way of an alternative use for my talents.'

Maude frowned. 'I do not wish you to fight. Yours will be a more difficult task.'

When Richard looked nonplussed, she continued.

'When Geoffrey left for Anjou, he took our sons with him. The oldest is Henry, and although he is only fourteen years old, he seems to regard himself as a warrior. He insists on travelling alongside his father, clad from head to foot in battle armour. I need hardly advise you of the danger he courts by such rash behaviour, and I wish you to journey to his side and prevent him from getting himself killed. He will inherit England and Normandy on my death and will no doubt then amply reward you for your service. Until then, he will merely resent it.'

Richard smiled. 'I seem to recall being similarly inclined towards exposing myself to death on the battlefield at an impossibly young age, and only my father's stern discipline prevented me from the consequences of my folly.'

'How is Father?' Elinor asked anxiously. 'John told us that he was injured when they broke out of Oxford.'

Richard's face fell. 'He lies on my estate at Chalfont, half a day's ride from here, and he is likely to die from poison that entered the wound he sustained on that occasion. He has been asking for you — also for our mother, but clearly only you can fulfil his dying wish.'

On the verge of tears, Elinor turned towards Maude with a pleading look. 'Might I be excused in order to journey to bring comfort to my dear father, Maude? He suffered his injury in your service.'

'Of course you may,' Maude replied kindly. 'Since Richard has graciously undertaken to see to the safety and welfare of my own firstborn, I could not in all conscience prevent you from making such a charitable journey. But not until the weather improves, surely? In the meantime, Richard must remain here and learn what I can tell him of the nature of the headstrong young man to whom he will be acting as protector. Now, I see the board being set for supper, and Richard will no doubt be pleased to learn that his brazen impudence has once again borne fruit. We are having venison.'

Three days later the snow had abated, leaving behind a cold, hard frost. The ground crunched under their horses' hooves as

Richard and Elinor made their way slowly across the land until Chalfont Manor came into view.

The group huddled at the front door seemed to become aware of their imminent arrival, and Brother James gave a welcoming wave. Richard waved back, then slid swiftly from his saddle, strode urgently towards him and whispered, 'My father?'

Brother James shook his head and muttered something in Latin, before nodding towards Elinor. 'That is your sister?'

'It is, but sadly we would seem to have arrived too late.'

'Do not blame yourself,' Brother James consoled him. 'He has been gone these several days past, on what would have been only your second day away. I did what I could to ease his suffering, but you must advise me regarding the final resting place for his earthly remains. We are fortunate that the weather is so cold.'

Elinor remained on her mount until Agnes, frustrated beyond endurance, sent a groom to assist her from her saddle. She then walked over and embraced her.

'You must be my husband's sister. You are much alike in appearance. I am sorry that this occasion of our first meeting should be in such sad circumstances.'

'My father is dead, isn't he?' Elinor croaked.

Agnes nodded. 'Two days since. His body is laid out in the private chapel, and we have packed ice around it.'

Richard walked over with a gloomy countenance, trying to frame the necessary words, but Elinor pre-empted him.

'I know that Father has passed on to his eternal life. We must consider how we can convey him back to Walsingham.'

Richard looked at her in disbelief. 'Walsingham would be a week away, travelling with a corpse. Even in this cold weather, he would be in no suitable state by the time we got him there. I never heard him express any wish to be buried where his father was. Our family links with that place were surely severed some years ago?'

'You forget two young men in the orphanage there,' Elinor replied coldly.

'I did not forget them. The last time I saw them, they were at the abbey school in Ely. Walsingham belongs in our past, not our future.'

Two days later, Richard and Elinor stood, heads bowed and arm in arm, while Thomas's corpse, wrapped in a winding sheet, was lowered into a space beneath the floor behind the altar of Missenden Abbey. The generous donation towards the work of the holy house that had been made by Agnes had also secured the services of the abbot for the funeral.

As the abbot finally pronounced '*Requiescat in pace*', Richard recalled with total clarity the final words of advice given to him by Thomas: 'Take what steps you can to be on the winning side, and ask yourself where the crown would best lie in the next generation.'

XXVI

'I don't need a bodyguard,' Henry muttered resentfully. Richard had been admitted to the chamber in the castle at Rouen in which the putative heir to England, Normandy and Anjou was repairing a gash in his leather riding jerkin.

'I'm not here as a bodyguard,' Richard advised him curtly. 'I'm here to ensure your continued life.'

'That is surely the same thing. I'm still alive, even after my father and I have re-conquered the whole of Normandy to such a degree that Louis of France wishes to parley with us.'

'The main reason why you are still alive,' Richard pointed out as he pulled the sewing from Henry's hand in order to command his full attention, 'is that your so-called "conquest" has been a succession of sieges and surrenders. So far as I have been informed, there has not been a single clash of arms in the open field. Even if there had been, you would no doubt have been held in the rear, surrounded by men at arms from your father's personal bodyguard.'

'Give me back that jacket, or I'll cut off your arm,' Henry threatened as his face grew red with anger.

'Assuming that you can get past my defence,' Richard goaded him.

Henry leaped to his feet with a roar of anger, grabbed his sword, and swept towards Richard with an arcing swing. Richard used his hand to block the swinging arm with a well-practised blow to the nerve that served the fingers, and the sword fell uselessly from Henry's hand.

Only then did Richard draw his own sword and point it directly at Henry's barrel chest. 'No wonder your mother feared for your life,' he muttered as he lowered the sword point. 'Now sit down.'

'I am Henry of England, and drawing a sword on me was an act of treason!' the young man insisted, outraged and embarrassed.

'You are not yet Henry of England. In fact, you are not yet even Henry of Normandy. That title belongs to your father, although Louis of France disputes that, or so I am informed by your mother. It is that same mother who now insists that I preserve your impetuous neck for long enough for her to leave you the disputed crown of England.'

'Must my mother be obeyed in *everything*?' Henry enquired in exasperation.

'I find it the best policy,' came a quiet voice from the doorway. Geoffrey walked in with an apologetic smile in Richard's direction. 'I am sorry that I was not here to effect the introductions, but I was delayed by another messenger from Louis of France. He invites us to the Île de France in order that I might be acknowledged as Duke of Normandy. Anyway, it would seem that you two have made each other's acquaintance.'

'He drew a sword on me!' Henry complained.

'In self-defence,' Richard explained. 'Your son tried to hack my head off in a very unwise action that would have left him with a gushing throat had I not held my hand.'

Geoffrey chuckled. 'It was just as well that it was you, and not an enemy soldier.'

'You intend not to punish him?' Henry demanded, outraged.

Geoffrey's face hardened. 'Not only do I not intend to punish him, but I intend to underline the serious lesson that you have clearly not learned — namely that this man can best you in swordplay. If he can, then so can others, so he will teach you what he knows of skills with a blade.'

'But he's an old man!' Henry objected.

Geoffrey raised his hand to silence him. 'This "old man", as you insultingly call him, recently saved the lives of your mother and that companion of hers who you are constantly lusting after.'

'My sister,' Richard reminded him, and both Henry and Geoffrey squirmed. It was Geoffrey who broke the embarrassed silence as he glared at Henry.

'This man also has a name, and it would be a mark of respect were you to employ it. He is Earl Richard de Chalfont, and he will be accompanying us through the Vexin all the way to Paris. But not until you have learned both more manners and greater skill with a sword. Now, let us see if we can command an early supper, shall we?'

For the next few weeks, Richard swallowed his desire to strangle the arrogant teenager who seemed fated to die by his own impetuosity. He was short in the leg but long in the arm, with a barrel chest and a paunch that reminded Richard of the voracious appetite that had killed King Henry. But little by little, he seemed to grudgingly accept and apply the lessons that Richard taught him.

As master and pupil cut and thrust at each other day after day, in the inner bailey of Caen Castle, they began to forge a relationship, first of begrudging tolerance, and then of mounting mutual trust. By the time the day arrived when Richard advised Geoffrey that they might safely head south to visit King Louis of France, Henry was no longer in danger of dying by his own rash stupidity.

The plans to travel south to the French Court were then delayed by a series of significant events. The first was the death of Robert of Gloucester, Maude's half-brother and lifetime counsellor. He was in his late fifties, and had been in indifferent health ever since his capture and imprisonment, so his death came as a surprise to nobody.

However, it was a serious blow to Maude, who had relied on his sage counsel for most of her adult life. Given that matters in England had now reached a miserable stalemate, she opted to journey back to Caen along with her close retinue, including Elinor. However, rather than enduring the constant hustle and bustle within the seat of Norman government, she opted for a set of private apartments in the nearby Priory of Notre Dame du Pré. Both she and Elinor were now approaching fifty years of age, and the hushed sanctity of a holy house was preferable to the constant clatter of horses' hooves and the coming and going of clerks and messengers.

The other great event was the calling of a Second Crusade. The lands in the near east conquered during the previous Christian expedition, and in particular Jerusalem, had been ruled by Frankish and German overlords for over half a century, and were known collectively as 'Outremer'. But the Turks had recently begun to fight back, and when the Christian settlement at Edessa fell to the Saracen armies led by the Islamic warlord Zengi, Pope Eugenius published a papal bull that was a call to arms by all Western monarchs to come to the aid of the Christian communities in the Holy Land.

One of the first to respond was Louis VII of France, anxious to purify his soul after a massacre carried out by his army at a village called Vitry-sur-Marne during a campaign in Champagne almost a decade ago. He and his queen, the beautiful Eleanor of Aquitaine, were gone for over two years, and it was in an atmosphere of humiliating defeat and mutual acrimony that they had returned to Paris. Louis appeared to be a broken man, and was anxious for a peaceful northern border. He therefore sent his constant mentor and guide, the revered, spiritual and scholastic Bernard of Clairvaux, to Caen with a renewed invitation to a meeting in Paris.

It was an extended family counsel of war that met around the table in Maude's private quarters in the Priory of Notre Dame du Pré. Henry, at eighteen, had lost some of his early hormonal bluster and arrogance, but had been warned in advance by his father that if he wished to persuade Louis to recognise his title to Normandy, then he would need to display more humility than he was accustomed to. Henry was still outraged by the suggestion that he was obliged to bow the knee to a soft fop who had the reputation of being more of a monk than a monarch.

'He's just returned from a failed Crusade, and when his army last challenged our southern border, he was obliged to seek peace terms because he had a chill,' Henry observed contemptuously.

Maude gave him a look that combined concern with admonition. 'You really *must* learn that the world does not turn at your every whim,' she chided him. 'The sun does not rise with you, or set when you take to your bedchamber. It is by being magnanimous in victory that true men are measured. If you are to inherit all the lands that your father and I can bequeath to you, then you need more lessons in statecraft, humility and charity than you do in warfare.'

'I merely point out that King Louis is in a weak bargaining position, and that we should turn the screw even tighter in order to extract the greatest concessions from him,' Henry replied with irritation.

'All the more reason to be seen to give something in return,' Richard said quietly, and all eyes turned to him. 'Your mother speaks wisdom,' he added. 'Louis may be weak, but he is also proud. Nothing could be more guaranteed to turn him against any meaningful concession than the fear that he is displaying weakness. If you were to offer him some token of concession on your part, he would be so grateful for the saving of his face that he would be likely to grant you whatever you desire in return.'

'I desire nothing less than to be acknowledged as Duke of Normandy,' Henry announced.

'By Louis, or by me?' Geoffrey enquired with a penetrating stare. 'I am the current Duke of Normandy, as you seem to have overlooked. I was acknowledged in that title two years ago, before Louis left on Crusade. Before you can ask Louis to grant the same to you, it will be necessary for me to cede the lands to you.'

'But surely you will?' Henry asked, for once lacking his customary over-confidence.

'I will, *only* if you agree to listen to what your mother and Richard are urging upon you. That is, greater humility and a small concession.'

'But what have I in my possession that I can concede?'

'Again, nothing, unless the father whose advice you seem to regard as beneath you offers something on your behalf.'

'Something in the Vexin, perhaps?' Maude suggested.

Geoffrey nodded. 'That is precisely what I had in mind. The estate of Evreux would be a good start.'

Elinor looked pleadingly across at Richard, who sought clarification.

'You do not propose any armed action against the current *seigneur* of Evreux?' he enquired fearfully.

Geoffrey shook his head. 'In no way. In fact, I am advised that the current *seigneur* holds it in right of his dead sister, and only then because his brother-in-law is the de Montfort who holds estates within proximity of the Île de France, and has never failed to bring men at arms to Louis's side when called upon.'

'Would I be correct in believing that the current *seigneur* is the former Poitevin adventurer called Guy de Garlande?' Maude asked as she reached out and laid a comforting hand on Elinor's arm.

'The very same,' Geoffrey confirmed, completely unaware of the significance of this information. 'He became the *seigneur* upon the death of his sister, who in turn acquired it as the dowager of the previous de Montfort lord. It is quite a complex situation, but there is little doubt that Garlande will do whatever his powerful de Montfort brother-in-law demands, and he in turn is close with Louis of France. By conceding Evreux, and similar Vexin estates on the Norman side that will always ally with Louis anyway, we offer him what looks like a valuable prize while at the same time relieving ourselves of the need to enforce our rule there from year to year.'

'That's agreed, then,' Henry announced with a smile as he rose to his feet. Maude and Geoffrey exchanged glances, and it was Maude who spoke for them both.

'Never forget that it was your father's generosity and regard for your future welfare that enabled this step forward to be taken. And where are you going? Supper will be served in here shortly.'

'It will also be served in the Rising Sun,' Henry replied as he walked towards the door. 'I deem it appropriate to keep company with those men at arms who will one day serve their king with what I hope will be unswerving loyalty.'

In the stunned silence that followed his departure, Maude looked at Richard. 'You taught him that?'

'No, Your Highness,' Richard replied with a grimace. 'I taught him only how to fight. How to associate with rough men at arms is something he taught himself.'

As they trotted, three abreast, down the wooded path that led to the front gates of the Evreux estate, with six men at arms in two lines behind them, a group of twelve mounted knights eased their horses out from under the trees and sat awaiting their approach. Henry's hand went instinctively towards his sword hilt, but he withdrew it with a frown when Richard spoke.

'We come in peace, and we are preparing to concede overlordship of this estate anyway, so why would you foolishly risk your neck in a show of arrogant defiance?'

Henry muttered a blasphemous obscenity as Richard gave a cheery salute to the man in the centre of the welcoming party, who called out, 'I take it that you come in peace? For one, you are outnumbered, and secondly you betrayed your approach an hour since. How goes your sister?'

'She is well, and remains unmarried, before you ask,' Richard grinned back.

Guy de Garlande's face clouded slightly as he replied, 'Sadly, so am I. My wife died of a swamp fever over a year since. It is prevalent in these parts, due to the pestilential insects that plague our abundant fish ponds. We will escort you to the manor house, since you must be in need of rest and sustenance.'

Once a very rich and generous dinner had been disposed of, Geoffrey announced their business.

'We are bound for the *Île de la Cité*, there to meet with King Louis. He seeks terms upon which these borders between our lands can enjoy perpetual peace, instead of being used as a dedicated battlefield. You will no doubt eagerly endorse that prospect?'

'Most definitely. But I anticipate that this requires more on my part before it may become what we here call a *fait accompli*?' Guy responded.

'Indeed, but it will, I imagine, entail little hardship on your part. You simply abandon any pretence of being loyal to Normandy, and accept that King Louis is your overlord, as in practice he has been for as long as I can recall.'

Guy looked both confused and slightly alarmed. 'You wish me to demonstrate my obeisance to Louis in order to justify an attack by you on my estate?'

'No, no,' Geoffrey reassured him. 'It is simply the case that when we proceed to Paris, I shall be conceding suzerainty of Evreux to Louis, along with other estates in the Norman Vexin, in return for Louis's kiss of peace to Henry here as the new Duke of Normandy. We would be grateful if you would accompany us to the French Court, in order that your formal consent to this transfer can be recorded.'

It finally became obvious to the remainder grouped around the table, as it had been obvious to Richard almost since they had sat down, that Henry's attentions were elsewhere. Guy's daughter Claudine was approximately seventeen years of age, and blessed with both a fulsome figure and flowing, fair locks. She was becoming increasingly uncomfortable and restless under Henry's overtly lustful stares, and gave Geoffrey a smile of thankful relief when he dug his son in the ribs.

'We are talking about your inheritance,' Geoffrey admonished. 'You might at least do us the courtesy of paying attention.'

'I've heard it all before,' Henry muttered, 'so I am unlikely to learn anything new to my advantage. Gazing at this beautiful daughter of Evreux, however, is both a new and a delightful experience.'

'Is he always like that?' Guy enquired of Richard as the company broke up, and Henry declared his intention of joining their escort as they watered and bedded down their mounts.

'Henry?' Richard answered. 'Regrettably, it would seem so. If a lady is only passing fair, then she has all of Henry's attention. His importunate behaviour towards your daughter was nothing out of the ordinary, although she *is* very comely. In your youth you commanded the stares of all the ladies, so if your late wife was beautiful, then little wonder that your daughter is likely to inspire romantic lays from troubadours.'

'She certainly would in my native Poitou,' Guy smiled reminiscently, 'and you are correct in your supposition — her mother was indeed very pleasing to the eye. But not so heart-stopping as your sister in her day. Is she still entrancing to behold?'

'She wears her years well, certainly,' Richard smiled, 'although those long black tresses are now threaded with silver in places, and the years of attendance upon Queen Maude have filled out certain former folds in her gowns.'

'She is still with her mistress in England?'

'She was until recently, but now that the war between Maude and Stephen seems to have degenerated into a stalemate, they have transferred to Rouen.'

Guy gazed thoughtfully into the distance before enquiring tentatively, 'Our sons?'

'They were thriving when last I saw them, in the abbey school at Ely. But Elinor has never once visited them — whether by design or through force of circumstances, I know not.'

XXVII

A week later, Richard suppressed a sneeze as they were admitted into the presence in the *chambre de Roi* of the royal palace of Louis VII, and their noses were assailed by heavy perfumes. The palace was located on an island in the middle of the Seine, and the perfumes were clearly intended to cover up the smell wafting from what was no doubt a convenient flowing midden. Although it was mid-afternoon it was still stiflingly warm, and a fresh breeze would have been welcome.

King Louis sat on a throne in the centre, looking every inch the monk he was said to be by his detractors, which made the lady sitting next to him seem even more beautiful. Queen Eleanor was Duchess of Aquitaine and heiress of Poitou in her own right, and had just returned with Louis from the crusade that they had both helped to lead. Although she was rapidly approaching thirty years of age, her regal beauty seemed, if anything, to have become enhanced by her years, and red-gold hair still flowed promiscuously from under her plain white cap. Although seated, the way in which her limbs were drawn back in order to maintain her comfort betrayed the fact that she was tall of stature, and the neat fit of her elegantly styled gold robe left little doubt that she was slim of form. The jewels that dripped from her throat and arms had been specially selected to contrast with the burning ochre of her garment. Only Geoffrey and Richard kept their eyes on her husband as they approached the dais and bowed from the waist. Guy had seen it all before, and concentrated on acknowledging, with polite nods, his friends and acquaintances among the others in attendance.

Henry's eyes did not wander from Queen Eleanor as he stood, transfixed, behind his father. Richard was obliged on several occasions to nudge him roughly. Henry was about to become infeft of one of the largest duchies in the old kingdom of Francia, but this seemed to be of minor importance to him compared with drinking in the beauty of his host's wife.

'You are welcome at our court,' Louis advised them all in a piping voice that seemed reluctant to be expelled from his throat. 'Assuming, that is, that you come in peace.'

'Both in peace and in accordance with our obligations as vassals of France for the Duchy of Normandy,' Geoffrey oozed.

Richard looked urgently at Henry's face, fearing that his expression might reveal either anger or resentment at his father's servile words, but it was obvious that Henry had eyes only for the queen. This was also obvious to Eleanor herself, who dropped her gaze modestly to her feet, but from time to time she looked furtively back at Henry. Eventually she rewarded him with a coy smile, and his eyes flashed back a grateful and fascinated response.

'What aspect of your feudal obligations brings you to us?' Louis asked.

Geoffrey gave him the much practised response. 'Unlike yourself, I find that my advancing years sap my natural vigour, and in consequence I am not as able as I once was to manage the affairs of the duchy that I hold in seisin from you. There are also several estates within the Norman Vexin and elsewhere on our mutual border that I find increasingly onerous to control. I therefore come with a twofold request. The first is that you recognise my son Henry as the new Duke of Normandy, and the second is that you take seisin of the estates of Evreux, Gisors, Mantes and Bray as part of the French Vexin.'

Louis's mouth sagged open slightly as his eyebrows rose in disbelief. 'You are prepared to offer such strategically important estates solely in exchange for my consent to a father passing on a duchy to his son?'

'I am, sire,' Geoffrey confirmed. At this point, a silver-haired cleric leaned forward and caught Louis's sleeve, whispering urgently in his ear. Louis nodded, whispered something back to his adviser, then turned to address Geoffrey.

'Abbot Suger reminds me that in due course, in right of both of his parents, your fortunate son will be lord of most of northern Francia — if I grant your wish. I think that my adviser suspects something unworthy and underhand in your request.'

'How can it be either unworthy or underhand for a vassal to seek, from his liege lord, the formal acknowledgement of what every father must wish for his son — namely the smooth accession to all that the father has striven to bequeath him?'

At this point Guy de Garlande held his breath in case Geoffrey had gone too far, and was subtly mocking Louis, who was known to be perplexed and distraught at the failure of Queen Eleanor to bear him a male heir. But Louis appeared not to have picked up the allusion as he smiled benignly at Geoffrey and nodded.

'Indeed. I see that you are accompanied by the lord of Evreux, whose name escapes me for the moment. How does this proposal sit with you?' he enquired of Guy.

Guy bowed and replied, 'Guy de Garlande, sire, and I rejoice that by his generosity Duke Geoffrey has made it possible for my feudal obligations to be aligned with those of my kinsman Simon, the *seigneur* of Montfort-l'Amaury.'

At this point he smiled across at a tall, bearded and fierce-looking warrior standing among the assembled company down one side of the salon, who returned the smile and gave a slight bow of recognition.

'This is excellent!' King Louis announced as he clapped his hands. 'We shall take our ease now, until the banquet that I have ordered in honour of our guests.'

Louis rose and held out his hand to Eleanor, who bowed to the company, then leaned down and whispered something in the ear of one of her attendants before being led out of the audience chamber on Louis's arm. Geoffrey turned to Henry with a frustrated grunt as he followed the line of his fixed stare.

'You have just been granted one of the most powerful duchies in northern Europe, and all you can do is chase a pretty tail.'

'"Pretty" is too weak a word, Father,' Henry replied absentmindedly. 'She is perhaps the most beautiful woman I have ever laid eyes upon.'

The lady in waiting who had received the brief communication from the queen had not yet left the chamber, but was waiting discreetly to one side as the party from Caen began to leave. As they passed where she was standing, she pulled gently at Geoffrey's tunic sleeve and whispered something in his ear.

'Go on ahead and see to our apartments,' Geoffrey commanded the rest of his party. 'It seems that the queen wishes for an audience with me.'

'What do you know of Eleanor of France?' Guy asked of Richard as they walked down the hallway to their allocated chambers, Henry having opted as usual for the company of their armed retinue in the stables.

'Only that she is most comely, and that young Henry was undressing her with his eyes. Why, is there something I should know?'

'Something that Henry should know, and perhaps something that Duke Geoffrey is about to discover for himself, if rumour be correct.'

'What rumour?'

Guy pulled Richard into an alcove, where they halted as he lowered his voice. 'She is of course Duchess of Aquitaine and heiress to Poitou in her own right, which makes her both my liege lady when I am there on my family's estate, and my fellow Poitevin. Even before she beguiled King Louis with her beauty, there were tales of her wild and indiscreet promiscuity among the young courtiers in Poitiers, where she was raised. As you may be aware, the Languedoc is the land of romance, poetry and courtly love, which has a chaste form but a sensual substance. Those who are raised under its influence have a moral character that exposes them to sexual intrigue and renders them accomplished in the bedchamber.'

'As my sister learned to her cost,' Richard replied sourly, but Guy was not about to be silenced.

'She therefore came to Louis's bed with something of a cloud of indiscretion hanging over her head, but this was as nought compared with her fabled antics during the Crusade.'

'There is some purpose in my learning of this?' Richard asked testily.

'It is said that while in Antioch she lay with her uncle, Raymond of Toulouse. King Louis chooses to ignore the rumours, such is the power of Eleanor to bewitch men. But she is said to be restless in the marriage, and unsatisfied in the marriage bed due to Louis's constant renewals of his vow of celibacy. In short, the Queen of France is a passionate and wanton creature who burns with lust and is seeking to have her marriage to Louis annulled on the grounds of consanguinity. They are cousins in some degree, it is said.'

'And why are you making these disclosures?'

'Your master Geoffrey of Anjou is probably in her clutches even as we speak. The lady who stopped to speak with him is Angelique de Beaurevois, the most promiscuous woman at the French Court. She is the one who governs the queen's apartments, where all manner of comings and goings are rumoured to take place in conditions of utter secrecy. If your lord has a smile on his face on his return, you will now know why.'

When Geoffrey did return, there was barely time for him to change his attire ahead of the banquet that droned on for several hours. Henry as usual ate and drank far more than was good for him.

'What business were you conducting with the queen?' he asked his father.

'Nothing of which your mother would approve,' Geoffrey replied with an enigmatic smile.

XXVIII

'I must assume that we are about to become enemies for a second time,' Guy remarked to Richard as they rode alongside each other on the well-worn track leading back towards the Normandy border.

Richard nodded sadly. 'It will of course depend upon when, and if, our two ultimate lords resume their battle for dominance of everything on this side of the Channel, but in broad terms you are correct. I shall take little comfort in bombarding your manor defences with rocks launched by trebuchets, or setting fire to your thatch and slaughtering those who run from under it.'

'As I shall be reluctant to bring down, with a well-aimed bolt, the man whose family I once hoped to be joined with by marriage.'

'Do you still miss Elinor?'

'With all my heart.'

It fell silent as the same thought ran through both their heads. Finally, Richard asked, 'Do you wish me to convey a message to my sister when I return to Caen?'

'The message I would most like her to hear is that I am awaiting her in an adjoining chamber,' Guy replied. 'Please forgive my forthrightness.'

'Honesty should always carry its own rewards,' said Richard. 'When we reach the side track that leads back to Evreux, please regard yourself as my guest on the road that will take us to Caen.'

He experienced little difficulty in gaining Geoffrey's agreement to his proposal. He was still overcome with gratitude for the part that Guy had played in their joint contrivance that had delivered half of Francia to 'Henry FitzEmpress', as he was popularly known.

Upon their return to the Norman capital, Guy slipped silently from his horse and used it as a shield against his identity being revealed when it became apparent that the ladies had been advised of their return, and were awaiting them by the doors to the hall. He reached the safety of the stables and slipped coins to a groom who would unload his baggage and take it up to the guest chamber. Then, given the lateness of the hour, the remainder of the returning party adjourned to the hall in anticipation of a celebratory supper.

There were congratulations all round as they recounted the ease with which they had persuaded Louis of France to place Henry in possession of a collection of estates that greatly exceeded those governed by Louis. 'That just leaves England, and I shall then become the most wealthy and powerful potentate in the discovered world,' Henry boasted as he slurped down his fourth mug of *vin de pays*.

'Do not ever forget those who made this possible,' his father reminded him, 'and that includes our new enemy, the *seigneur* of Evreux, who bravely volunteered to be on the losing side in our next encounter with Louis.'

A look of alarm flashed across Elinor's face as she dropped her knife and stared at her brother. 'Is this true, Richard?' she quavered.

He nodded with a smile. 'That may be why he sought sanctuary somewhere closer to both his loyalties and his heart,' he replied. He then rose from the board and walked to the doorway, where he threw open the double doors to admit a tall grey-haired man dressed in the fine attire that had last seen service in the French Court. 'Do come in,' Richard invited Guy with a bow.

The visitor strode towards the supper table with a warm smile, his eyes fixed on Elinor. She gave a loud squeal, then turned to Maude.

'You must forgive me, Your Highness, but I seek your leave to either burst into tears or swoon with sheer delight. In truth, I believe that I am about to do both *without* your leave.'

The unbridled joy with which Guy and Elinor were reunited all but eclipsed more mundane matters of politics. However, they came to the fore again barely three weeks later when word was conveyed to Richard by a messenger from Westminster that an important man was waiting to meet with him in a nearby monastery. Intrigued, and with the blessing of his patrons, Richard followed the messenger to the Abbey of Saint-Étienne, in whose chapter house he found another ghost from his past.

'You have clearly prospered since your desertion,' Waleran de Beaumont grinned in mock condemnation as he rose from the bench to shake Richard's hand. 'The good news is that King Stephen has forgiven you, and sends you the greetings due by an uncle to a nephew. For myself I am sworn to depart on Crusade, but I promised that in return for the wealth with which to do that I would seek you out on my travels and sound out the prospects for an enduring peace between our masters.'

Richard eyed him suspiciously. 'We are all over here licking our wounds, while my uncle is securely installed on the throne of England. Why would he need to sue for peace?'

Waleran's face fell. 'England is in a state of chaos. There have been repeated famines, the barons have taken advantage of the uncertainty of who is their monarch in order to disregard royal authority completely and fight among themselves, the Treasury is all but bare, the currency is debased and Stephen has fallen out badly with Theobald of Canterbury, who refused to crown the older son Eustace as heir apparent. Since Eustace's recent unexpected death, there has been no suggestion that the younger son William will succeed. It is believed that a very public peace treaty with Maude that recognises Stephen as the legitimate King of England will do much to restore calm and stability within the realm.'

'And what does he offer in return?'

'If the young Henry will do homage to him as the legitimate king, he will adopt him as his son and name him as his successor.'

'And William?'

'He has undertaken to do homage to young Henry.'

'So Maude must relinquish her claim to the English crown?'

'Does she still desire it? She must recently have attained her fiftieth year, and has spent most of those years running from one castle to another. A woman of her advanced years must be thinking in terms of ending her days in the peaceful surroundings of a convent and arranging her affairs with a view to her death. What better legacy could she leave her precious son than the throne of England?'

'I will of course put the proposal to her, although I am uncertain of her response,' Richard advised him. 'You have somewhere to abide until I bring you her answer?'

'This holy house will suffice for my simple needs,' Waleran assured him. 'My fortunes have ebbed as yours have risen, and the guarantee of regular meals, albeit of a modest nature, is more than sufficient to satisfy me. Until your return, I wish you good health and continued favour with your mistress. She is perhaps not as fickle as my master.'

Maude's reaction to the proposed peace terms was more enthusiastic than Richard had expected. As they sat around the dinner table later that day, she attempted yet again to give Henry advice.

'This is a perfect opportunity for you to grasp what is rightfully yours,' she beamed, but Henry responded by banging his wine mug down on the board and subjecting her to an angry stare that seemed intended to blast her across the chamber.

'Why should I be required to grovel at the feet of a usurper who denied our family the crown for so many years?'

'Henry!' Maude gasped. She looked across at Richard, who shook his head.

'This is not the time, Your Highness. He is in no mood to acknowledge the reality of the situation.'

'The reality of the situation,' Henry thundered as he grabbed a dish of crayfish tails and hurled them at the wall, 'is that I would prefer to eat my supper in the company of those who truly have my best interests at heart — my future men at arms — and not an assembly of spineless puddings who would have me bow to a traitor!'

With that, he stormed from the chamber and slammed the door behind him. There was a shocked and embarrassed silence, broken by Maude as she made a great display of selecting a pear from the fruit bowl with a trembling hand. 'If only his father were here, instead of inspecting his castles in Anjou. *He* would make the ungrateful boy see sense. In the meantime, Richard, it would seem that you have to advise the messenger from Stephen that Henry declines to accept the kiss of peace. But please do so in more courtly language than Henry chose to adopt.'

Several days later, word came from Château-du-Loir that Maude's second husband had died of a fever brought on by bathing in an icy cold lake on a hot afternoon. Maude retreated for a week in mourning, and Elinor took the opportunity to plan her wedding to Guy.

It took place in late October 1151 in the local cathedral, with Richard standing in for their dead father. Maude came out of official mourning in order to attend, and made her faithful companion a marriage gift of the moderately wealthy estate of Escoville. The motives behind the gift were threefold. First of all, Maude had made a promise to herself that she would now withdraw from public life, and did not require even a companion to attend her. Secondly, such loyal service over so many years deserved its own reward. But, perhaps most important of all, Elinor and her new husband would have somewhere to live if hostilities ever broke out again with France, given that the *seigneur* of Evreux would then become an enemy of the nation to which his wife belonged.

Witnessing the new-found, and long-delayed, happiness of Elinor and Guy reminded Richard that his return to Chalfont was long overdue. He had not intended to dwell for so long on this side of the Channel. Maude was more than happy to allow him to depart, while Guy and Elinor smiled their approval, asking only that he enquire after the welfare of their two sons.

'We had thought that perhaps we might visit them ourselves,' Guy explained, 'given that we are now united in marriage. But then we came to appreciate that they are now young men without need of parents, and they would probably resent our appearance in their lives. But be sure to advise them that we think lovingly of them every day, and wish them all the happiness and success that life can offer.'

Only Henry proved obdurate, when Richard finally managed to pin him down. The prince had been missing from Caen for long periods of time when no-one knew where he might be, and even the small armed escort that he took with him were sworn to secrecy. When he did reappear at his ancestral base, it was only for long enough to acquire changes of clothing, fresh horses and enough coin to enable him to roam freely across the countryside again.

Richard was obliged to push past several guards in order to force himself into Henry's chamber. The prince was stripped down to his hose, holding several tunic jackets up to his reflection in the long glass. He looked round angrily when he saw Richard lurking in the doorway.

'I came to enquire whether or not I might return to my own estate,' Richard announced, 'since you do not seem to have required my presence these past weeks.'

'That is one of the hardships of being in the royal service,' Henry replied coldly. 'One never knows when one's master may demand one's attendance.'

'I was not aware that I was in your service,' Richard bridled. 'I came here at the request of your mother, in order to preserve your neck from the consequences of your foolhardy actions. That was almost three years ago, during which time I have missed three harvests on my own estate. For all I know, my wife may be dead.'

'Consider yourself in the royal service,' Henry advised him in a warning tone as he held up the purple tunic and admired his reflection. 'I shall take it ill should you desert me at this critical time. Let me see — a suitable office might be that of "Capitaine de la Garde Royale". How does that appeal to you?'

'That means "Captain of the Royal Guard" in English, does it not?' Richard asked. 'My father occupied a similar role at the court of your late grandfather.'

'Then you are merely maintaining a long family tradition, are you not? Clearly, given your duties, it would not be appropriate for you to leave my side at this crucial moment.'

'*What* crucial moment?' Richard demanded.

Henry smiled craftily. 'I am about to turn the landscape of these northern lands upside down by actions that will also bring me great satisfaction.'

'You are to invade England?'

'Would it be safe to do so at present?' Henry asked. The prospect momentarily distracted him from admiring himself in the mirror.

'You will not know unless someone with lengthy experience of warfare returns to England to assess the current state of affairs. Someone such as the Captain of the Royal Guard, perhaps?'

Henry thought for a moment, then nodded. 'Six months, and no longer. Spy out the land, put your estate in order, bed your wife, then get back here.'

Richard bowed and saved the oaths under his breath until he was safely outside in the hallway. He could now make plans to return home — not that he was entirely convinced that he needed the permission of such an arrogant young cockerel.

XXIX

'There is much here that requires your urgent attention, including me,' Agnes advised Richard as she hugged him. 'I had feared you dead — where have you been, and when must you desert me again for no good reason?'

'I have been engaged on business for a queen who no longer seeks to be queen, and a quarrelsome and unruly oaf who regards himself as king by right, without the need to earn it. But tell me, how went the past three harvests?'

'Better than they did for most, since our land is well drained and we were able to marshal the beasts onto higher ground during the worst of the rains. But there were lines of starving tenants at our kitchen door for most of the past winter. Now, do not seek to evade my question — for how long may I expect you in my bed this time?'

'Until either I am able to fully advise myself of the strength of King Stephen's position, or I am summoned back to Normandy. I may of course refuse to return, but I have a strong belief that the young Henry will find his way back over here with an army, whether I assist or not. Then I would end my days dancing from a rope.'

'Are you hungry?'

'Not if you have other plans for me.'

'Then your first task must be to put out a slow burning fire. We still have the same bedchamber.'

The following morning, Richard made up for the lack of supper by consuming enough breakfast for three. He then stood gratefully under the weak January sunshine, admiring the surrounding countryside and basking in the silence.

Agnes appeared beside him and slipped her arm into his. 'Thinking of deserting me again already?'

'No,' Richard reassured her, 'but I must make some effort to learn of the disposition of the royal forces, and who remains loyal to Maude and her son Henry.'

'I made it my business to attend Court during your long absence,' Agnes revealed, 'and I can advise that most of the barons would welcome certainty in the nation's affairs. It is rumoured almost every week that Maude will return with a great army, assisted by the King of France, and that King Stephen will be swept from his throne. The Church has fallen out with him badly due to his insistence on taxing them as if they were laymen, and appointing his own favourites to vacant offices. By these processes, we have some very strange bishops and other clerics whose own sins are likely to bring thunderbolts down on their congregations. Church attendance has dwindled, and there is violence and rapine in every corner of the realm.'

'So the people of England would welcome someone who could promise them stability and resumed prosperity?'

'Without a doubt. Do you now serve someone who might achieve that?'

'Not without a good deal of assistance, wise counsel and downright brutal adjustment to the realities of kingship.'

'The young Henry?'

'The same. The prince has been handed his privileged future on a golden platter, but he regards it as merely his due. He has grown spoiled, selfish and boorish, with a foul temper and an overpowering sense of his own importance.'

'Perhaps it would be as well for the nation were he to remain abroad.'

'Perhaps. But then, he may be the only hope for England, if he can kick it back into shape with his own stubborn determination. However, he needs someone who can persuade him to act in the best interests of the nation, while making him believe that it is what he selfishly desires anyway.'

'I would prefer you to remain in Chalfont,' Agnes murmured as she hugged him tighter. 'At the very least, you owe it to me to delay as long as possible in discovering for yourself if the time is right for invasion.'

'Perhaps you can assist me in that,' Richard suggested. 'The nearest castles of any note are Oxford and Wallingford. Do you know who currently occupies them, and in whose name?'

'The garrison at Oxford surrendered to Stephen once you had secured the escape of Maude and your sister. I have not heard of any change there. But Wallingford is still held in Maude's name by Brian Fitzcount so far as I am aware, and it is said to be impregnable.'

'No castle is impregnable. Its walls may be ten feet thick and forty feet high, with oak doors that would withstand the heaviest battering ram, but it can always be overcome by a siege from the outside or treachery from within. I might begin the task I have set myself by calling on Brian Fitzcount.'

For the next two months, Richard travelled the length and breadth of the land, learning what he could of the likely response to any invasion by Henry. He was richly entertained by his former patron Hugh Bigod of Norwich, who assured him that he was in regular communication with the powerful northern baron Ranulf of Chester, and that Henry could count on over three thousand fighting men once he crossed the Channel. In the Midland counties Richard was surprised, and not a little suspicious, to be advised that the Earl of Leicester,

Robert de Beaumont, was similarly inclined, despite his brother Waleran still being notionally loyal to Stephen. But from him he also learned that the former heartland of Robert of Gloucester's West Country had fallen to Stephen following Robert's death. Malmesbury Castle now housed several thousand royalist soldiers and was being used as a rallying point for all those who still acknowledged Stephen's claim to rule England.

While in East Anglia, Richard finally braced himself to complete the mission he had promised to undertake for Elinor and Guy. Late one blustery March day, he presented himself at the abbey school in Ely, where he was obliged to explain who he was to the recently appointed new master, Brother Clement.

'You are fortunate that at this time of year both young men are back here at Ely,' Brother Clement advised him. 'For many months of the year, they are accommodated in our college hall in Oxford.'

'They have moved on from studying here at the abbey school?' Richard asked.

'They are two of the finest scholars we ever had the privilege of nurturing, but in very contrasting ways. Alain is destined for holy orders, while William appears to have a promising future in the law, to judge by the talents he displayed in our rhetoric and classics classes. You must be very proud of them.'

'I'm only their uncle, not their father,' Richard reminded him, 'but no doubt my sister and her husband will be heartened to hear of such success. However, are there not fees to be paid for such an excellent education?'

'Ordinarily, there would be,' Brother Clement replied, 'but we established a fund many years ago for the benefit of indigent scholars or orphans who show great academic promise. We had thought them to be orphans, and I admit to having been somewhat taken aback by your disclosure that they have parents. However, I am obliged to record my disappointment at their seeming lack of regard for their welfare. To the best of my knowledge, they have never visited. Until today, I was not even aware that they had an uncle. I have been here for three years now.'

To cover his shame and embarrassment, Richard undertook to ensure that Elinor and Guy sent a generous donation to assist in the work of the abbey school, and to defray the cost of the excellent education that both boys had received.

'I assume that you wish to see both of the young men?' Brother Clement asked.

A few minutes later, Richard rose from his bench by the front door of the school and turned to meet the two young men who were total strangers to him. However, he recognised that they had maintained the obvious differences in their appearances. For one thing, the smaller of the two — who must, Richard deduced, be Alain — was already displaying the tonsure that went with his declared dedication to the Church. Around the bald centre was a fringe of fair hair that was a legacy from his father. The taller of the two seemed equally determined to record his debt to his mother, and his flowing black locks would need regular attention from a barber if they were not to become unruly. This was clearly William, and it was he who broke the silence.

'I seem to recall that you visited on a previous occasion. What brings you back now — your conscience?'

'Your mother and father wish to know how you are faring,' Richard replied, painfully aware of the weakness of his response.

William pierced him with a stare that would no doubt stop men in their tracks, once he became a fully grown adult.

'Would it not have been better for them to attend in person, rather than send a messenger?'

Richard swallowed hard. 'They are unfortunately trapped across the Channel by the seemingly endless war between the two rival claimants for the English throne.'

'A pity that they could not sit down and negotiate some sort of peace treaty,' William observed dismissively. 'They are simply drafted, and it requires only goodwill and honesty on each side.'

'While in the meantime, honest but misguided men are dying needlessly,' Alain added in a pompous voice that would serve him well as he progressed through the Church ranks.

'I share both of your opinions,' Richard was happy to advise them, 'and I hope to work towards same, since I serve one of the current rivals.'

'The useless King Stephen, or the strident Lady Maude?' William enquired, heedless of who might overhear his treasonous words.

Richard was shocked, but didn't allow it to show. 'Neither. My master is Henry, Duke of Normandy and Count of Anjou, who is Maude's son.'

'So this is destined to continue into the next generation?' William asked censoriously. 'There will be nothing left of this fair land by the time they resolve their differences, if they ever do. But clearly we must not keep you from your appointed task of feeding the ambitions of the latest claimant, thereby sealing the fate of our once prosperous land. You may return to our alleged parents, who we would not recognise if we passed them on the road, and tell them that you have faithfully discharged your onerous duty. Then you may return to ruining the nation. Good day to you, sir.' With that, he turned and walked swiftly back inside the school building.

Alain hesitated for a moment as he gave Richard an apologetic look and whispered, 'You must forgive him, but the affairs of fighting men cause him great suffering in his mind. When you place your trust in God, all that burden is lifted from one's shoulders. And so I wish you all the blessings that God can bestow upon you, and thank you for coming here today.'

Once he too had disappeared back inside, Richard turned sadly and walked back to where he'd tied his horse. Without thinking he urged the horse to the left, towards the track that headed north, rather than back south. He was an hour into his seemingly pointless detour, reflecting on the circumstances that had reduced what should have been a happy family into a group of strangers, when he realised where he was subconsciously heading. He wondered if perhaps God had answered young Alain's request, and was guiding him to where he would find balm for his tortured thoughts.

It was fully dark the following day as Richard nudged his horse through the open gates of Walsingham Manor, but this suited his purpose, since he didn't wish to explain himself to those who were living here now. He slipped from his horse but kept its bridle firmly in his hand as he walked down the grass slope that housed the original shrine. He stood silently before each of the Walsingham family graves, sending those who lay in them such loving thoughts as he could muster.

Richard had been back home at Chalfont for two more weeks, and he was just beginning to believe that perhaps God continued to smile favourably upon him, when he awoke late one sunny spring morning to see Agnes standing by the bed with tears rolling down her face. When he asked what had upset her, she mumbled that there was a messenger down in the hall who claimed to have been sent by someone called 'Henry of Normandy and Anjou, shortly to become Henry of England'. He was insisting that the message he had to impart was for Richard's ears only, and it had not been put into writing lest the messenger be captured on his journey.

Cursing loudly and enthusiastically, Richard slipped into some clothes and descended to the hall, where the messenger had been provided with bread, cheese and beer.

'Your message?' Richard demanded.

The man rose to his feet respectfully. 'My master Duke Henry advises that he is to be richly married one month from now. He requires you to attend upon him to ensure that the event remains a secret to the rest of the world.'

Richard was still cursing as he made his way out into the weak April sunshine. He steeled himself against the possibility that he might never see this manor again, that he might never again know the pleasure of lying with Agnes, and that he might not even remain in life beyond another month.

It was almost too much to bear, and he was getting far too old for this sort of thing.

A NOTE TO THE READER

Dear Reader,

Thank you for taking the time to read this third novel in a series of seven that between them cover the twelfth century, a period during which England was transformed beyond recognition. I hope that it lived up to your expectations. Once again, the basic plotline was written for me by the events that took place during one of the most unsettled periods of that tumultuous age.

The tragic death, in 1120, of the heir to Henry I's throne sparked eighteen years of bloodshed, uncertainty and internecine strife that historians would later label 'the Anarchy'. The two rivals for the throne of England, Henry's daughter Matilda of Anjou and her cousin Stephen of Blois, set about each other with a disregard for family loyalty that served as a benchmark for the noble families of half of northern Europe. Brother fought against brother, cousin against cousin and father against son, and this breakdown is hopefully reflected in the main plotlines of this novel.

Two aspects of this sad and confused period of English history became obvious to me as I researched the known facts. The first was the extent to which the notionally English nobility were still jealously guarding their estates across the Channel in what we today call 'France', while the nation proudly bearing that name under the Capetian dynasty was confined to an area of some five thousand square miles based on Paris. It was smaller than some of the duchies by which it was bordered, most notably Normandy and Anjou, and the French kings strove to maintain their power base by luring the dukes and counts of those provinces into disloyalty against the English monarchs to whom they owed allegiance.

The warlike barons who held the balance of power in England, but who also enjoyed vast tracts of land across the Channel, were therefore torn in their allegiance between the Kings of England and France. When the right to rule England was being contested by two ill-tempered rivals whose constant warfare was bringing England to its knees, it was all too easy for Louis of France to stir the pot for his own territorial interests.

The second, and closely related, feature that emerged from my research was the devastating effect that the Anarchy had on the ordinary people of England. Apart from natural disasters such as poor harvests and endemic disease, their land was being plundered by one army after another. The castles — which were in many ways the hearts of the towns that were in turn the centres of commercial life — were being besieged, plundered, demolished and left in ruins by wave after wave of men at arms employed by each side.

Richard Walsingham could not have picked a worse time to seek to earn his spurs and establish himself as a nobleman. By entering the service of one of the rivals for the throne while his father and sister served the other, he was courting early extinction.

This novel ends with the prospect of yet another descendent of William of Normandy bending England to his will. In the next novel in this series, *The Lion of Anjou*, we enter the autocratic reign of Henry Plantagenet, England's Henry II, whose steely stubbornness resulted in the assassination of an Archbishop of Canterbury, the breakdown of what began as an idyllic marriage, and the bitter rebellion of all his sons in turn. England might have acquired only one monarch as the

Anarchy came to an end, but he was not one who it was wise to annoy.

I hope that you are sufficiently encouraged to acquire this next novel, but whether you are or not, I'd love to get feedback from you on this one — or perhaps even a review of it through the agency of **Amazon** or **Goodreads**. Or, if you prefer, send your thoughts to me on my author website, **davidfieldauthor.com**.

David

Sapere Books is an exciting new publisher of brilliant fiction and popular history.

To find out more about our latest releases and our monthly bargain books visit our website:
saperebooks.com

Printed in Great Britain
by Amazon

31162003R00150